PRAISE FOR

WELL READ, THEN DEAD

"A terrific new spin on the culinary cozy—with a great story, plenty of heart, and compelling characters. Sassy—who really is sassy—and her cheeky roster of friends sparkle as brightly as the sun on the Gulf of Mexico."

—Laura Childs, *New York Times* bestselling author of *Steeped in Evil*

"BOOKLOVER ALERT: *Well Read, Then Dead* celebrates books, food, laughter, friendship, and, oh yes, dark dire doings. Clever, original, and sure to please."

—Carolyn Hart, national bestselling author of *Death at the Door*

"Solving crime with Sassy and Bridgy is nothing short of delightful."

—Laura Bradford, national bestselling author of *Shunned and Dangerous*

"I've long enjoyed the short fiction of Terrie Moran, and I'm thrilled to see her expand her talents to the novel with *Well Read, Then Dead*. Set in a paradise Florida island town, with lovable and quirky characters and a combination bookstore/café that I wish was in my own hometown, Terrie's well-plotted novel tells a tale of murder, old secrets, and friends-for-life who will do what it takes to protect their loved ones and way of life. Very much recommended."

—Brendan DuBois, two-time Shamus Award–winning author of *Fatal Harbor*

Well Read, Then Dead

TERRIE FARLEY MORAN

BERKLEY PRIME CRIME, NEW YORK

THE BERKLEY PUBLISHING GROUP
Published by the Penguin Group
Penguin Group (USA) LLC
375 Hudson Street, New York, New York 10014

USA • Canada • UK • Ireland • Australia • New Zealand • India • South Africa • China

penguin.com

A Penguin Random House Company

WELL READ, THEN DEAD

A Berkley Prime Crime Book / published by arrangement with the author

Berkley Prime Crime Books are published by The Berkley Publishing Group.
BERKLEY® PRIME CRIME and the PRIME CRIME logo are trademarks of
Penguin Group (USA) LLC.

For information, address: The Berkley Publishing Group,
a division of Penguin Group (USA) LLC,
375 Hudson Street, New York, New York 10014.

ISBN: 978-0-425-27028-8

PUBLISHING HISTORY
Berkley Prime Crime mass-market edition / August 2014

PRINTED IN THE UNITED STATES OF AMERICA

10 9 8 7 6 5 4 3 2 1

Cover illustration by S. Miroque.
Cover design by Rita Frangie.
Interior text design by Kristin del Rosario.

Emelia, Billy, Katie, Madeline, Abby, Shane and Juliet:
best grandkids ever

Chapter One ‖‖‖‖‖‖‖‖

"Oh, pu-leeze, Rowena, Anya Seton never measured up to Daphne du Maurier's elegance. I'm shocked you would say such a thing." Jocelyn Kendall, pastor's wife and book club gadfly, crossed and recrossed her legs in perfect tempo with the ever-increasing meter of her rant. Our discussion of *Green Darkness* was deteriorating rapidly.

"For example, in *Rebecca* . . ."

Recalling last year's "Battle of the Brontë Sisters" completing ruining one meeting of the Books Before Breakfast Club, followed by minor skirmishes flaring up during the next two or three, I interrupted with a feigned look at my watch and as much cheer as I could muster.

"I'd no idea it was so late. We need to select this month's book." I tried for a smile bright enough to encourage participation. "Does anyone have a suggestion?"

Jocelyn pushed a hank of hair, the color and texture of

straw, off her forehead and glared at the other four women sitting in a semicircle, as if daring anyone to answer me. She certainly didn't intimidate the oldest member of the book club, Miss Augusta Maddox, who glared back, shoved her own copy of *Green Darkness* into a faded denim tote and zipped it shut. Then, tilting to her left, Miss Augusta nudged my favorite club member, Miss Delia Batson, who leaned in and handed me a piece of paper, edged by two sharp creases where it had been doubled and doubled again. As always, Delia avoided eye contact, gazing instead at her veined and mottled hands, now primly resting in her generous lap, fingers tightly interlocked.

"Well, thank you, Miss Delia"—I flipped opened her note and was relieved she was moving us in a completely different direction—"for suggesting the lighthearted Sheriff Dan Rhodes series by Bill Crider. Has anyone a particular favorite we might try?"

From the far side of the café, my BFF and business partner, Bridgy Mayfield, shot me a wink and a thumbs-up.

Irritated by our conversation, Judge Harcroft harrumphed and rattled his copy of our local broadsheet, the *Fort Myers Beach News*. He was sitting at the Dashiell Hammett table, right next to the café's book nook, not exactly a haven of peace and quiet during book club meetings, but he refused to sit anywhere else. His erect posture, immaculate white collared shirt and impeccably groomed, albeit thinning, gray hair gave the impression that he was merely on a short break from presiding over a momentous, legally significant trial, instead of being retired from traffic court for less than a year. The judge's ongoing routine drove everyone crazy. "I'll have just a *Dash* of milk, thank you." Or, when he finally folded up his newspaper, getting ready to leave, "Enjoy your day. I must *Dash*." His strident chuckle left everyone in hearing distance gritting their teeth.

Ignoring me, Jocelyn hammered her point. "You can hear the lyricism in *Rebecca*'s opening line." She rolled her hand in figure eights while reciting, " 'Last night I dreamt I went to Manderley again.' How does that compare to"—she opened her copy of *Green Darkness*—" 'Celia Marsdon, young, rich and unhappy, sat huddled in a lounge chair . . .'?" Jocelyn slammed the book shut. "Not even a hint of cadence."

Rowena Gustavsen's head snapped high. Shoulders ramrod straight, she jutted her chin directly at Jocelyn. Before she could toss a rejoinder that would no doubt launch a full-fledged melee, Miss Augusta Maddox boomed, "Delia's got a fine idea. I like Sheriff Dan. He had me chuckling all through *The Wild Hog Murders*. Sassy, can you find out if there's a new book and get us copies right quick?"

At my swift nod, Miss Augusta stood. "Thank you kindly. Delia and I are going to have our breakfast." And she walked to the Emily Dickinson table, with Miss Delia at her heels.

I jumped up and so did our newest member, Lisette Ortiz, who waved a halfhearted "so long" and practically ran for the door. I wondered if we'd ever see her again. Jocelyn stayed in her seat, determined to continue the argument, but Rowena gathered her things, ignored Jocelyn and looked directly at me.

"I have a new client from San Carlos Island coming to the Emporium in a few minutes. Got to run. Money to be made." And she hustled away with an evil backward glance clearly meant to tell Jocelyn the dispute would be settled another day.

Relieved as I was that the meeting ended without fisticuffs,

I took pity on Jocelyn, whose frustration was evident in her grim expression, so I offered her a cup of tea.

She accepted with a stiff nod. "Make it green, decaffeinated."

A tinny thump followed by the jangle of metal on metal signaled that we had customers hitching up to one of the bicycle racks on either side of the double doors. Bridgy tucked a golden tendril behind her ear and, menus in hand, walked to the front of the café to greet the two helmeted, backpack-toting cyclists tugging the screen door handle. An energizing morning breeze was drifting in from the Gulf of Mexico. Still, it was barely the beginning of November, so we'd probably need to turn on the AC before noon.

Bridgy seated the cyclists at Agatha Christie. They looked at the tabletop with the Christie quotes, stories and photos protected by layers of heavy-duty lamination. The bearded cyclist, wearing a shirt in the red and blue stripes of the Barcelona soccer team, with Lionel Messi's name in shiny gold letters across the back, asked, "Who else you got?" They picked up their gear and moved to Robert Frost. Bridgy pointed out the specials board and left them with their menus. The chubby blond wearing a faded black tee shirt said, "Hey, look at all the bookshelves. Like a bookstore."

Exactly. The Read 'Em and Eat Café and Book Corner. Breakfast. Lunch. And all you can read. Anything from *Wuthering Heights* to the newest graphic novel by Alan Moore or Neil Gaiman was readily available on natural rattan shelves lining two walls. The subdued color of the bookcases complemented the glossy white and yellow café décor. All of our gleaming white tables were decorated with pictures of famous writers along with snippets of their work, melding the café and the book corner perfectly.

Three years ago Bridgy caught her ex-husband—the Bonehead—fulfilling his Mrs. Robinson fantasy with a Botox babe from his mother's mahjong group, and the very next day my bosses Gordon and Nina Howard announced that they were moving Howard Accounting from Manhattan to Connecticut. We were barely twenty-five and life had dealt us death blows. Ever since ninth grade, whenever the sky fell in on one of us, we had a sleepover, cried it out, talked it out and put it behind us. "It" being anything from Bridgy's squad losing the soccer championship to a team from Staten Island to that creep Marjory Haskins stealing my worthless boyfriend in tenth grade. Over the years we'd graduated from cola and chips to mojitos and whole grain crackers, likely served with gorgonzola cheese or hummus. It may have been mojito courage, but during the Bonehead sleepover we made a pact to head south and follow our dreams. It turned out that Bridgy's dream was to own a breakfast/lunch café while my dream was to own a bookstore. Can you say fusion?

We loved putting together book-related events, such as the Potluck Book Club, which focused on cookbooks and foodie novels like *Julie and Julia*. The tea and mystery afternoons featuring novels by twentieth-century greats like Josephine Tey and Dorothy L. Sayers were a major hit. We were constantly experimenting with various combinations of food and books. Our clientele, comprised of both year-round residents and returning snowbirds who came south every autumn, increased month by month.

As I served Jocelyn's tea, she barely grunted her thanks,

so I was grateful Lionel Messi waved me over and ordered Miss Marple Scones with strawberry jam and two Robert Frost Apple and Blueberry Tartlets. I finger-tapped the table beside the copies of Frost's fruit poems and went to get their food. I was behind the counter, putting jam in a dark green leaf-shaped bowl, when their conversation got animated.

"It's an omen, bro." The blond was rubbing his hands together, his voice tingling with anticipation. He bent over the tabletop, reading. " 'I took the one less traveled by, / And that has made all the difference.' That's us, dude. How many wreckers do you know? We're gonna be the big dawgs, oh yeah." He slammed his fist on the table.

His buddy flapped both hands to quiet him, but it was far too late. Miss Augusta blasted across the room. "Wreckers! What do you know about wreckers?"

Tiny as she was, with a face that was all sharp beak nose and skin shriveled from a lifetime in the Gulf Coast sun, you'd expect Augusta Maddox to chirp like a parakeet. But, no. Her thunderous baritone bounced off every surface in the room, shaking the tops of the sugar bowls. She was the direct opposite of her lumpy, cuddly cousin Delia Batson, who rarely spoke and never above a whisper.

Lionel Messi glared at his pal as if to say, "Now look what you've done." Then he turned to the Emily Dickinson table with an apologetic smile. "Sorry, ma'am. We're on vacation. A friend is taking us out on the water. Said he'd show us some places where the Spanish galleons are rumored to have been sunk by hurricanes."

"Been sunk by pirates, more likely. We been here more'n a hundred years." She pointed to Miss Delia and let her index finger snap back and forth between them. "Our families come when the Florida Everglades and Islands was the only frontier left in these United States. And we still own the family land. As to wreckers, we got salvage maps older than me. Didn't need no wrecker permit to hunt treasure years ago. Grampas did what they did." Now she waggled the finger in their direction. "You boys have a nice time on the water, but don't go looking for treasure what don't belong to you anyway."

Trying to avert calamity, I pulled the calendar off the wall and stood directly in the firing line between the two tables. "Miss Augusta, Miss Delia, the end of hurricane season is coming up fast. Could you help me pick a date? Plan the End of Hurricane Season party?"

Miss Delia offered me an uncommonly direct look. I'd swear her rheumy gray eyes twinkled a bit. Then she lowered her eyes, folded her hands neatly and buried them in the fabric of her palm frond and bird of paradise muu-muu. Clearly she was waiting for Augusta to answer.

Miss Augusta looked thoughtful for a while. Absently, she twirled the fragment of rope tied at her waist to keep her sun-faded jeans from sliding off her frail hips when she stood. Then a near smile broke through her face, shifting her wrinkles from vertical to horizontal. "I suppose if you need the help, we're obliged to help you. Give it here." And she snatched the calendar out of my hands.

I glanced at the Robert Frost table. The cyclists were long gone. My practiced eye spotted two ten-dollar bills crossed over each other, clamped down by the salt shaker. They hadn't even waited for their food. Still, the money they left would more than cover what they'd ordered and a generous tip besides.

"Need to get past Thanksgiving. Give some of them

7

snowbirds a chance to land." Augusta's skinny finger couldn't quite cover the single digit of the date she chose. "First Saturday in December should do."

Of course we'd held our End of Hurricane Season party on the first Saturday of December each year since Bridgy and I opened the Read 'Em and Eat. Still, I beamed.

"Perfect, absolutely perfect." I slid the calendar from under her bony finger and made a huge production of writing in the date. Then I circled it for good measure.

Miss Delia stretched out her hands on the table, a sure sign that she was working up the enthusiasm to speak. I waited, patiently counting, *one Mississippi, two Mississippi*, in my head. I was at twenty-nine (and halfway through *Mississippi*) when she opened her mouth. I leaned in to hear her whisper. "When do you want us to meet, dearie? You know, to plan?"

Well, I'd set myself up for that one, hadn't I? Before I could answer, an enormous crash echoed from the kitchen, along with a bloodcurdling scream. Then, dead silence.

Bridgy and I both ran, bottlenecking at the kitchen door like a *Saturday Night Live* skit channeling Lucy and Ethel. With a little adjusting, we pushed through the doorway.

Miguel, our chef, was lying on the white tile floor, with a large metal tray covering his stomach, broken crockery scattered everywhere.

As always when excited, he spoke Spanish.

"Chicas, me rompí la pierna."

Pierna—leg. My eyes darted south of the tray and sure enough, Miguel's khakis couldn't hide the fact that his left leg was bent at an odd angle. He had indeed broken his leg.

Bridgy was hyperventilating into her cell phone, urging

the 911 dispatcher to send help. I picked up the tray and was moving the broken dishes away from Miguel when I heard a strange voice from the counter behind us.

"I'd like to pay for this." A wiry man held the current issue of *TIME* magazine up in the air while he dug in one pocket of his fisherman's vest for some cash. I rushed to give him change, anxious to get back to Miguel. As I turned away he spoke again.

"In your parking lot, two ladies were getting into an ancient, beat-up Chevy. One looked a lot like a friend of my mother's from years back. Do you know their names?"

I swiveled my head and took a hard look. Not much to see. Graying stubble on a narrow chin and gaunt cheeks. Under a faded green bucket hat, his aviator sunglasses revealed nothing but the reflection of my own brown eyes, puzzled by his question.

"I'm sorry, but as you can see . . ." I indicated Miguel, lying on the floor, clearly visible through the kitchen doorway.

He took the hint and left.

I looked around. The café was empty. Miss Augusta, Miss Delia and one or two other regulars, although neighborly enough, had packed up and gone home, deciding to stay out of our way while we tended to the mayhem in the kitchen. I walked to the front door and was flipping the sign from "open" to "closed" when a green and white Lee County Sheriff's car pulled in.

Smokey Bear hat in hand, Ryan Mantoni waved as he was getting out of the driver's seat. A native Floridian, born on Pine Island, he was always bragging that he'd been conceived while his parents were fishing on Lovers Key. His mother denies it, but that doesn't stop him from spinning the tale.

Ryan pushed his hat down over his sun-streaked brown hair and said something to the new deputy climbing out of the passenger side of the cruiser. Even at this distance I suspected the deputy had washboard abs. He took off his sunglasses and seemed to inspect me intently. I felt myself flush even as my hand rose to twirl a lock of my always unruly auburn hair. *Good Lord, with Miguel writhing in pain on the kitchen floor, please don't let me get all flirty.*

They walked toward me in military lockstep, and, judging by the way the short sleeves of his uniform shirt hugged his well-developed biceps, I became more convinced that my suspicion regarding his physique was spot-on. Even from half a parking lot away, I could see he would tower over my five feet seven inches. Not many men can make me feel petite.

I was hoping for a quick introduction, but Ryan asked, "What happened?"

I told them about Miguel's fall.

"Sassy Cabot, meet Lieutenant Anthony. He's a new boss in the district, learning the islands."

The lieutenant's smile lit up the parking lot no matter it was broad daylight. "Make it Frank. They really call you Sassy or is that Ryan being Ryan?"

I sighed. "My parents have a sense of humor. My given name is plain old Mary, but my middle name is—"

"Sassafras!" Ryan shouted gleefully, as he opened the café door.

"Hmm." The lieutenant was still eyeing me. "Time will tell if you live up to your name." And he followed Ryan into the café kitchen. I hurried after them, willing myself not to start the hair twirl thing again.

Chapter Two

Sirens blaring, the ambulance rushed toward the mainland. I tried to follow, my rusty, trusty Heap-a-Jeep bobbing and weaving through the traffic on Estero Boulevard. When the ambulance turned onto San Carlos, heading for our anti-quated one-lane-in-each-direction bridge to Fort Myers, cars pulled onto the embankment to let the ambulance pass but immediately filled in behind it like the Gulf washing over the sand at high tide. I fell hopelessly behind.

By the time I got to Health Park Medical Center and found the emergency room, Miguel was on a gurney in a cur-tained alcove, wired to an IV drip. As soon as he saw me, he clawed at my arm and pleaded, "Take me to Miami, mama. I wan' go home."

The attendant assigned to take Miguel up to the OR must have been used to dealing with the power of pain meds. He pulled the gurney away from the wall and said in a soothing voice, "Little Havana, here we come. *Vamos a Miami.*"

Miguel let go of my arm, gave a cheerful wave and went off with his new friend. His heart was bound for home and family; no matter that his leg was going to the operating suite.

Hours dragged by. I alternated between thumbing through old magazines and pacing around the visitors lounge until a surgical intern came to tell me Miguel was out of surgery and doing nicely in the recovery room. And no, I couldn't see him.

I finally got back to the Read 'Em and Eat right after closing. When I opened the door, Bridgy jumped up, planting her hands on her hips. "I've called you a half dozen times. No answer, voice mail, voice mail."

"I turned off my cell at the hospital. I guess I forgot to turn it on again."

"And you never thought to call me? I've been worried sick about Miguel. How do you think I felt when Ryan stopped back after work to ask about Miguel and I had no information?"

She and Ryan were eating Miguel's mega-aromatic *Old Man and the Sea* Chowder. Think red pepper flakes, onion and tarragon slathered on the planks of a fishing pier. Ignoring us, Ryan reached for the plate of crackers set mid-table and crumbled a few into his bowl. He wore his off-duty uniform, baggy shorts and a Fort Myers Beach tee shirt. This one read: "Deputies Do It Safely."

"The hospital called Miguel's sister in Miami, and during one of his more lucid moments, Miguel gave me his cousin Rey's cell number. Remember him? Last Fourth of July? Anyway, he's driving down from Lake Butler."

"Can he cook?" Ryan asked, raising a spoon brimming with bits of grouper and carrots.

"Cook? I don't know." Then I understood. Who was going to make breakfast when we opened in the morning? "Oh. The kitchen."

I folded my arms and looked straight at Bridgy. The café part of Read 'Em and Eat was her idea, and she did fancy herself quite the gourmet cook.

"I can manage for a few days, but with snowbird season right around the corner . . ." She hesitated. "We'll be awfully busy. And I don't know most of Miguel's specials."

I sighed, knowing what was coming.

In her tiniest indoor voice, Bridgy said, "Aunt Ophie."

"Who?" Ryan's eyes swung from Bridgy to me and back again, slightly alarmed by the dread mixed with resignation crossing both our faces.

"My Aunt Ophelia is the best cook on planet Earth, but, well, she's a little different."

"What kind of different?" Ryan rested his spoon on the table.

"Let me," I said. "Three years ago when we first opened, Bridgy's aunt Ophelia offered to come down from Pinetta to help with the cooking until we found a chef. You know how folks round here say that north Florida thinks it is really south Georgia with that y'all southern charm mindset? Living barely south of the Georgia border, Aunt Ophie takes her role as Antebellum Grande Dame to heart."

Ryan gave a "no big deal" shrug.

Bridgy took over. "Get ready to have your cheek patted and be called 'honey chile,' and I wouldn't wear that shirt unless you're willing to sit through a thirty-minute lecture about gentlemanly appearance and behavior. The happy news is you can bring your appetite for southern. We'll have grits and hush puppies aplenty on the menu." She turned to me. "As I recall, you had one of your cutesy book names for the hush puppies. *To Kill a Mockingbird*?"

"Close. Harper Lee Hush Puppies. And don't forget True Grits."

"Like the movie?" Ryan knew his westerns.

"Like the book."

Bridgy laughed at my response. "Sassy doesn't know movies. She only knows books."

"Do so know movies," I retorted. "Both movies. The forty-some-odd-years-ago *True Grit* with John Wayne as Rooster Cogburn and the recent one starring Jeff Bridges. That one revived interest in the 'based on' novel, *True Grit*, by Charles Portis. The movie tie-in edition of the book hit the best seller lists."

Bridgy wrinkled her forehead, gave me her "whatever" look and moved on. "Your boyfriend was here. He heard about Miguel and wanted the 411."

"Boyfriend?" I panicked, afraid Ryan had noticed my getting lost in the dreamy blue eyes of the new lieutenant.

"You know. The reporter with the feminist name. Cady."

Cady Stanton. Irritated as I am by having Sassafras as a middle name, *his* mother named him after nineteenth-century women's rights activist Elizabeth Cady Stanton. I'd often wondered if she'd married Cady's father for the sole purpose of having that last name for her children, Cady and his sister, Elizabeth.

"He's not my boyfriend," I protested automatically.

"You spent a weekend with him in Key West. If he's not your boyfriend, what does that make you?" Bridgy was doing the hands on her hips thing again.

"It was a literary seminar." I waved my arm at the book-shelves. "Books, authors, readings. Anyway, we only traveled together. We had separate rooms."

Ryan guffawed. "You were right, Bridgy. She's all about the books."

There was a loud bang on the door, and as we turned toward it, the face pressed up against the glass window pane screeched.

"I can see you're in there. Open this door."

"Sounds like that lady with the poufy lilac-colored hair. The one who runs the consignment shop."

Ryan nailed it. Rowena Gustavsen. Remembering this morning's book club, I thought, *This can't be good.*

I opened the door and Rowena barged past me, her face nearly as purple as her hair. She dropped a huge lemon-colored purse on the Hemingway table and growled, "Which one of you sent that derelict to me? I demand to know." Chunky plastic bracelets clattered on her wrist as she flung one arm high in the air and dropped it to a dramatic rest on her forehead. "I cannot have such riffraff in my shop. What will my clients think?"

She finally stopped for a breath, followed by a deep sigh.

"Rowena, sit down. Have a cup of tea."

She pulled out a chair, crumpled heavily onto the seat

and propped her elbows on the table. I scurried to put on the kettle, hoping to keep her calm at all costs.

I was reaching for the tea canister when she bellowed, "Sweet tea, if you have it."

I brought a tall glass of sweet tea, with a couple of sugar cookies on a doilied plate. From the moment Rowena came through the door, Bridgy and Ryan were frozen in place. I signaled as discreetly as I could for them to join her, but Bridgy gave an infinitesimal shake of her head, confirming my suspicion that she was at the bottom of Rowena's dilemma, be it real or imagined.

I sat opposite Rowena. After watching her drain the glass dry, I went back to the kitchen and brought out a pitcher of sweet tea and a tray of empty glasses. This could take a while.

I was pouring her refill when Rowena sprang to life again. "I almost called the sheriff." She turned to Ryan. "You know how you're always saying to call if I think something is wrong." She swung back to me. "But he said you sent him, so I decided to ask you first. Glad Ryan is here nonetheless." Her head bobbed an emphatic nod.

"Rowena, who are we talking about?"

"Who did you send to my shop?"

Round and round we go.

"We all support one another's businesses. Could have been anyone."

"Not anyone. That old man. Smells like seaweed. The one who carried the human head around all last year. You sent him to me." The accusation was forceful.

Skully. What would he be doing in the Sand and Shell Emporium?

Bridgy stood up and cleared her throat. "Actually, Rowena, I sent him." She was fidgeting, the fingers on her right hand tugging on her left. "I ordered some earring posts and jeweler's wire from a website and encouraged him to stop using fishing line for the things he makes. I'm convinced his lovely shell and fish bone jewelry will be top sellers. I thought you'd want to market such exquisite items, but if you don't . . ."

"We'll sell them here," I finished.

Bridgy's eyes widened in surprise, but I was not about to waste my night on Rowena's histrionics, so I called her bluff.

"Not so fast." Rowena must have had a vision of dollar bills flying out of her cash register and into ours. "I need time to decide."

"Well, what did you tell Skully?"

"He said his name was Thomas. Thomas Smallwood. I told him I'd think things over and he should come back tomorrow. That way I could have Ryan around if needed."

"And what did you think of his jewelry?"

"Oh, it's magnificent. His wire and shell pendants are elegant; the handiwork is extremely intricate. They are guaranteed to jump off the shelves. He can't possibly make pieces as fast as my clients will buy them."

Ryan spoke for the first time. "Ms. Gustavsen, believe me, Skully is a decent man, just a little out of touch with this century. A few decades after the Civil War, lots of folks began traveling up and down the Gulf, stopping their boats at this island or that, plying their skills. Fishermen. Toolmakers. Tradesmen. It was how they earned a living, and passed down father to son for generations. Times have changed. Skully prefers the old ways. Nothing wrong with that."

Rowena knew the history of the islands better than most. It was part of the sales pitch for her merchandise. I could see she was 95 percent convinced.

"Why do you call him Skully? He said his name is Thomas."

Ryan touched each side of his head with his index fingers and rocked from side to side. Before Rowena realized Skully got the nickname when Lee County deputies found the fifty-year-old skull he'd dug up on Mound Key and stashed in his duffel bag for a few months last winter, Bridgy tapped Ryan on the nose with a rolled-up magazine as if correcting a naughty puppy.

Rowena reached over and poured another glass of sweet tea and began muttering, almost to herself, "Now if only Delia would part with some of the old bric-a-brac cluttering up her house, I could have a banner year; make a nice commission. Stubborn as a mule, she is. Why, she won't even sell her island. Not like she ever spends any time there."

"Island?" I was mystified.

"Down in Ten Thousand Islands. Did you think all that 'we been here forever' talk was blather? Delia's and Augusta's families came here, claimed and settled land forever ago. Long before the E.J. Watson brouhaha, and that happened right after the hurricane of 1910. Between Delia and Augusta, they probably own at least a hundred islands. Most not more than patches of mangroves. Maybe a shell mound or two. Anyway, some resort company took a fancy to one of Delia's islands. She won't even talk to them." Rowena shook her head at the folly of Delia's decision and reached for the last cookie.

"Except for Chokoloskee, those islands are all in one

state or national park or another," Ryan countered. "No one can own them."

Rowena placed her palms on the table and pushed herself to standing. "That might be what you think. Might even be what the government thinks, but I guarantee that Augusta and Delia have papers that say different. And they aren't the only ones. Say, maybe my new jewelry supplier has a deed or two tucked away in that scruffy bag he carries."

At long last we shut the door firmly behind Ryan and Rowena, who were still chattering about the islands and the Everglades. After we wiped down the tables and chairs, I ran the electric broom over the floor while Bridgy did the end-of-the-day kitchen checklist. Stove burners off? Check. Freezer door shut? Check.

I put the broom away and was wiping a barely visible speck off the countertop when I decided to put on my happy face. We'd talked Rowena into consigning jewelry from Skully. Miguel's cousin Rey would be at his bedside tomorrow morning. The worst was behind us.

Bridgy was quick to erase my imaginary smile when she poked her head in the kitchen pass-through and said, "I guess I'll call Aunt Ophie first thing in the morning."

Chapter Three

Thunder rat-tat-tatted like gunfire. I opened one bleary eye. Not thunder. Bridgy banging on my bedroom door.

"We have kitchen duty. The café opens at seven sharp. We've got to go. Put on the coffee. Fire up the grill."

I reached for my night table and smacked the button on my projection clock. Like the Bat Signal in Gotham City, a circle of light beamed on the ceiling, but instead of the shadow of the Caped Crusader my light circled three numbers. 4:45. In. The. Morning.

I threw a pillow at the door. It bounced once and floated silently to the floor. I should've thrown the clock.

"Come on, Sas. Get out of bed."

I grumbled, nothing intelligible, but Bridgy took any sign of life as acquiescence.

"Glad you're up. We going to ride our bikes or are you too tired, poor thing?"

I buried my head in my one remaining pillow. I so wanted to close my eyes for another hour or two, but I accepted my fate and flung back the covers.

"I'm up," I announced to the door. "And I seriously wish we'd bought two tiny but very separate condos instead of sharing this palace you swore would be a growth investment. If I had my own place, you couldn't come wakin' me whenever you feel like it."

"But then you wouldn't have that mind-blowing view. Look out the window. That'll chipper you right up." And I heard her trot away from my door, feeling pleased, I'm sure, that she'd got me to my feet.

Okay, she was right about the view. From here on the fifth floor, my not-quite-floor-to-ceiling bedroom window faced north, showing off the whole of the Gulf of Mexico. Brooklyn girl that I am, I never quite got used to the Matlacha Preserve, with its foliage, green and dense from January through December. Dead ahead, the fishermen on Pine Island already had their lamps lit and were probably filling their thermoses about now. Across Pine Island Sound, other barrier islands— Sanibel, North Captiva, Cayo Costa—jutted into the Gulf with far less electric sparkle. Past those familiar islands, land masses were mere dots to the naked eye, but I knew they led a path straight to the Florida panhandle. I opened the window and stretched my arms high, bent to touch my toes, all the while taking deep breaths of that salty/sweet Gulf air.

It had been a long time since Bridgy and I did the morning setup at the café, but we fell into the old rhythm, Bridgy as the chef, with me as scullery maid.

Fortunately, the breakfast rush was steady but not heavy. Not until January would we have folks waiting in line for tables. Right before eight o'clock someone pulled the chain on the old bronze ship's bell hanging beside our door. It clanged loud enough to wake half of Fort Myers Beach. At a table for four, the two ladies gave a yelp but one of the men laughed. "Don't know a ship's bell when you hear it? Reminds me of my days in the Navy."

The door flew open and Aunt Ophie breezed in, tottering on bright pink heels so high and stylishly strappy that I'm sure I'd know the brand if only I paid attention to such things.

She patted my face with a white gloved hand. "Y'all must be so relieved to see me." She swung a pink patent leather purse right at my stomach. It took a second for me to realize it was my job to take custody. Well-mannered ladies didn't carry purses indoors. It had been a while, so I'd forgotten the "well-mannered ladies" conventions. Bet I'd be reminded of all of them within two, three hours, tops.

"I would have been here sooner, but the Publix on San Carlos don't open 'til seven. I didn't 'spect y'all to have the ingredients for my buttermilk pie." She looked around, pleased that she had the attention of the entire room. "No one makes it good as I can." She winked at the retired sailor. "My dear departed and most sainted husband always said it tastes like kisses from heaven."

I was so busy wondering which husband, the one who departed for the great beyond, or the one who departed for Mobile with his manicurist, that I almost missed her hand fluttering in the direction of the door.

"Sassy, my things are in the car. Bring in the supermarket bags first. Freshness, you know. And where—there she is!"

Bridgy came out of the kitchen, plopped a couple of hot breakfasts on the counter and practically sang. "Did I hear my dazzling Aunt Ophie? How did you know? How did you know we need your help? Do you have a crystal ball? Tarot cards?"

Ophie blushed and opened her arms wide. While they were doing the big ole bear hug thing, Bridgy pointed to the plates and mouthed, *Christie. Pancakes for the lady.*

There's a strong family resemblance in the way they order me around. I stashed the pink purse under the counter. While I was serving the food at the Christie table, I heard Ophie say, "Facebook, you darlin' girl. I saw your status last night about Miguel's broken leg. I knew you'd need me to come a'running. I packed up my things and left Pinetta not long after midnight. I-75 was empty. Only me and a string of long-distance truckers. Would have been here earlier, if that sorry excuse for a Publix had been open. And of course that bridge. One lane on, one lane off the island. Need a new bridge is all I'm saying." She primped her oat-colored shoulder-length hair, confident that one word from her and the town council would widen the bridge in a week or two.

When I struggled through the door lugging the bounty of Ophie's shopping, she was seated at Emily Dickinson, sipping a glass of sweet tea. Taking no notice that my arms were filled with her grocery bags, she smiled. "Sassy, honey, could you get me a sprig o' mint?"

Without so much as a "hey," a gray-haired man with

bronze leathery skin wearing torn cutoffs and a rumpled camouflage tee shirt followed me in and placed his thermos on the counter. He dropped his duffel bag next to his feet. The duffel gave me the creeps. He'd carried that human skull around for months, and when he finally gave it up, I never understood why he didn't trash the bag. I headed to the kitchen to unpack the groceries but gave him a cheery "Be right with you." Skully shook his head and pointed to Bridgy coming through the door carrying mint sprigs on a dish.

After I put away Aunt Ophie's groceries (did she really think we needed twelve quarts of buttermilk?), I crossed back into the dining room and roamed from table to table with an orange-topped pot of decaf in one hand and a brown-topped pot of regular in the other. Standing at the counter, Skully and Bridgy were deep in conversation, while, from her seat at Emily Dickinson, Aunt Ophie was watching them intently. Hopefully, she was admiring her niece; Skully didn't strike me as husband material if she was looking for number three.

I was distracted when Judge Harcroft came in. Even though each and every morning he ate the Hammett Ham 'n Eggs over hard, I still had to wait, order pad in hand, while he pretended to decide. The day may come when he asks for the Agatha Christie Soft-Boiled Eggs over *Catcher in the Rye* Toast, but it won't be in this century.

The cook was still sitting with her aunt. I pulled the judge's order off my pad and held it out to her.

"Here you go."

"Duty calls. You sit here and rest, Aunt Ophie. I'll be right back."

I followed her, wondering aloud about her conversation with Skully.

"Poor guy. He wanted to tell me Rowena seemed a little distant when they spoke. I told him to go on over to the Emporium because we straightened it all out last night. He's on his way to see her now. Here comes Miss Augusta. I wonder where Miss Delia is. I'd love to ask her about the island Rowena mentioned."

Augusta stopped short when she saw Aunt Ophie sitting at Emily Dickinson. I ran over to do a quick introduction before Augusta could start booming about "her table."

"Here you go, Miss Augusta. Have a seat. You remember Bridgy's aunt Ophelia. She's helping us while poor Miguel is recovering from his fall."

"Don't look like much help, sitting around drinking sweet tea." Augusta's baritone filled the room. The regulars paid no attention, but the vacationers were startled and turned to glare at the great hulk who was shouting querulously. The disbelief on their faces when they realized all that noise came from diminutive Augusta was comical.

"And where is Miss Delia, this morning?"

Augusta shook her head. "Delia knows what's expected. If we're going out in the morning, we decide the time the night before. I drive because her eyes are good for nothing but the big-screen TV." She emphasized with her arms spread wider than a fisherman lying about the one that got away. "We give up our bikes the year she turned seventy-three and I turned seventy-six. Knees gone. Anyway, I expect she stands on the porch. I pull up. She gets in the car. If she ain't on the porch, I tap the horn. Count to fifty and pull away. Used to count to twenty but we move slower

25

now. Guess she changed her mind." She pointed to me. "You know how Delia is—flighty."

Aunt Ophie patted Augusta's hand. "Honey chile, I understand. I have a friend like that back in Pinetta, that's up in Madison County, you know. Few miles south of the Georgia border. Sassy, get my friend—Augusta, is it? Lovely name—get my friend Augusta a glass of sweet tea."

I'd never seen Augusta drink sweet tea, but when she didn't demur, I went to the kitchen. I placed the glass in front of her, and Ophie offered the plate of mint. "Have a sprig. Adds a little zing to the tea." On my way back to the kitchen I heard a rap on the window. I looked over and Cady Stanton was waving frantically for me to come outside. I shook my head and signaled him to come in, but he was insistent that I come out. Cady is way too gentle to insist on anything, so I wondered what could be so earth-shattering. Still, I signaled I'd be right there. I pushed the kitchen door, told Bridgy I'd be in the parking lot and hurried away without listening to her questions and objections.

Cady was pacing back and forth with his hands behind his back, and his chin buried so deep in his chest that his hunched shoulders grazed the tips of his earlobes. A gust of wind tossed his sandy hair this way and that, but he didn't reach up to slick his hair back in place, something he normally does a hundred times a day. He stopped in front of me. His face was so unnaturally pale that his freckles stood out like freshly painted dots on a Raggedy Andy doll. He threw his shoulders back and stretched to his full six feet. His thin frame looked a tad scrawny. Absently, I wondered why I suddenly thought him scrawny, and unbidden, the biceps of Ryan's new lieutenant flitted through my mind.

"Sassy, Miss Delia is dead and Miss Augusta is missing."

I actually laughed at his rude joke. "Sometimes that newspaper reporter's humor of yours is a little too dark for me." I pointed through the window. "Miss Augusta is sitting right there, talking to Bridgy's aunt."

Cady peered through the window, and a look of relief swept across his face just as the wind blew, and this time he did slide his hand over his hair to push it back in place.

"Don't be coming around with your tall tales, Cady. I don't like it." I tucked a stray hair off his forehead, one he'd missed. I hoped my touch would soften my words.

Cady put his hands on my shoulders. "Sassy, you have to be strong. The sheriff notified the *News* about Delia's death a few minutes ago and said they can't find Augusta. I came here because I know how much you care about those two old ladies. Thank God Augusta is okay. But Delia is definitely dead." He pulled me to his chest, and, as I noticed a time or two before, his shoulder was comforting, and not a bit scrawny. He kissed the top of my head and said, softly, "And now someone has to tell Augusta."

Chapter Four ||||||||||

I wiped my eyes on the hem of my apron and took a couple of deep breaths trying to compose myself. Cady was still talking about ways we could gently break the horrible news to Augusta, but I was grappling with the newly empty space in my heart and the agitation swirling in my stomach. I prayed I wouldn't heave.

The four vacationers came outside, laughing and joking as if nothing out of the ordinary had happened. And I supposed that to them, nothing had. As they lifted their bikes off the rack, the onetime sailor yelled to Cady, "You're a lucky man, fella. Your girlfriend serves a great breakfast. We'll be back; you can bet on it."

They mounted their bikes and looped toward the boulevard in a crooked semicircle, waving as they glided down the driveway. I managed a halfhearted salute in return and whispered to Cady, "I guess it's time."

As we came through the door, Bridgy, who was clearing tables, raised an inquiring eyebrow and I head-nodded toward the kitchen.

Aunt Ophie was chattering away, and I was surprised that Miss Augusta seemed engaged in the conversation. At least she hadn't fallen asleep or shouted at Ophie to stop rambling, both things she'd done more than once in mid-conversation. The judge's newspaper rustled as he turned a page. A couple of honeymooners who had turned up for a late-ish breakfast every morning for the past three days were holding hands and gazing soulfully into each other's eyes at Barbara Cartland in the far corner. I was grateful for the quiet.

Cady and I followed Bridgy into the kitchen. I waited for her to scrape the dishes and deposit them in the soaking sink. One look at my face told her I had bad news, which may be why she braced her back against the sink, elbows tucked over the metal lip.

I started to tear up again so I choked out the words. "It's Miss Delia. She's dead."

Bridgy slumped, leaning more heavily on the sink. "Her heart? A stroke?"

Cady shook his head. "Not sure yet. The mail carrier saw her lying on the floor through the screen door this morning when he delivered the mail. He called 911 and the EMTs declared her at the scene."

He was speaking in newsman shorthand but we got the message. Miss Delia was dead before the emergency medical technicians arrived.

"Augusta?"

"We're going to tell her now. Could you call your aunt in here, so we can speak to Augusta privately?"

Bridgy stuck her head out the kitchen pass-through, called Ophie and ducked back into the kitchen. "She'll know something is wrong if she gets a good look at me."

Ophie walked into the kitchen asking how soon we wanted buttermilk pie on the menu, but when she took a look at us she whispered, "Dear Lord."

Cady took my hand for the short, dreadful walk to the dining room so we could break the devastating news to an unsuspecting Augusta.

As we sat down, Augusta boomed, "Nice enough, that Ophelia. Says she's been here before, not that I remember her. Look at you two, like death warmed over. Must have something awful serious to say."

I reached out to pat her hand and she didn't pull away.

"Miss Augusta, you know how much we love you and Miss Delia." I blinked back the tears that welled up, unbidden. "It is really hard for me to tell you but, well, there's been an accident. It's Miss Delia."

We watched her face change from puzzled to concerned. "Delia? Delia's hurt? Please say she didn't break her hip. At our age . . ."

I squeezed her hand. "It's more serious than that."

Always sharp as a crab's claw, Augusta said the words I couldn't. "Delia's dead?"

I nodded and started to cry. Cady spoke in a sweet, comforting tone. "We don't have any details yet, but she was in her own home, which is where I think she'd want to be."

Augusta looked directly at him. "Did this happen before I stopped by her house this morning?"

I could see guilt starting to mix with the sorrow in her face. I wanted to cut it short before it gripped her entirely.

"We don't have any details."

She nodded.

Bridgy came out of the kitchen with a plate of muffins and silently set them in front of Augusta.

"So you heard about Delia." Augusta started to stand, wobbled and sat back in her seat.

Bridgy leaned down, gave Augusta a kiss on her cheek and squeezed her shoulder. Then she asked the honeymooners if they needed anything else.

The new husband tore his eyes away from his bride long enough to pay the check, and they walked out with arms entwined around each other's waists.

We sat wordlessly at Emily Dickinson until Augusta said, "Well, I guess I better get on home."

Cady took charge.

"Sassy will drive your car, and I'll follow along, if that's all right." He rose and stood next to Augusta's chair and offered his arm.

Augusta rested a tentative hand on his wrist and then gripped with determination. She stood and Cady began to slowly shepherd her to the ancient blue Chevy parked outside.

I stayed a few steps behind and threw a question mark to Bridgy, who shooed me along with a flap of her hands, saying, "Aunt Ophie will help me here. Call if you need anything."

Augusta surrendered her car keys but not before saying, "You take it careful, Sassy. Car's a bit delicate."

When we pulled out of the parking lot, Cady was still sitting in his car, chattering into his cell phone. I hoped he wouldn't be too far behind us. Augusta was looking more and more tired, and I feared I'd need help getting her up the porch stairs and into the house.

We drove a few blocks in silence. The shocks and struts had long given way, and the car bounced and rocked if it rolled over as much as a pebble. I could feel my fists tightening on the steering wheel, but I knew it wasn't the car that had me agitated. When we turned onto Augusta's block, I was surprised to see a sheriff's car parked alongside her mailbox. Ryan Mantoni was leaning on the fender, and we watched him turn his head to speak into the two-way radio he wore on his shoulder. Then he walked toward us as I turned in to Augusta's driveway. He gave me a quick nod, went to the passenger side of the car and opened the door for Augusta, offering his hand in the process.

I heard him say how sorry he was for her loss, and he kissed her gently on her cheek. For the first time, I saw a tear glisten in Augusta's eyes.

We climbed the four rickety stairs to the weather-beaten porch as if they were the final steps to the top of Mount Rainier. Ryan pulled open the old wooden screen door, and I handed Augusta's key ring back to her.

She put the keys in her pocket and pushed the house door open. "Don't ever lock it but at night. Nothing worth stealing. And keys get lost, you know."

She pointed left. "There's the parlor. Have a seat."

Then she shuffled farther along the hallway to a scarred pigeonhole desk leaning against the back wall. I watched her rummage in a compartment and pull out a book.

I'd only been in Augusta's house a few times before, usually dropping off books for a club meeting. Once I came by to pick up donations for the flea market supporting the

Christmas Toy Fund. This was the first time I had a chance to look around the outsized but sparsely furnished living room. A couple of rattan settees piled with flowered cushions, a lone recliner and a small box-shaped television all touched the edges of a beige sisal area rug. A coffee table of etched glass with a base made of driftwood sat atop the rug.

"Sit down, sit down." Augusta gestured to the settees and settled herself into the recliner. I was plumping a cushion to support my back when there was a soft knock on the screen door. Ryan offered to answer and came back with Cady carrying takeaway boxes.

"Bridgy sent your lunch." He raised the box in his left hand. "She wants you to keep your strength up. And the other box is cookies and pastries for your friends who stop by. Where's the kitchen?"

I jumped up and reached for the boxes. "I'll take care of it. Miss Augusta, can I get you anything?"

No response. Since we'd arrived at the house, Augusta seemed to have gotten even smaller. Once she'd sunk into her seat, she looked for all the world like a child sitting in a grown-up's chair. I thought her skin was losing color, and I could see the energy had faded from her eyes.

I touched Augusta's shoulder. "Perhaps you'd like a drink. Water? Tea?"

Augusta leaned her head forward as though it was reaching for a thought. "Look in the dining room breakfront. Ought to be a bottle of Buffalo Trace corn whiskey. I'll take a couple of fingers."

Ryan quickly covered his guffaw with a cough.

"Either of you boys want a taste?"

Cady and Ryan politely declined. Augusta told me to

33

feel free to help myself, cautioning that I might want to add some water if I wasn't used to "likker."

I easily found the half-full bottle with the pale gray label featuring a fiercely charging buffalo and brought it into the kitchen. The drinking glasses were in the third cabinet I tried. I took one, wrapped two fingers around the base and poured the amber liquid to about a finger and a half. More than enough.

I was putting the bottle back in the breakfront when I heard a new but vaguely familiar male voice and wondered if I should have left the whiskey in the kitchen to serve to folks stopping by to console Augusta.

I stepped into the parlor just as the vaguely familiar voice expressed sincere condolence to Miss Augusta.

Lieutenant Frank Anthony.

He was standing with his back to the doorway but turned at the sound of my step, gave me a curt nod and continued speaking.

"The sheriff's department is sorry to intrude at such a difficult time, but we have a few questions to ask you."

I slid past him and handed Augusta her glass of bourbon. She set the book she'd been holding on the coffee table and reached for the glass. Examining it with a critical eye, she said, "You must have a child's hands if you think this is two fingers of corn likker. I might be needing a refill."

Cady jumped in. "I've always thought Sassy had elegant hands."

Frank Anthony shot Cady a look as if seeing him for the first time and not really liking what he saw. Then he said, "Miss Maddox, we'll let you know all about Sassy's hands as soon as we take her fingerprints."

Flustered, I automatically clasped my hands behind my back.

Ryan started a hoot, remembered why we were here and cut himself off but couldn't quite contain a wink and a grin.

Miss Augusta sipped her bourbon, ignoring us all. Finally she picked up the black notebook and held it so we could all see the faded gilt letters on the front that spelled ADDRESSES.

"I'm sorry but I got family and friends to telephone, arrangements to make. Questions'll have to wait for another time."

The lieutenant and Ryan exchanged a nearly invisible glance, and from the look of it, Augusta was about to lose control of the discussion. I took a step closer to her chair, ready to help her cope.

Frank gave a nearly imperceptible nod, and Ryan cleared his throat. "Miss Augusta, it pains me to tell you that Miss Delia's death was not an accident. She was killed by person or persons unknown. We are here as part of the official murder investigation team, and as such, we need to speak to you alone. And that needs to happen right now."

Augusta closed her eyes, and for a second I feared we might lose her there and then. When she opened her eyes, she drained her glass dry and asked, "You sure?"

Ryan nodded.

Augusta turned to me. "Sassy, I'm going to need that refill now. One finger'll be plenty."

Chapter Five |||||||||

I picked up her glass and left the room. When I brought it
back, Frank was sitting in the seat I had previously occupied near Augusta and Ryan was standing at attention next
to the doorway, as if ready to block the exit if she tried to
escape. Cady was nowhere to be seen. I handed Augusta
her one finger of bourbon then stood at her side, uncertain
where I should sit, what I should do. Frank looked out the
front window, just over his right shoulder.

"Your reporter friend is on the lawn. No sense you keeping him waiting."

He was sending me packing. Nice. I hesitated, not willing to leave Augusta, who quickly resolved my quandary.

"Sassy, could you stay around until we're done here?
I'm going to need a little help sorting things out."

I flashed a triumphant look at Frank Anthony.

"Of course."

But when I moved to sit down, he went all official on me. "This interview is private. You have to leave. If you wish, we'll let you know when we're done."

I couldn't resist telling Augusta that I'd be right outside and would come back in an instant if she needed me.

As I walked past Ryan, he whispered, "Sorry," which didn't help my battered ego one bit.

Cady was leaning on his car, cell phone glued to his ear. As I came closer, I could see that he was listening intently, his brow knitted in a furrow of concentration.

He thanked whoever was on the other end and stuffed his phone into the tan leather case threaded on his belt.

"It's pretty bad." He opened the passenger door of his car. "I'll tell you what I can on the way back."

"I'm not going back. Augusta wants me to stay."

He nodded. "Makes sense. Okay, here is what we know so far. Someone knocked Delia to the floor, smothered her with some kind of fabric-y thing and ransacked pretty much her entire house. No one has a clue as to why, but the inquiry only just started."

My stomach pitched like a twelve-foot sailboat on a stormy sea and I felt my knees buckle. Kind, sweet Delia Batson was pummeled and suffocated. And for what? To steal the family silver? If there even was family silver. Cady caught me as I started to fold and guided me to the passenger seat of his car. He reached into an ice chest on the rear floor and offered me a bottle of coolish water. I accepted gratefully.

I took a long drink then heaved a deep sigh. "It doesn't make any sense."

Cady agreed. "I always wanted to be a newsman. Freedom

of the press. Keep the world informed. But when the story hits this close to home . . ."

He shook his head. There was nothing left to say.

We shared the silence for a while and then he asked, "What about Augusta? She and Delia always seemed a pair of harmonizing opposites. Filling in each other's gaps, as it were. How will Augusta manage?"

Mourn the dead; help the living, I thought. Always a compelling challenge.

"We'll comfort her. All of her friends will get together and form a support group."

Cady shook his head. "You know how independent she is. Augusta would never take to having anyone interfere with the way she lives her life."

"Believe me, she'll never know," I boasted with more confidence than I felt. It wouldn't be easy to fool Augusta, but I knew it would be necessary to keep her on track.

Cady looked at his watch. "Listen, I hate to leave you alone out here . . ."

"I know. You have to hit the keyboard. Get going. If anyone is going to write this story, I'm glad it's you. Delia knew you liked her. She once whispered to Bridgy that she thought you had the ways of an old-fashioned gentleman. She meant it as quite the compliment."

Cady doffed an imaginary hat then furled and flourished it through the air with the deep bow of a seventeenth-century courtier.

"Thank you, m'lady."

In spite of the horror of the day, he brought a smile to my lips. That was Cady's special gift.

"Not quite that old-fashioned. I think she was aiming a few centuries closer in time."

"I'll stop by the Read 'Em and Eat after work. See you there?"

I nodded. "By the time Ryan and his crony leave, Augusta will probably be tired and pushing me out the door to follow along behind them, but I think I should offer to stay with her, at least for a while. There's so much to do."

Cady climbed into his car and drove off. He waved when he reached the corner and then disappeared around it, leaving me standing alone on Augusta's lawn. I looked up and down the street, which migrated east toward the placid water of Estero Bay. Like most residential streets in Fort Myers Beach, the lawns were neat and the houses summery. The porches tended to have a pastel Adirondack chair or two, backrests fitted with oversized pillows decorated with a seashell or palm tree motif. Typical cozy Florida, the colors were muted and sandy soft. As a Brooklyn girl, I still found it hard to believe that life could be so comfortably low-key. Leisurely and serene . . . until now.

I took another sip of water, tightened the cap on the bottle and decided to sit on Augusta's front steps. Her porch swing was right outside the living room window, but it wasn't worth the comfort of a cushiony seat to risk taking guff from Frank Anthony, who'd surely accuse me of listening in where I wasn't wanted. I'd sit on the creaky wooden steps until long after my butt fell asleep before I'd give him anything to say.

I kept myself occupied by composing a to-do list and was on number three—help the choirmaster pick out appropriate hymns—when Augusta got tired of speaking softly.

"I can't waste no more time talking with you. There's lots of work to be done, folks to call."

I could picture Augusta waving her address book in Lieutenant Anthony's face.

I heard the murmur of both men trying to soothe her into continuing to cooperate, but she wasn't having it.

I jumped to my feet when I heard her yell, "Sassy. Get Sassy in here. And you two can leave."

I suspected Frank Anthony wasn't used to being dismissed. Personally, I thought it would do him good.

I was still standing at the bottom of the stairs when Ryan opened the door and head-nodded me inside.

I couldn't quite suppress a triumphant grin. Ryan responded with a quick wink, and then we both resumed our somber faces and walked into the living room.

Frank rose from his seat and placed a business card on the coffee table in front of Augusta, who was still hugging the address book for dear life. She turned her head away, clearly indicating that she was done with him, but he persisted.

"We'll need to continue this conversation when you are feeling up to it. Maybe later in the day."

"Ain't talking no more without a friend by my side. Or do I need one of those television lawyers?"

Ryan and I exchanged glances. The fleeting vision of Augusta negotiating with one of the countless expensively dressed attorneys who solicited business during the commercial breaks on daytime television boggled the mind.

Frank Anthony stood a little straighter, like he was

stiffening his spine, and then proceeded to put on the most bureaucratic show I'd ever seen. As if Augusta were an errant child, he explained every American's right to counsel, the difference between a lawyer and a friend, and most insultingly, said he was sorry to inform her that until they narrowed the pool of suspects, it was wisest to interview all the friends and family members of the victim separately.

Augusta inhaled until her face turned nearly purple.

I heard Ryan mutter, "Uh-oh."

And then, just as quickly, she deflated and gave a slight nod. "I suppose we have to do what's right for Delia, even if it's a waste of your time. Delia wasn't killed by any friend or family. I'm sure of that."

The two deputies said their good-byes to Augusta, ignored me and left. As I closed the screen door behind them, I heard Ryan say, "Well that wasn't so bad."

I couldn't hear the lieutenant's response, but it was a safe bet that he wasn't as sanguine as Ryan. Frank Anthony didn't strike me as a man who was used to not getting his way.

I stepped into the living room and Augusta was holding up her glass.

"Sassy, I could use a glass of water. There's a pitcher in the fridge."

I was relieved she wasn't looking for more Buffalo Trace. I went to the kitchen, found two clean glasses and filled them with ice cubes and water. There was half a lemon in the vegetable drawer. I cut it and put a slice in each glass, then I took out a stem of grapes and a few strawberries, washed them, rolled them in a paper towel and arranged the fruit on a paper plate. I found a round blue tray with a pink flamingo painted in the center and carried our fruit and water, along with a few paper napkins, into the living room.

Augusta looked tired but she brightened at the sight of the fruit, and for the first time she let go of the address book, placing it to the right of the tray.

"Thanks for fixin' us a nice snack. I am feeling a might peckish."

We sat in silence, eating fruit and sipping water. Suddenly an earsplitting *kee yarr* shattered the peace. I remembered when Bridgy and I first met Ryan. He'd come into the Read 'Em and Eat and was introducing himself as our local deputy on patrol when a *kee yarr* exploded in the parking lot. I thought someone was being attacked and screaming for help. I couldn't understand why Ryan hadn't run out the door to see what was going on, but he explained the piercing screech was nothing more than the cry of the red-shouldered hawks who nest all over the island in the coastal woodlands. Now when I hear the hawks cry, it's a welcome sound of home.

Augusta picked up a napkin and wiped her mouth with more grace than I'd noticed her use in the past, and sat back in her chair.

She looked thoughtful. I wondered if she'd fully absorbed all that had happened or if it was now beginning to sink in.

"I'm going to need a bit of help. With Delia gone so quick, there's lots to do."

She noticed my eyes slue to the address book and took my meaning.

"Nope. I can make the calls. Better that way. Delia's

nephews wouldn't take kindly to getting a call from a stranger."

Nephews?

"But I'm going to need you to take on the important chores. Things I can't do because I'll be tied up with the paperwork and the funeral and such."

I nodded, not at all sure what could be more important than seeing Miss Delia laid properly to rest surrounded by family and friends sadly saying good-bye. But whatever Augusta wanted, I'd make sure it was done. I had a vague idea that she'd need help with shopping, cooking and perhaps I could even lend a hand hostessing the post-funeral meal. Food wasn't my area of expertise, but Bridgy would help. And Ophie.

"Of course. Tell me what you need. I'm available for whatever you want me to do. Everyone is."

It was important that Augusta knew she wasn't alone. Her friends and neighbors would do whatever we could to make this tragedy bearable. In my wildest dreams I never could have imagined what she wanted.

"I need you and Bridgy and whoever else you think can help us to search the island and find them who killed Delia. Then we'll show those rascals some of grampa's island justice.

"Now let me get to who needs calling."

Chapter Six |||||||||||

The next few hours were such a blur I barely had time to wonder what "grampa's island justice" could possibly entail. Tarring and feathering crossed my mind, along with an old-fashioned wooden stockade.

Augusta moved resolutely from one chore to another as if she were ticking off the items on a mental list of things to be done. I hovered around, responding to her modest requests. She asked me to look up some phone numbers and to check the kitchen for finger foods, make a shopping list, things of that sort. When she was occupied, I was free to wander off to do anything I thought would be helpful, like making a pitcher of sweet tea and giving the company dishes a rinse in case they hadn't been used for a while. The china pattern reflected Augusta's sharp personality. The stark white dinner plates were nearly round but had twelve straight edges that met at tiny points with a raised rose design. I flipped to the back of one plate. Rosenthal. Germany. Maria pattern. Somehow I expected even Augusta's best tableware to be more contemporary and certainly less expensive. Bridgy would love these dishes.

I kept one ear open, following Augusta's phone conversations, so I could appear instantly if she got rattled. Apparently there were two nephews down in Everglades City, neither of whom seemed to respond with any great sorrow to the news of their Aunt Delia's death. At least that was the impression from Augusta's end of the telephone calls. Still, Augusta bullied them until it was agreed that one would say the eulogy and the other would sing a hymn, which pleased Augusta to no end.

"The young one sings in his church choir. I heard him a few times. Nice strong voice. Not feeble-voiced like Delia."

After speaking to family members, Augusta dialed the Michael J. Beech Funeral Home, colloquially called the "Rest in Beech" by longtime island residents. I was thankful Fern Lester answered the phone. Fern was a regular at several of our book clubs and knew Augusta well enough to give the help she needed without bumping up against Augusta's crusty independent streak. They were chatting about floral arrangements garnished with seashells when I heard footsteps on the porch. Pastor John Kendall was balancing a covered glass casserole dish firmly against his chest and holding a bouquet of flowers. He was about to tap on the wooden frame of the door with an elbow when he saw me through the screen.

"Jocelyn made a seven bean salad. Said it will last in the refrigerator for any number of days." I took the casserole dish, and he thrust the flowers toward me.

I shook my head, pointed to the living room doorway and whispered, "She's talking to Fern. They've been on awhile. Should be wrapping up soon. Would you like to wait in the dining room? I made some sweet tea."

His head gave one quick bob up and down, which I took to be a yes, especially when he followed it with, "Hotter than usual for November."

When I brought in his glass of tea, he was still holding the flowers and Augusta was still on the phone. My thought was to have him present the flowers directly to her. Hopefully she'd admire them, and then I'd take them into the kitchen, find a vase and take my time arranging them, giving Augusta and Pastor John a chance to talk. Pastor looked uncomfortable holding the outsized bunch of white and yellow flowers that were nearly overwhelmed by a profusion of island greens. I took the bouquet and laid it sideways on the table, with the blossoms hanging over the edge.

"Thanks." He sounded a wee bit chagrined. "I was afraid I'd crush them if I put them down, and those are the last of this year's asters and yellow buttons. We struggle to keep the church garden filled with native wildflowers."

Proud of the churchyard that perennially won the Natural Public Garden Award from the local Rotary Club, he puffed his chest like a bantam rooster; then, remembering why he'd brought the flowers, he raised one bushy gray eyebrow and lowered his voice. "How is Augusta doing?"

"Needing a prayer or two with Delia dead and all," Augusta rumbled from the doorway.

I hurried to her side and tried to steer her back to the living room and her comfortable chair, but she jerked away with a strength that contradicted her size. "I can sit right here, thank you."

She pulled a chair out from the dining table and plunked down hard on the seat. "Glad you're here, Pastor. We got work."

Pastor John struggled to express his condolence, but Augusta brushed him away like a swarm of no-see-ums. "Lots to do. We need to get Delia's funeral service exactly right."

Not one to give up, Pastor tried to hand her the large yellow and white spray of flowers, but Augusta pushed them off to me and started outlining her plans.

As I took the flowers to the kitchen, I heard Augusta telling Pastor to have the organist practice "I'll Fly Away." I smiled. As if practice would be needed. I'd listened to that plaintively joyful hymn at nearly every funeral I'd attended since coming south.

I puttered around the kitchen, checking supplies and making lists until I heard another knock at the door. Augusta boomed, "Come on in."

John's wife, Jocelyn, opened the screen door, and I was surprised to see that she was carrying a straw basket covered with a gaily striped dish towel.

"The muffins weren't quite ready when John came over with the bean salad so I had to stay behind for a bit." She sounded contrite, as if not showing up with two courses of a meal at the same time was a severe failing. However contentious Jocelyn might be at book club meetings, when circumstances required, she habitually slipped right into her role as docile pastor's wife.

"I wanted to bring everything at once, but John was in such a hurry. Pastoral duties and all. Still, a clergyman's wife gets used to having to rush when the unfortunate happens."

"What's all that whispering out there?" Augusta banged her hand on the table like a schoolteacher demanding silence.

Jocelyn startled. "It's me, Miss Augusta. I brought some muffins."

"Thanks for your kindness, but Pastor and me have plans to make. We need quiet."

I nearly giggled at the stricken look on Jocelyn's face. She was having trouble staying in her clergy spouse role. I pushed her into the kitchen and closed the door.

"If we keep it low, we should be able to sit in here. Can I get you a glass of tea?"

Jocelyn set the muffins on a placemat in the center of the scarred wooden table and sat gingerly on the edge of a rickety chair. She glanced at the door as if she feared Augusta would barrel through and toss us out into the road if we disturbed her again. I moved the pitcher of sweet tea right in front of her and she nodded.

I set out glasses, poured the tea and sat, grateful for the opportunity to relax for a few minutes.

Jocelyn took a sip or two and then leaned back in her chair. She pulled a bright blue fan out of her purse and slid it open, revealing a large white ibis holding its head high, with its long, thin beak pointing majestically to an orange sun. She flapped the fan in front of her face while using a tissue to tap at her brow.

She dropped the tissue on the table and gave a wry smile. "Soon enough, Sassy. Soon enough you'll be flashing and sweating and wondering where your waistline has gone. Count your blessings for the years between now and then. The day will come when an hour in the kitchen with the oven on is like working in a blasting furnace."

I nodded in sympathy. I'd often heard these same complaints from my mother. I bit my tongue before I said that out loud.

After a moment of silence in memory of her declining estrogen, Jocelyn folded her fan and leaned across the table whispering as though we were coconspirators.

"I know you were close to Delia. Tell me what happened?"

My mind sifted through the bits I'd picked up from Cady and sorted what I could comfortably say. "Well, the mail carrier found her this morning. She was . . . she was already beyond help."

I hesitated, still trying to decide what to reveal, but Jocelyn heaved a loud, impatient sigh. "That's old news, Sassy." With a flutter of her fan, she dismissed my reluctance to say more. "I want to know how she died." She snapped the fan shut and tapped my forearm sharply. "Everyone knows you're on the friendly side with the newspaper reporter." She arched her eyebrows to let me know her definition of "friendly." "If he knows something, you know it, too. Now tell me." And she rapped my knuckles with the fan.

Much as I cherished living on this island paradise, the lack of personal privacy often drove me crazy. If you sneezed in Bowditch Point Park, people as far south as Lovers Key were soon calling to say *Gesundheit*.

Searching for a response less vague than *Cady's just a friend. Why would he tell me anything?* I was saved by

Augusta's summons. She had me call Fern to let her know that she and Pastor were ready to leave for the funeral parlor, but Fern was finishing up with another client and said she'd call Pastor as soon as she was free.

Back in the kitchen, Jocelyn had drained her glass and was standing by the table smoothing her beige linen skirt with both hands; the fan was no longer in sight, which, since I was starting to view it as weapon, was fine with me.

"Never let it be said that a pastor's wife is less than honest. You may be tight with information, but I am obligated to tell you what I know. That skull man? The itinerant? He's been hanging around Delia's house more often than not. Does your news-writing beau know about that? And the sheriff? Did anyone bother to tell the sheriff? I'd say you have some work to do, Sassy. You owe it to Delia."

And she turned on the clunky heels of her open-toed tan sandals and charged through the kitchen door. I followed in time to hear her say to the pastor, "See you at home, John." It sounded more like a threat than a welcome. Poor man.

I was wiping the kitchen tabletop when Augusta called me back into the dining room. Her face was sunken as if she had suddenly lost all her back teeth, and there were cavernous shadows under her eyes. In the few hours since Cady and I told her about Delia, Augusta had aged ten years. I prayed the next few days wouldn't kill her. Augusta asked Pastor to give us a few minutes alone. He excused himself, saying he'd be on the porch if we needed him. Augusta offered me a chair.

"Sassy, you've been a true friend and I'm sure going to call on you again, but me and Pastor have to make the tough arrangements with Fern and Mr. Beech down at the funeral parlor. I'm going to be busy, so I need you to take care of things for me."

I squeezed her hand and nodded gently. I would do whatever she needed to help her get through these trying times. Of course I was still thinking more in terms of notifying folks and keeping the house neat and the kitchen well stocked during the wake and funeral. But Augusta continued to focus on finding the killer, or killers. Worse, she was sure she knew exactly who they were.

"Find me them wish-we-were-wrecker boys and the man that's running them on these islands. They're looking for treasure, no matter it's not theirs to find or to keep. Delia knew a lot about the old days and where things are hid. I think them boys tried to find out from her and the talking moved to pushing and shoving."

I gasped. If Jocelyn had left me unsure of what to say, Augusta left me downright speechless.

From the porch Pastor John called through the screen door, "I spoke to Fern. They are ready to see us, Miss Augusta."

She put her hands on the table and pushed herself up with the exhaustive effort of a crew hoisting a beached whale back to the sea. She grabbed on to me so suddenly that I feared she'd lost her balance. I leaned in to steady her. Then she whispered in my ear.

"Find them wreckers."

Chapter Seven ⅲⅲⅲⅲⅲⅲⅲⅲⅲⅲ

I walked Augusta outside and handed her over to Pastor John, but not before I insisted she lock her front door. After they drove away I sank down on Augusta's front steps for the second time in a few short hours. I pulled my cell out of my pocket to check the trolley schedule. Like magic, as soon as I touched the phone, it rang. Bridgy's face popped on the screen. She must be having quite the day with me MIA and Miguel in the hospital. OMG, Miguel's surgery. I tapped the line open and started talking.

"How's Miguel? I forgot—"

"He's doing better. I ran over to see him about an hour ago. He's thrilled to have family members around and he's loaded with pain meds, so he thinks he's in Miami and no one wants to tell him he's not. His cousin came down last night, his sister arrived this morning and an aunt is on her way from Orlando."

Aunt! I thought of Ophie. "Speaking of aunts, how did—"

Bridgy cut me off, told me she was ready to pick me up and asked when I would be able to leave Augusta's house.

My "now" was so forceful that I was both surprised and dismayed by my overwhelming relief that Pastor John had slipped into the job of "helper of the bereaved," leaving me free to move back into my own life, even if only until tomorrow. I needed a stress break.

Back in my Brooklyn days, life was frantic, frenetic even. Our first months in Florida were even more chaotic. Finding a place to live. Opening the Read 'Em and Eat. We had to decide which books our clients would be dying to read, not to mention developing a menu that would bring folks back time and again. I remember a day I was feeling like Dorothy tumbling through the tornado on her way to Oz, when a teenager wearing oversized sunglasses and an undersized tank top came in to ask if we had a copy of *The Handmaid's Tale*. We'd made a decision not to stock merely the usual "beach reads," and I was excited that, apparently, the word was beginning to spread. Vacationers who can't quite let go of their need to be productive often want to exercise their brains while their bodies recline in pillowed lounge chairs. Even with a "thinking person's book" in hand, most readers often wound up nodding off to the sound of waves cresting no more than a few feet west of their blankets and umbrellas. As long as they felt they were doing something purposeful with their lounge time, they'd buy lots of books, heavy in both content and size.

I led the girl to the corner shelf where I had stashed the dystopian novels a few days before. Awwk! In my unending quest to make the books orderly and accessible, I must have moved them. Now that shelf was filled with various texts on learning to speak foreign languages. My head swiveled, eyes wide and searching.

The teen flipped her sunglasses atop her sun-streaked hair. "Don't get all cray-cray. You look like you're trying out for a remake of *The Exorcist*. If you don't have the Atwood book, it's no biggie."

I kept searching but I couldn't find the book, and I felt myself shredding like confetti right in front of the poor child.

I was astonished when she grabbed my shoulders. "Chillax. Take a breath. Now another. Slow. Your. Breathing." I felt myself relax even as I was wondering—who is this kid?

Now sitting on Augusta's steps, I thought about the enduring lifeline Holly, the girl I met that day, and her yoga instructor mom, Maggie, had tossed to Bridgy and me during our first year in Fort Myers Beach. I closed my eyes, turned my face to the sun and slowed my breathing.

By the time Bridgy pulled up in front of the house, I was calm enough to start thinking about Augusta's final command. She wanted me to find the wreckers. And then what?

We'd barely walked through the door of the Read 'Em and Eat when Aunt Ophie began hovering, her hands fluttering around me like butterflies searching for a welcoming branch to sit on.

"Why, gracious me, you poor chile! How did you survive all these hours dealing with such an awful, awful tragedy? Come sit down over here. This eye-catching gentleman has been fraught with worry waiting for you."

And she led me to the Alex Haley table, where Cady sat hunched over his laptop. He folded the top down, stood and pulled out a chair for me, asking precisely the right question as he did so.

"How is Augusta?"

I told them everything that happened at Augusta's house. Hearing about my being set out on the front porch, so to speak, Ophie clicked her tongue and opined that law enforcement officers should be taught decent manners right at the start of their career and get refreshers from time to time. When I mentioned Jocelyn, Bridgy rolled her eyes and said, "For all the virtuous works he does, John's passkey to heaven will actually be earned by living with that woman."

After more questions and answers than I thought the situation required, my interrogators finally ran out of steam. Bridgy and Aunt Ophie began the usual close-down tasks, leaving me to sit, restfully and conversationless, with Cady. After a few golden moments of silence, he gently patted my hand and asked, "Are you okay?"

I nodded and then looked around to see how much privacy we had. Bridgy and Ophie were cleaning the kitchen. Still, I decided to whisper for fear that if they heard us talking they'd come back to the dining area afraid to miss any gossip.

I reassured Cady that I was fine and then shared my concerns about Augusta.

"She is set on bringing Delia's killer to justice."

Cady leaned in to pat my hand sympathetically.

"The thing is . . . she wants me to help her find the killer."

Cady pulled his hand away as if mine had turned into a burning coal.

"Of all the scatterbrained ideas! You and Augusta trying to find a murderer! How would you even start?"

Even though I knew the question was rhetorical, I lowered my head ever so slightly until I'd arranged my features to look like a puppy pleading for one more treat. Then I raised my head and looked him straight in the eye.

He got my message and rejected it instantly.

"Absolutely not. There is no way I am going to help you put yourself in danger. And Augusta! At her age she shouldn't be considering anything more strenuous than . . . than . . . a book club meeting."

His face was bursting with finality, but I wasn't one to give up easily.

"We wouldn't actually *investigate*. I thought that with your help and Ryan's we could let Augusta know how the inquiry is progressing so she would know things before she read them in the paper." I watched him soften. "And when she has a question, I'd ask you or Ryan and get her the answer."

His eyes were hardening again.

"Unless the information is confidential. Naturally we couldn't expect to learn any confidential information."

As I watched his face, always transparent, I could see the side of his brain that labeled my plan foolish and ridiculous wrestling with the side that strived to be Boy Scout helpful.

I held my breath, then his expression changed and I knew the Boy Scout had won.

I exhaled even before he started laying out ground rules. Half listening to Cody's safety list, I haphazardly nodded now and again while preparing to casually ask what he knew about any wrecker crews working in the area. I was willing to bat an eyelash or two if it would help get the information I wanted.

Cady wrapped up with, "I mean it, Sassy."

I lowered my eyelids as meekly as I could and planned to gaze through my lashes while I agreed to obey, thus lulling him into a false sense of security before I brought up the wreckers.

Aunt Ophie came bursting through the kitchen door, shattering the mood I was working so hard to build.

"I think this awful day has left every one of us worn." She stood with her hands on her hips and rocked back and forth on the impossibly high heels that she'd pranced in on so many hours earlier. "I told my darlin' niece that a relaxing dinner would do us all a world of good. And she agrees. We're going to enjoy a leisurely meal at that gorgeous restaurant with the great seafood. You know, the one set right on the water."

Unaware that she had described most of the restaurants in Fort Myers Beach, she gave a "that settles that" clap of her hands and turned back toward the kitchen, untying her long white chef's apron as she walked.

The always logical Cady opened his mouth, and I could see the question coming. He'd be asking which seafood restaurant Ophie was planning on visiting. I shook my head to stop him. He threw me a quizzical look and I explained.

"No point in starting a Q&A. Ophie'll only confuse you. She'll play some combination of Charades and Twenty Questions for the fun of making us dizzy. Besides, I'm too tired for dinner. I want to go home."

Cady stood immediately and offered to drive, but that wasn't what I wanted.

"You are sweet but I need exercise. I think I'll walk, and if I want to speed things up, I'll jump on the trolley."

I tiptoed across the room, barely slowing at the kitchen pass-through to declare my intention. Then I slipped out the front door before Bridgy and Ophie could delay me with a barrage of objections and/or questions. Poor Cady—they were sure to hold him accountable for my vanishing act, but I needed to spend time by myself.

I turned off my cell phone as I crossed Estero Boulevard and zipped along until I found myself on the sun-bleached sand bordering the always vibrant Gulf of Mexico. I slid out of my sandals and buckled them around a belt loop on my shorts. I meandered around the late-day sunbathers and a few energetic volleyball players, until I reached the wet sand at the water's edge. Peeking out of the foam-encrusted seaweed dropped by a fresh wave was a pink twirled sea-shell looking for all the world like a spiral of strawberry frozen yogurt curled up in a Menchie's cup. I was fairly certain it was a tulip shell. I shook it to make sure that it was empty and put it in my pocket for Bridgy, who was becoming quite the expert on all things related to mollusks. As the salty water stroked my feet, I stood and looked across the Gulf to the sun floating above the horizon. It didn't take a brainiac to anticipate a magnificent sunset was on its way. Dazzling southwest Florida sunsets are as predictable as shells and seaweed along the beach.

I backpedaled and sat on the dry sand, wiggling my fanny until I was comfortable enough to concentrate on the horizon, one of my favorite focus points for meditation. No verbal mantra. No physical yoga or tai chi. Just the horizon, always present and always endless. It never failed to settle my mind into peaceful contemplation of nothing other than the meeting of sky and sea. The gentle lapping of the waves provided a cadence of serene harmony.

After twenty or so minutes, I closed my eyes, let the horizon recede while the events of the day slowly resurfaced in my freshly ordered mind. I stood, brushed the sand from my shorts and walked north toward the pier, my sandals bobbing and banging against my hip. I was a few yards away from the pier when the sun glinted off the gold letters on a red and blue striped shirt. There were bound to be any number of Messi fans roaming the island. Still, I noticed this Messi fan was part of a group surrounding a man in a bucket hat. I hurried closer, and as I stood next to the pier in a spot right below them, I recognized a voice from yesterday. Bucket Hat.

"Don't worry about idle threats from silly old women. I told you, I know where the ship is and I guarantee no one is going to get between me and this treasure, especially not a broad so old that she could easily be dead and buried before we ever leave port."

I gasped and took a quick step back from the pier. I looked up, hoping to memorize the faces of the men I hadn't yet seen, and was startled to see Bucket Hat staring directly down at me. Without the mirrored glasses, his eyes were dangerously penetrating.

I ducked under the pier and out the other side, hurried up to the street and headed for home, looking over my shoulder the entire time.

Chapter Eight |||||||||||

The apartment was happily quiet. Who knew how long that would last? Bridgy and Aunt Ophie were bound to be back soon. My cell! I turned it off when I began taking my walk, and I never turned it on again. By now Bridgy would be calling every five minutes, and getting more frantic each time voice mail picked up the call. As soon as I turned it on, the phone rang. I pushed "Talk" and began speaking without looking at the caller ID.

"I'm sorry. I know you hate when I turn my phone off. I needed time alone. But I have climbed the turret and am in for the night so I'll be here when you get here."

"Turret? Oh, I get it. Some sort of code for Prince Charming like in Rapunzel." I couldn't quite recognize the male voice. "When you feel like Cinderella, I guess 'glass slipper' is the code." Ah, the mocking tone. Lieutenant Frank Anthony.

I was grateful he couldn't see my reddening cheeks. I

almost explained that I thought he was Bridgy but decided he didn't deserve an explanation or even a conversation after he unceremoniously ordered me out of Augusta's house. I settled on a crisp, no-nonsense, "How can I help you, Lieutenant?"

"Actually, I was calling to thank you for your assistance today. I think it was easier for us to talk to Miss Maddox because you stayed nearby. I got the impression from Ryan that she could be quite difficult if anyone stirred her feathers. So I'm grateful that the interview was no worse than it had to be under the circumstances."

A few hours before I was some kind of annoyance and now he's all nicey nice? I wondered what he really wanted.

"Miss Augusta is a unique and treasured friend, the same as Miss Delia was. I thought it was fitting that I stay with her." I sniffed, hoping I sounded frosty rather than defensive.

"I'd like to interview you sometime tomorrow morning. I know you have a business to run . . ."

Interview? Like I was a suspect? What was I supposed to respond *No problem, stop by anytime?* Fat chance.

"Actually, we're shorthanded at the café . . ."

"But you do want us to catch the killer."

He had me there.

"How about elevenish? We usually have a lull between late breakfast and early lunch. But if we get busy . . ."

"I'll see you at eleven." And he hung up without as much as a good-bye.

I tossed my sandy clothes into the hamper, used a wet paper towel to wipe up the grains of sand scattered on the tiles of the bathroom floor and jumped into a hot, relaxing shower. In a few seconds I washed away Lieutenant Frank Anthony's commanding attitude. Then I snuggled into my

Winnie the Pooh pj's, snatched up the latest issue of the University of Florida magazine, *Subtropics*, and settled on the patio with a fresh cup of lemongrass tea.

I was reading a soothing poem about horses and dogs when the peace and quiet was shattered by Bridgy and Ophie clattering into the apartment laden with suitcases, assorted totes and multiple plastic bags.

Ophie opened the slider and thrust a plastic bag at me.

"We brought you dinner. Mind you, I would have broiled the snapper rather than . . ." She stopped abruptly and I watched her face morph as though something had shocked her into silence. But of course silence was never Ophie's strong suit. "What ARE you wearing? Come in here before someone sees you."

Behind Ophie's back, Bridgy stood in the center of the living room. She tilted her head and stuck out her tongue while making a hanging motion with one raised arm. We both knew I was done for.

When I didn't hop up immediately, Ophie pointed her finger at me and shook her entire arm as her voice changed into strict schoolmarm, a tone I hadn't heard since the last time she came to town.

"Well-mannered ladies do not appear outdoors in their nightwear. What on earth has gotten into you?"

It did me no good to point out that we were on the top floor of the highest building for miles around. I tried to soften her by joking, "That's why we call this place the turret. It is high and private. No one can see us."

Ophie wasn't having it. "Every boat pilot in the Gulf from here to Sarasota need only train his spyglass up at the light and you and your nightwear are on full display." With that she flicked the light switches, leaving the living room and the patio bathed in nothing but moonlight. "And what kind of nightwear is that? Well-mannered ladies wear feminine gowns, not children's footie pajamas."

I closed my magazine with a sigh and decided I was too tired to defend Winnie and Tigger as an adult clothing motif, so I obediently got up and walked into the living room, turning on the light as I headed to the couch. I would have flopped into a cozy corner but didn't want another well-mannered ladies lecture on how to sit.

Of course Ophie followed behind me, the bag holding my dinner still in her hand.

"You have to eat. In times of sorrow we need to keep up our strength."

Bridgy ran interference skillfully. Taking the package out of her aunt's hands, she offered to heat up my fish and tactfully suggested Ophie get herself settled in the guest room, which was little more than a home office with a futon covered by a shocking pink quilt and a half dozen flowered pillows.

I followed Bridgy into the kitchen. While she tossed a salad and nuked my fish and veggies, I told her about the conversation I'd overheard on the pier.

She remembered the two young bicyclists, but of course in the midst of all the angst about Miguel, I never did tell her about the man with the bucket hat inquiring about Miss Augusta and Miss Delia.

I sat at the kitchen counter, and as she placed my dinner in front of me, Bridgy said, "Surely you don't think . . ." and stopped dead as Ophie spun into the room wearing a bright yellow caftan with mangroves along the hem and sparkles scattered around the V-neck collar.

"Don't think what?" Ophie looked at Bridgy, and when she didn't get an instant response, she turned to me.

"Come on, honey chile, whatever game's afoot, don't have me be the last to know." She sat opposite me and propped her elbows on the table, determined that all further conversation would include her.

Bridgy raised an eyebrow and I gave a slight nod, then I cut an oversized piece of baked snapper and shoved it in my mouth, signaling that the discussion could go on without me.

When Bridgy finished her brief rundown of the events involving the wreckers, Ophie clutched her chest as if in the throes of a massive coronary.

"The sheriff. You call right now, hear?"

Bridgy glanced back to me for guidance, but I kept stuffing fish in my mouth. I couldn't decide whether Bucket Hat and his cadre of wreckers were all full of bluster or if they were dangerous. I decided to let Ophie and Bridgy battle it out. But there was no disagreement. In a split second they were staring at me, each with that single-minded gaze that runs in their family. It was as though they took a solemn vow, right then and there, to poke and prod me until I told them what little I knew about the treasure hunters.

They were somewhat placated when I told them I had an appointment with the sheriff's department the next morning. I was relieved they let me crawl off to bed with my magazine, without having to pinky-swear that I would tell Frank Anthony about the wreckers.

The morning setup was easier with three pairs of hands instead of two. I spent my time in the dining area taking breakfast orders and refilling coffee cups. I was quite happy to leave the kitchen to Bridgy and Ophie, thus avoiding their constant reminders to "tell the sheriff's office about the wreckers." In the fresh morning sunlight, the memory of Bucket Hat and his hard stare seemed a lot less ominous than it had yesterday.

I always enjoy the breakfast rush, some folks back from a long walk or bike ride, others eager for a swim or a long session in a lounge chair on the sand.

I'd finished helping a snowbird grandma pick out a few books to send north to the grandkids when Rowena Gustavsen came through the front door, making an entrance that even Ophie would envy. Rowena's usually bouffant lilac hair was sticking out wildly in all directions as if someone had taken a leaf blower to her head. She was struggling with a large suitcase in one hand and a cardboard box balancing precariously on the other. She dropped her keys and her ten-gallon purse on the floor with a clang and thump demanding, "Why are you standing there? Help me."

Her command was directed toward me but was so loud and disruptive that several breakfasters jumped up to give her a hand.

I ran to the doorway, barely beating out an octogenarian who probably weighed less than the suitcase. He certainly weighed less than Rowena.

Bridgy came out of the kitchen, her hands covered in flour. "What in heaven's name . . ."

When she saw the source of the noise, she tried to head back to the safety of the kitchen, but it was too late. Rowena caught her on the turn.

"Don't run away. I need help. I'm locked out of the Sand

and Shell and I have to go home for my keys. My car won't start. Don at the service station says the tow truck is busy over by the Mound House. I have to open now. I can't lug my merchandise back and forth on the trolley, and I can't leave it in the car. Who knows what kind of people the winter season brings? Thieves? Vandals?"

It didn't help that in a dining room filled with winter residents, her voice rose at least two octaves on those final words. There was only one solution. Get her out and get her out fast.

"Here, give me that." I took the suitcase and began to slide it behind the counter. "You can leave your things here, nice and safe. I'll drive you home to get the keys to your shop, and you'll be open in a heartbeat."

Bridgy tossed me a look of sympathy and quickly volunteered to take over serving. Anything rather than be trapped in a car listening to Rowena whine.

Rowena lived in a condo on the south end of the island near Lovers Key, a short enough trip, but I'd have to drive her back and forth. I gritted my teeth and moved Rowena out the door and into the Heap-a-Jeep.

Channeling Aunt Ophie's comments from our early-morning ride to the Read 'Em and Eat, Rowena sniveled, "You really need to think about getting a new vehicle. And this one could certainly use a trip to the car wash."

I was sure Ophie would have given me well-mannered ladies points for not dumping Rowena out on the street right then and there.

"It's this thing with Delia. Her dying and all. It's so up-setting. I've known her and Augusta since I first opened my consignment shop, nearly fifteen years ago. I've been begging her to allow me to sell some of the piles and piles of bric-a-brac strewn all over her house. But, quiet as she was, that's how stubborn she could be."

I had trouble thinking of Delia as stubborn, but even I could see that she was deeply attached to all things related to her past.

"What happens to all her old junk now, I wonder. It'll probably be tossed to the curb and go out with the trash. Such a waste." Rowena sighed. "We could have made a fortune. Not to mention the island. Did I tell you that World of Luxury Spa Resorts sent a vice president here all the way from California to buy Delia's island? Delia wouldn't even meet with him. I tried to help smooth a path to conversation, but she wasn't having it. I could have gotten quite the tidy commission brokering that deal. Now I suppose he'll have to talk to Augusta, and we both know that she's far more mulish than Delia.

"Here we are. Make a left in the driveway and head to the building on your right. Anyway, trying to reason with Augusta isn't going to be easy. You can wait here. I'll be right down."

I could have mentioned the nephews, but Rowena's soliloquy was so self-absorbed, so irritating, I decided not to give her the teensiest bit of information. She'd only run back to the Spa Resort guy and try to curry favor by being first to tell him the latest gossip. She'd find out soon enough.

I sat in the car thinking that I could chalk this ride up as the worst part of my day. Then I had a dark thought. Lieutenant Anthony was coming to interrogate me. That would be worse. Still, I managed to plaster a smile on my face as I watched Rowena walk out of the building and back toward me.

Chapter Nine

By the time I dropped Rowena in front of the Emporium the tow truck was on-site. The driver, a young, skinny guy in surfer shorts, had popped the hood of her boxy Ford Flex and was running cable from one of those portable battery chargers to her car battery. I offered to deliver her suitcase and package rather than have her follow me back to the Read 'Em and Eat. I needed to be done with her, at least for the day. I parked the Heap-a-Jeep, ran into the café, and dragged Rowena's clumsy box and overweight suitcase across the parking lot. I dropped them by the front door of the Sand and Shell Emporium where Rowena was still yammering at the mechanic while he was putting away his tools. His eyes pleaded for a rescue, but Bridgy needed me more.

"Rowena, here's your stuff." I pointed to the doorway. "Enjoy your day." And I turned on my heels and half jogged back to the café before she could stop me. I heard her yell something. I pretended it was "good-bye." I knew it wasn't "thank you."

The breakfast crowd was pretty much gone except for three surfers who'd worked up huge appetites out on the Gulf this morning, judging by the piles of food on their table, and the lovey-dovey newlyweds who'd become late breakfast regulars.

I took one look at the kitchen and realized that there were worse things than driving up and down the island listening to Rowena's mercenary drivel.

It seems Ophie'd been cooking up a storm of her own special recipes ever since the early morning rush died down. One glance and I remembered from past visits that Ophie's razzle-dazzle in the kitchen ended at the stove. It's like she was appearing in her own cooking show on the local public television station. She added ingredients and chucked the dirty bowls, spoons and whatnots wherever they might land. There were no sinks and sponges, no brooms and dustpans and definitely no dishwashers in her methodology. Cleanup was strictly for minions, not for master chefs. Bridgy was ecstatic to see me. I imagined she'd been running in circles like a Roller Derby queen trying to keep the customers satisfied while encouraging Ophie to at least try to meet minimum Board of Health standards in the kitchen.

If we weren't in southwest Florida, I would have thought we were mid-snowstorm in Brooklyn, that's how white the kitchen was—the floor, both work counters, the stove, even a swath of wall. My first thought was food fight. But no. A food fight would require cooked food. This mess looked like someone took bags of flour, slit the sides, held them at arm's length and shook. Crushed eggshells and spilled liquids added stringy globs of stickiness, and there were food containers of assorted sizes and shapes strewn everywhere, some empty, some not.

Ophie looked up from her culinary task and brandished a sharp-looking boning knife in my direction.

"Sassy, bless your heart, I'm glad you're back. Bridgy is, what do you northerners call it, a bit 'wired' without you, although I can't imagine why, seeing as how I'm here to help." Completely clueless to the havoc she was causing, Ophie went right on filleting chicken breasts, no matter that our freezer held a half dozen boxes of easy-to-cook, evenly sized chicken cutlets.

I gave her a wide berth, gathered my cleaning supplies and started with the wall. Then I moved on to the work space Ophie wasn't using. I rubbed and scrubbed. I was making real progress when Bridgy called me into the dining room. I grabbed a dish towel and was drying my hands as I pushed the swinging door. There, all official in his uniform, stood Lieutenant Frank Anthony.

I frowned at Bridgy. She couldn't have given me a hint? She couldn't come into the kitchen and whispered? Her grin told me that she knew I was annoyed and she didn't care a whit. She picked the coffeepot off the warmer and walked over to the surfers, offering to refill their cups. And if, later, I complained, she'd say, "You made the appointment." And she'd be right.

Frank Anthony's smile was close to a smirk, and the crinkles around his eyes shimmered as if he'd read my mind and was a wee bit pleased with himself for being the source of my irritation. He brushed some flour off the sleeve of my baby blue tee shirt and said, "I can see you really do throw yourself into your work. You wear it well." Then the smile disappeared and he was all business. "Is there somewhere we can talk?"

The minuscule office in the back of the kitchen is the café's only private space, but with Ophie reigning supreme from counter to stove and back again, the office was out of the question. I looked around the room and then suggested we go outside and sit on the benches our customers used when they had to wait a few minutes for a table. It was the only spot where we'd have a modicum of privacy. As I followed the lieutenant out the door, I heard Bridgy hiss, "Don't forget the wreckers."

He signaled me to sit, and so I did, directly in the middle of one bench so that he would have to sit on the other.

We sat without speaking long enough for me to start to feel squirmy, and finally he started talking, more gently than I would have expected.

"Sassy, I know this is really difficult for you, as it is for all of Miss Batson's friends, but the more information we can gather, the more likely we are to catch her killer."

Killer! A shudder went through me at the dreadful word. No living soul would have any reason to harm Miss Delia, much less murder her. I shook my head, then realized that the lieutenant might think I was disagreeing, so I said, "I'll help in any way I can." *For Delia*, I added silently.

He had me start at the beginning. I told him that when Bridgy and I opened the Read 'Em and Eat, Miss Delia and Miss Augusta were semi-regulars for breakfast, and then one morning Augusta boomed, "Delia keeps reading

71

in the *Fort Myers Beach News* that you hold book club meetings here." I remember her head swiveled for thirty seconds or so, then she commented, "Don't look like you have the room for it, but you sure got a lot of books."

I explained to Lieutenant Anthony that Augusta and Delia added the Books Before Breakfast Club to their schedule and occasionally sat in on one or two others, especially the Potluck Book Club.

"Neither of them seemed to be interested in cooking, but they enjoyed the books and the talk. It may have helped that we usually serve snacks, sometimes made from recipes from the current book. And who doesn't like a mid-afternoon snack?"

Bit by bit Frank moved me forward in time, until we were up to the day before Delia was found on her living room floor.

He was a patient and skillful interrogator. I found myself wondering if he was that methodical in everything he did. And, as always when a thought like that came into my mind, I found myself twirling my hair. I forced my hand back to my lap. Better to stay with the progression of time leading up to the murder rather than allow myself to be sidetracked by Frank's determination to reach any and all of his goals.

"You mentioned that there was a book club meeting that morning. Did anything out of the ordinary happen that you can recall?"

I thought about mentioning the Anya Seton/Daphne du Maurier dustup between Jocelyn and Rowena but then decided that those two bickering would hardly be considered "out of the ordinary." So I shook my head.

"You have to realize anything that happened that morning was completely overshadowed when Miguel fell in the kitchen."

"Ah, the chef with the broken leg. How could I forget? After all, that's when you and I first met." And there it was again: the wide, smirky smile and the crinkly eyes. I didn't miss that his tone of voice made it sound like this was the story he was saving to tell our grandkids. Was that a sneaky interrogation technique he used on female suspects?

He leaned toward me, and clasping his hands, he rested his forearms on his knees. He seemed to be waiting for me to say something. And then I remembered I did have something to say. Something guaranteed to throw him off his game—whatever the game was.

"That was also the morning Augusta had words with two young wreckers who stopped in for breakfast. Delia was with her."

He straightened instantly, his whole demeanor changing back to no-nonsense official.

"Why am I only hearing this now? Shouldn't you have mentioned it yesterday? Tell me exactly what happened." There was a tad of accusation in his voice, as though I was shirking my responsibility as a star witness.

I recounted the conversation as accurately as I could remember it. Frank nodded, and I saw his shoulders relax ever so slightly.

"Well, doesn't sound like there was much to it. From what I've heard about Augusta Maddox, she's likely to scrap with anyone over anything. Still, I'll have the deputies be on the lookout for a couple of kids trying to scrounge up some four-hundred-year-old Spanish coins."

73

I shook my head. "No. No. They weren't talking about walking metal detectors along the beach after hurricanes. They were talking about ships. Sunken treasure ships. That's what got Augusta so wound up."

"You mean they want to salvage a Spanish galleon? Most of that action is on the east coast right now. Off north Florida, I think." He shrugged. "Of course hundreds of millions of dollars' worth of treasure from the *Atocha* was salvaged back in the eighties somewhere between the Keys and the Dry Tortugas. But that was forever ago. Even the lawsuits are finished. Haven't heard any rumors about another treasure hunt being planned. We usually hear; the hunt brings jobs and money. And the occasional bar fight."

He shrugged indifferently as if bar fights were the normal course of doing business, and I guess in his line of work that was true.

"Well, anyone who wants to salvage treasure from ships sunk in Florida waters needs a license from the State. I'll check with Tallahassee, see if anyone is looking at wrecks between Sarasota and Key West."

He saw the hesitation in my face and went ramrod straight again.

"What?"

"There was a man . . ." And I told him how strange it was that Bucket Hat insisted on questioning me about Augusta and Delia, even with Miguel writhing on the kitchen floor.

"That is . . . out of place. Are you sure he could see Miguel? Knew there was a problem?"

"There's more." When I finished telling him about my accidental brush last night with Bucket Hat and the wrecker boys all talking about treasure and old ladies who could soon be dead, Frank stood towering over me, with a cloud-less sky as background.

"Tell me again. As close as you can remember, repeat exactly what he said."

And I did. In my memory, the threat in Bucket Hat's words was magnified by the fierce glare he sent my way when he caught me eavesdropping. I wouldn't want to come face-to-face with him again.

Frank took a few steps away from me and spoke quietly into his shoulder radio. Then he pulled out his cell phone and made a call. When he was done, he came and stood over me again. He leaned back, crossed his arms and stared directly in my eyes. We'd moved back to not speaking. Was this an interrogation technique? I wondered. Too bad. I'd told him everything I could think of; besides, I had so much work waiting for me in the café. I cleared my throat, gave as sweet a smile as I could muster and stood.

"I guess we're done here. I've told you all I know."

"Sit. Down," he ordered.

Wondering what else we could possibly have to discuss, I decided to comply although I'd already told him everything I knew. I reached for my cell phone to check the time then realized I'd left it on the counter. I started to fidget. The lunch crowd would be gathering soon.

Finally, he broke the silence, his voice dripping with accusation. "This conversation you overheard on the pier. That was last night?"

I nodded. "I know it was after Delia . . . but I thought it might be important."

"Thought? Thought? You saw these men before I called, didn't you?"

I was starting to see where this was going.

"The problem is you didn't think. If you weren't so completely thoughtless and irresponsible, you would have told me this last night. You've cost this investigation valuable time."

Abruptly, he turned away, throwing a curt "we'll need to speak again" over his shoulder.

As I watched him stride to his car, I determined that from this point on, the only person I'd speak to from the sheriff's office was Ryan. This new lieutenant had far too much 'tude for me.

I was barely through the café door when Bridgy hurried toward me holding my phone in her outstretched hand. "You left your cell. It's been ringing constantly."

"Who's been calling?"

"I don't know. I didn't look."

As if, I thought. I took the phone from her hand and pressed the "Missed Calls" button.

Chapter Ten

Two calls from Cady one minute apart. As was his habit, he called then re-called instantly, assuming I hadn't reached the phone in time to catch his first call. Next, Pastor John. He probably needed help dealing with Miss Augusta. The fourth call was from a number I didn't recognize, which my phone unhelpfully named "Wireless Caller." Still, it was a 239 area code.

I decided to return that call first. I suspected that both Cady and Pastor would undoubtedly require more of my time than Wireless Caller. I hit the "Call" button and in half a ring a woman screeched over the earsplitting sound of something like a lawn mower or edger.

"Are you with my husband?"

"Pardon me?" Oh Lord, don't tell me. Smilin' Eyes Frank Anthony has a jealous wife. Perfect, just perfect. I wonder if she calls all his witnesses.

The whirling motor stopped and her voice dropped to more reasonable decibels.

"Sorry. I grabbed the phone so quickly that I didn't quite shut down the vacuum."

"Jocelyn?"

"Sassy, who else would be calling you looking for her husband? Isn't John there with you and Augusta?" She rattled on before I could answer, "Vince Crowley called about some committee meeting and John seems to have turned off his phone. Anyway, he's not picking up. And I was hoping you could let him know that Vince needs an answer about . . . whatever it is. John will know."

"If I talk to him, I'll certainly tell him."

"If you talk to him? Aren't you with him?"

"No. I'm at the café."

"You aren't with John and Augusta?"

How many ways could I say it?

"No."

"Oh dear. Sassy, that will never do. I really don't think John can handle Augusta all on his own. Where do you think they are? Why aren't you with them?"

Never mind that neither Augusta nor Pastor John asked me to spend any time with them this morning. I grabbed for a workable excuse.

"I had a meeting scheduled with someone from the sheriff's office to discuss the case." *Discuss the case! Who am I, Jessica Fletcher?*

"Was it that new sheriff, the one I saw with Ryan? He's quite attractive. I bet all you single girls are swooning."

Swooning? Ha! Not exactly.

"It may be the same one. He's a lieutenant, not the sheriff, and he's new to the island."

"All the same, if I wasn't a happily married woman, I'd be hard-pressed not to go gaga over his looks." Still, Jocelyn seemed mollified by my excuse. "I guess helping the investigation has to take precedence over helping John. When you're done with the lieutenant, find John and Augusta before she drives him crazy."

I reluctantly agreed, hoping that if I returned Pastor's call, it would count as trying to find him.

"And one more thing, Sassy. Be sure to tell the hunky lieutenant that the crazy old man who found the skull has been lurking around Delia's house at all hours of the night. Don't mention my name, but I do think the investigating officers should be told. You'll take care of it? And don't abandon John."

With a click she was gone, and while I was grateful for that small favor, her assignments provoked me to no end. Oh well, I could at least take care of the one task that made sense. And I clicked my phone to return Pastor's call.

He answered before the second ring. Not quite as fast as his wife, but still not one to keep a caller waiting.

"Sassy, thank goodness. You know Augusta can be a handful. I'm afraid she has moved into territory where I can no longer assist. This needs a woman's touch. It's the clothes."

"What clothes?"

"The burial clothes for Delia. Fern showed us some lovely things that Mr. Beech is willing to include in the funeral costs for what I think is a reasonable price, but Augusta had a tantrum. Wants Delia buried in a blue silk dress she bought in Port Charlotte ages ago, and there is some sort of trinket. Oh, I don't know. Can you come over here and talk to Augusta, find out exactly the things she wants and then talk your way into Delia's house and get the burial clothes? Otherwise this funeral is never going to happen."

He sounded so exasperated that, without thinking it through, I agreed if only to decrease his stress level.

"Oh, Sassy, thank you. I'll tell Augusta. She'll be so pleased." I could hear the relief in his voice. Then to assuage whatever guilt he had about foisting this on me, he offered, "Don't worry. You find the things Augusta wants and I'll bring it all to Beech's."

Right, as if bringing the clothes to the funeral parlor was the hard part.

I put the phone down and sank into an empty chair at the Robert Frost table. Bridgy immediately appeared with my favorite midmorning pick-me-up, Greek yogurt and fresh berries.

I smiled my thanks and then asked if she had a minute.

"Sure, Ophie is doing her magic, messy may it be, in the kitchen, and we have a couple of minutes until the lunch crowd starts. What's wrong? You look drained. Was that lieutenant mean to you?" She looked at the door, ready to give him a piece of her mind if he dared walk through it.

"Frank Anthony was the easiest part of the past half hour. Surprisingly, Pastor John has me crazed."

As I explained the mission I had decided to accept, Bridgy rolled her eyes and hunched her shoulders.

"How do you propose to stroll into Delia's house, take whatever Augusta wants you to take and then waltz out again? You do know there is a sheriff's car parked right outside the house with a deputy sitting at attention, don't you?"

Of course I knew, but that was my second worst problem.

"Bridgy, we need to talk about Skully."

"Oh, stop. Not Rowena again! I'm starting to like your idea. Let's sell his jewelry here. We could set up a display over there." She gestured vaguely in the direction of the bookshelves.

"Not Rowena. Jocelyn."

"Ugh. Two sides of the same penny."

"After getting a lecture not twenty minutes ago from Frank Anthony about my 'withholding information,' Jocelyn called—"

"Do y'all need more pastries than this for lunch?" Ophie pushed through the kitchen door carrying a tray piled high with muffins, fruit tartlets and scones. "I can whip up another batch of lemon poppy seed muffins quicker than you can say delicious."

Looking exactly like a traffic cop in a busy intersection, Bridgy held up one hand ordering Ophie to stop while waving me forward with the other, as if we were two SUVs about to collide.

Ophie stopped instantly, pastry tray in midair. I grabbed the opportunity and my words tumbled out. "It's Skully. On the phone Jocelyn reminded me that yesterday she told me that Skully's been seen hanging around Delia's house."

Bridgy looked at the pastries and beamed a grateful smile. After lavishing praise on Ophie for the fresh-baked aroma that was filling the café, Bridgy asked her to check the freezer count for key lime pie, the number one dessert favorite with snowbirds and tourists. Fully expecting her will to be done, Bridgy turned her attention back to me.

"Come on, Sas. Skully is a sweet guy, not a killer. Jocelyn is a gossipy troublemaker. Exactly like Rowena," she added.

"Oh, I agree. The trouble is she keeps insisting I tell the sheriff's office. And, well, I didn't."

"You didn't? What were you talking about all this time you were outside with him?"

"The wreckers. You told me I had to tell about the wreckers, so I did. And why is everyone telling me what to report? Can't anyone else around here talk to the sheriff's office?"

Bridgy held her hands out defensively. "Don't look at me. I only told you to pass along what *you* saw and what *you* heard. Jocelyn's your problem."

My cell rang. I think Bridgy and I were both grateful for the interruption. Cady! In the chaos, I'd forgotten all about him.

"Sorry. I've been mega busy."

He told me that the newspaper had received Delia's obituary and offered to bring a copy by so I could take an advance peek before it went up in the online edition later today. We agreed he'd stop in after the lunch rush. By the time I had hung up, the café was half-full. I grabbed my order pad and got to work.

Within fifteen minutes we had a full house.

Bridgy was speedily bussing tables and I was serving key lime pie to some day-trippers from Cape Coral when Rowena Gustavsen rushed in and, as if there weren't another soul in sight, called across the dining room, "Sassy, what smells so scrumptious? Is there something new on the menu? I'm in a hurry."

She leaned on the counter, and I signaled I'd be with her in a minute. Ophie came out of the kitchen, all honey and smiles.

"Bless your heart, nothing makes me happier than to hear a cultured person such as yourself refer to my muffins as scrumptious, and you haven't even tried one yet. Here you go."

I couldn't see what kind of muffin Ophie offered, but Rowena's moan of ecstasy after she took a bite assured me that I had a couple of minutes to fuss over the day-trippers before Rowena would renew her demands for attention.

I offered refills of coffee to the remaining lunch customers, and as I moved closer to the counter, I heard Rowena say, "I knew it. I knew that man was nothing but trouble. How I let these girls talk me into doing business with him, I'll never know."

Darn. Ophie must have told Rowena that she'd heard us talking about Skully being seen near Delia's house. Now she'd never stop whining. I stepped up with my order pad, ready to take my verbal slap on the wrist.

I listened to Rowena fume for a couple of minutes, accusing us of putting a possible murderer right in her shop, before she finally ordered *The Secret Garden* Salad (hold the onions, extra tomato, vinaigrette on the side) and a side of sweet potato fries (extra crispy). I handed the order slip to Ophie with a pointed look at the kitchen door. Much as she hated to miss any gossip, duty called. She patted Rowena's hand and slipped into the kitchen, saying, "That's comin' right up, darlin'."

Rowena turned back to me, but I'd grabbed a spray bottle and a wad of paper towels and was busily scrubbing the counter, chair backs and bottoms, anything I could clean so as not to have to listen to her complaints about Skully, who was rapidly being transformed into a serial killer during Rowena's histrionics.

Rowena took her to-go bag and left, but not before issuing a general warning that "we're not done talking about this, not by a long shot."

The lunch crowd was thinning and I continued to clean, a mindless task that left me free to mentally organize the rest of my day. I had a lot to do. Get over to Augusta's and find out what clothes she wanted Delia to wear, then figure a way to get into Delia's house and locate everything. And Cady was coming with the obituary. Should we show it to Augusta, or had she helped prepare it? And if I didn't talk to Frank Anthony about Skully, how much trouble would Jocelyn cause? I was exhausted thinking about all that I needed to get done. I was sliding the spray cleaner under the counter when Bridgy said, "I know you have a lot going on, but don't forget the Potluck Book Club is meeting this afternoon."

Book club! I was completely blank. I couldn't even remember the name of the book we'd read this month. With everything else going on today, how could I lead a book discussion? Was it too early for a mojito? I stood in the center of the room not knowing whether to laugh or cry.

Then Ryan Mantoni walked in the door, looked me in the eye and said, "Sassy, come on. We need your help."

And he turned on his heel, expecting me to follow.

Chapter Eleven

I must have had a "what now" look on my face, because when Ryan glanced back to make sure I was behind him, he stopped in mid-stride.

"What's the matter? Miss Augusta needs you. We have to go."

"Augusta?"

"Pastor John told me he called you."

"About the clothes, yes, but . . ."

"Come on." He hitched a thumb on his gun belt and pointed his head toward the door. "Pastor got permission for me to take you into Miss Delia's house to find an outfit for the service. The techs are done and I can escort you through the house as long as I never leave your side and make sure you don't touch anything besides personal apparel and jewelry. Not that there's much in the way of jewelry, from what I saw."

"Ryan, I want to help but I don't know exactly what Augusta wants Delia to wear."

"No prob. We'll stop by her house and get a list. Can't be much on it." And he whisked me out the door.

We shared a quick and quiet ride to Augusta's house, while I tried to get my scrambled brain in order. When we pulled up in front, she was sitting on the porch swing, looked even tinier and more worn than she had yesterday. I guess the finality of the tragedy was beginning to sink in.

Pastor John came down the steps to thank me for bailing him out. Of course that wasn't the phrase he used, but that's precisely what he meant and we both knew it. I couldn't blame him for being uncomfortable at the thought of rifling through a woman's wardrobe, but couldn't Jocelyn have helped? Isn't that why Pastors have wives, to be helpmates? When I climbed onto the porch, Augusta gave me a wan smile and spoke in hushed tones I'd never heard her use.

"Come sit, Sassy." She patted the other half of the swing. As soon as I was settled, she handed me a picture.

"I was up half the night until I found this in an album. Don't Delia look nice all dressed in her finery?"

I looked at the picture. Delia had on a wide-brimmed straw hat that, given the angle of the sun, barely shaded her eyes. Her dress was a gentle teal blue, like the Gulf on a cloudless day. The empire waist hid her expanded midriff, and the puffed sleeves camouflaged the batwings I'd noticed when she wore sleeveless tops. The mid-calf length of the flowing skirt told me that the dress was a few decades out of style.

"She looks lovely, Miss Augusta, absolutely lovely." I

was struck by the joy and animation on Delia's face. Something I'd rarely seen. "Where was this taken?"

"Few years back, we had a celebration at the church, anniversary of some sort."

"Twenty-fifth anniversary of the choirmaster's service to the Lord," Pastor John injected, pointing to the edge of a banner partially hidden by Delia's hat.

"Well, Delia and I had a grand time. Lots of singing. Delia always liked to sing in church. Never could talk her into joining the choir. Too shy. You know about that."

I smiled, thinking of Delia at our last book club meeting.

"Anyway, Sassy, you take this picture to Delia's house and find that dress, with shoes to match. Service is coming up and we need to make sure Delia's as pretty as a picture. That picture. And don't forget the locket."

"Locket?"

"See for yourself." Augusta picked up a magnifying glass from the side table. "Here it is. It has a swamp lily etched on it signifying the Ten Thousand Islands. Our family home. She wore it on every special occasion, long as I can remember. And if this ain't a special occasion, I don't know what is."

The rounded glass enlarged the picture enough that I could see a small gold rectangle resting on the bibbed bodice of Delia's dress.

I sat for a few minutes, assuring Miss Augusta that we'd get the things Delia needed, then Ryan and I headed off to Delia's house and a chore I dreaded. Once we were in the car, I confided, "I feel funny doing this. I don't think I've ever been in a dead person's house before, and as for going through her clothes and jewelry, well, it doesn't feel right. I'm not a relative or anything."

Ryan cleared his throat. "About the jewelry. I didn't want to say anything in front of Miss Augusta, but when we were searching the house, a box with a cracked lid, seemed to be a jewelry box, was lying on the bedroom floor. Except for a couple of unmatched earrings, it was empty."

My head snapped in his direction, and he responded to my unasked question.

"Nope. I wouldn't bet on our finding the locket. Whoever killed Delia probably took it. And be prepared, Sas; the house was ransacked pretty thoroughly. Afterward our techs went through it with a fine-tooth comb, and they're far from neat."

Ransacked was one word for it. The first thing I noticed was that Delia's collection of bird figurines was shunted to one side of a bookshelf attached to the living room wall, and the books, well, they were tossed on the floor, scattered about; some had landed spine down, others had their dust jackets ripped off and dropped on top. Delia had always taken excellent care of her books. It broke my heart to see them left this way. And the furniture! Every piece was topsy-turvy. Why would anybody flip chairs, tables, even push the rolltop desk helter-skelter? It looked like a mess deliberately created by the stage crew for a murder scene in a television show. Except I knew better. This murder scene was real.

Ryan took my elbow and led me to the staircase.

"Come on. Let's get what we came for and get out of here."

I nodded.

Delia's bedroom was at the top of the stairs. I ignored the disarray and opened the closet door. Each item of clothing sat straight on its hanger, and the hangers were in a tidy row. My eye swept from the muumuus I was used to seeing Delia wear, moved past a few pastel dresses, things Delia probably wore to church and on special outings to downtown Fort Myers or Naples. On the right-hand side of the closet, separated by a few inches from the rest of her wardrobe, was her one special dress, teal blue with an empire waist. I checked the shoe rack tucked on the closet floor, and found sandals, water shoes and sneakers. Not one pair of dress shoes of any color, much less blue.

Then a thought struck.

"Ryan, can we check the other bedroom, the guest room?"

He hesitated, so I explained.

"Closet space is at a premium for most women. So we often stash things we don't wear frequently in places where they won't be in our way."

He nodded and led the way to a closed door a few feet down the hallway.

Sunshine filtered through lace curtains and brightened the room, which seemed to have escaped being torn apart like the rest of the house.

Next to the bureau opposite the daybed, a closet door stood slightly ajar. I opened it. Sharing the top shelf with some neatly folded quilts I spied a plastic box labeled "fancy shoes." I couldn't quite reach. I stepped out of the way so Ryan could take it down, and that's when I noticed the square pink leather box on the bureau.

I picked it up, opened it and was instantly disappointed. No locket. No gold at all. Curiously, I found two shell and fishing line bracelets. I didn't recall ever seeing Delia wearing any bracelets like them. In fact, I didn't recall ever seeing her wear any jewelry at all, not even the missing locket. I closed the box and set it back on the bureau. Perhaps the bracelets were keepsakes, gifts her nephews made for her when they were children.

Ryan handed me the shoe box, and inside I found a pair of barely worn teal blue shoes with sensible one-inch heels.

Back in Delia's room I found her undergarments neatly folded in the dresser drawer. I took out a set and then realized I didn't have anything to carry them in. I told Ryan we were ready to go but I'd need to stop in the kitchen for a bag.

Still carrying the shoe box, he led the way downstairs, took a few steps to the rear of the house and through an archway into the kitchen. That's when I saw the kitty litter box sitting in the hallway.

"Bow! Oh Lord. Where is Bow?" And I crouched close to the floor calling, "Bow, here kitty, kitty, Bow. Here sweet girl."

I saw her food and water dishes, little white bowls with a paw motif, sitting in a far corner. Neither was empty.

"Ryan, where is Delia's cat? Augusta doesn't have her. Where is she?"

Ryan looked at me as though I'd gone quite mad when I ran to the cupboard and took out a can of cat food and pressed it under the electric can opener.

"She'll come when she hears a fresh can being opened," I explained. But even when I sent the can spinning around the opener a second time, Bow didn't scamper into the room looking for a meal. We searched the entire house, upstairs and down, looking for any out-of-the-way space where Bow might be sleeping.

"Cats are nocturnal; they sleep a lot during the day," I told Ryan since I seemed to be the cat authority of the moment. Finally we ran out of places to look and gave up the search. Then I had an idea.

"Ryan, is it possible that one of your colleagues called Animal Rescue to come take care of Bow?"

He wasn't aware of any such call, but he told me he'd check at the district.

"Sassy, I was first on the scene, and even with everything going on, I'm sure there was no cat in the house. Don't forget, the front door was open when we got here."

I fretted all the way back to Augusta's house. How could I tell her that I couldn't find the locket and that Bow was missing as well?

Miss Augusta perked up a bit when she saw me get out of Ryan's car carrying the blue dress on its satin-covered hanger. Ryan grabbed the packages we'd put in the trunk and handed them to Pastor John. Then he took the dress from me and hung it on a planter hook screwed into the porch overhang. I took my seat on the swing once again.

Augusta patted my hand. "Thanks for taking care of this. Delia'll be so pleased to be dressed proper."

I took a deep breath and told her about the missing locket. She was quiet for a long time and then sighed. "You tried your best. Delia'll miss the locket, still, there's nothing to be done."

When I told her Bow was missing, too, I was shocked when she dismissed the idea.

"Missing, my foot. She's out gallivanting is all. Try the coral clapboard house directly across the street from Delia. Woman who lives there had a yen for Bow from the first day we found her in Bowditch Point Park, all hungry and scraggly-like.

"Delia brought her home, cleaned her up, got her healthy and gave her a place to live. But Bow liked to be on her own. Now and again she'd sashay down to the water's edge for some exercise. She'd leave with a green bow tied to her collar, and hours later she'd come home with a yellow one and a full belly to boot. I can't swear it was always the lady in the coral house fussin' over her, but I can swear it was her most of the time. I bet she took advantage of the situation to get what she always wanted—Bow."

Ryan tapped his watch. I gave Miss Augusta a kiss on her weathered cheek and reminded her that she had many friends willing to help. I was surprised to see a tear glide down her cheek, as she squeezed my hand in response.

I had scarcely enough time to get back to the café for the Potluck Book Club. On the way, Ryan promised he'd check with the owner of the coral house and call Animal Rescue to try to find Bow. I thanked him and jumped out of the car at the bottom of the driveway, hoping to get settled before the book club members arrived. At least I'd finally remembered the book we'd read, *The Long Quiche Goodbye* by Avery Aames, a cheese shop mystery that mixed murder with fine cheese and interesting recipes, guaranteeing our meeting would be great fun.

As I grabbed the handle of the café door, a bear paw–like hand clamped over mine.

"Saw you get out of the sheriff car. Causing more trouble, eh?"

Bucket Hat's eyes were far more threatening when we were nose to nose.

Chapter Twelve

I yanked my hand from underneath his and gave him as defiant a glare as I could muster. "Go away."

He maneuvered himself so that he was planted in front of the door and I couldn't brush by him.

"You listen to me, girlie, and listen good. You can't go around accusing folks of murder. Keep it up and there'll be consequences aplenty for you and your friends. You mind what I'm saying."

"Leave me—and my friends—alone."

"Sassy, is everything all right?" Cady was only a few feet away and walking right toward us.

"No trouble here," Bucket Hat called out, then he lowered his voice and growled at me, "Don't forget—consequences aplenty for all concerned," and he hurried away.

Cady could see how shaken I was. He put his arm

around me, walked me inside the café and plunked me in a seat at Robert Louis Stevenson.

"Bridgy, could you get Sassy a glass of water?"

She was busy setting up the book nook for the meeting, but she only needed one look at my face and she practically ran to the kitchen.

She came out with a glass of water and a slice of Ophie's buttermilk pie, set them on the table in front of me and sat down.

"What happened? Is it Miss Augusta?"

I shook my head and pushed the pie off to the side. "No, she's about as good as she can be. It's that wrecker, Bucket Hat. He grabbed on to me right outside our front door and threatened me. No, that's not right. He threatened us all."

She looked at Cady, who said, "He was blocking the doorway but he took off when I came along."

She stood up. "I'm calling Ryan."

"No," I said. "Please don't. He's spent so much time helping me today . . ."

"Sassy, that's his job, helping. He needs to know about this. Someone at the sheriff's office needs to know."

"Okay," I relented, suddenly too tired to argue. "Let's get the book club meeting behind us and then we can talk to Ryan."

She went in the kitchen and brought out a lace doily–covered plate of diced cheese, some pale yellow, some dark orange, along with a half wheel of brie. I snatched the sleeve of crackers that was dangling from her fist and followed her to the nook.

"This is a nice touch."

I noticed a couple of plum and gold paperbacks tucked

under the chair I usually sat in. "Thanks for remembering to put a few extra books on the side. Someone nearly always forgets their copy."

Cady came right along behind me.

"I have the obit. Do you want to take a look?"

I sat down and took the typewritten copy he offered. A few short sentences strung together in one paragraph summed up the life of Miss Delia Batson, fourth-generation Floridian, who was active in her church, the food pantry and the Animal Rescue League. She was survived by two nephews and her cousin and dearest friend, Augusta Maddox. Finally, it noted that donations in Delia's name could be made to the Animal Rescue League or the food pantry.

I was thankful there was no mention of how she died. Let the sensationalism stay on the front page. She would want her obituary to be dignified. I passed the paper over to Bridgy and thanked Cady for bringing it.

"Has Augusta seen it?"

"Sure has. Mr. Beech at the funeral home has a habit of showing each obit to the survivors before he okays it to go to print. I can only imagine he must have really screwed up an obit once upon a time, because it's a rule he never breaks."

He checked his phone.

"I have to get back. See you later?"

"I don't know. We have a book club and then, well, I haven't been very hospitable to Ophie. I thought I'd spend the evening with her." It was a big fat lie, but I knew I had plans for later; I just wasn't sure what they were. Bucket Hat's threats made me more determined to follow Augusta's lead and try to find out what happened to Delia. I'd wasted too much time already.

Cady took my hand and kissed the top of my head. He advised me to take care of myself and to remember this was a difficult time for everyone. I was struck again by how comforting it felt to have him around. Then he ruined it all by whispering in my ear, "And, promise me, no sleuthing."

I managed a feeble smile and a slight nod of my head. What he didn't know would keep us from arguing.

Two snowbirds had picked up the book club list the first time they came by for breakfast and said they'd be back for the Potluck Club. Sure enough they were the first to arrive.

I greeted them, led the way to the book nook and introduced myself.

"I'm Connie and this is Iris. Come from a little town a few miles north of Ottawa. We spent a few winters on the east coast. Much as I love the ocean, friends recommended we try the Gulf. Our husbands will go anywhere they can play golf in January, so here we are."

"Not happy about the murder, though." Iris shook her graying locks and her shoulders quivered as though a chill wind went by. "Does that happen a lot around here?"

"No. Of course not. Never, actually." I was relieved that the door opened and a couple of regulars bounded inside.

Maggie, dressed in her "I'm a yoga instructor" uniform of stretchy cropped pants and an oversized tee advertising her studio, Zencentric, was carrying a bouquet of greens tucked into a tall paper cup. "I brought some chervil, fresh from my garden. I thought we could talk about how nicely it goes with cheese in omelets and breakfast pastry."

That was what I loved about the Potluck Club; each book led us to delve into all the possibilities of the kitchen.

And after the Books Before Breakfast fiasco, I was delighted that Lisette Ortiz had decided to try us again. While tucking her sunglasses carefully in their case, she introduced herself to the two newcomers, confiding, "This book was such a fun read. I can't wait to talk about it."

The four ladies began chitchatting, which gave me a few minutes to consider my discussion points and decide how to present them, although it didn't look like this was going to be one of those rare meetings where I'd have to drag observations out of the participants.

The front door opened and we all turned to see who was going to join us. My smile faded the moment I saw her strawlike hair and determined thrust of chin. Jocelyn.

She tore into me the second she had me in sight.

"Aha! I knew I'd find you here. John is over at the funeral home right this minute with Augusta and where are you? At book club! I suppose it didn't occur to you that the poor man might need a bit of respite. Too self-absorbed, trying to sell your books, keep this rickety place afloat. Doesn't seem to bother you that one of your book club members has been murdered."

That triggered a rustling of chairs and a loud gasp from one of the snowbirds.

I wasn't slow to stand up and face her down. Jocelyn was the second person to rant at me in less than an hour. If this was "Pounce on Sassy Day," I was tired of it.

"Well, bless your heart, did you say you brought chervil?"

Aunt Ophie had charged out of the kitchen and grabbed Jocelyn by the arm.

"Let's wash it off and make something tasty from it. Not enough time for soup, but I'm sure we can have a flavorsome treat ready in two shakes of a sheep's tail." Ophie beamed a thousand-watt smile, as if we were all the best of friends.

Jocelyn sputtered, but before she could conjure up a response, Maggie jumped in.

"Pardon, ma'am, but the chervil is from my garden." She proffered the paper cup. "I brought it to share. Take what you need."

Ophie spun on today's impossibly high black sandals worn to match her tightly cinched tiger-striped shirtwaist.

"Well, aren't you a darlin' girl?" She patted Maggie's cheek, then she spun back to Jocelyn and gave her the same nose to nose treatment that Bucket Hat had given to me. Her southern drawl was softer, but her manner was every bit as intimidating.

"Seems like these ladies are ready to start talking about their book. You're welcome to join me in the kitchen or you can sit in on the meeting. Those are your choices."

Those were the words Ophie spoke, but we all heard her true meaning. Your *only* choices. Carrying on is not an option.

Even though she'd stopped sputtering, Jocelyn was agitated, and visibly annoyed that Ophie had outflanked her. We all watched as her determined chin weakened and began to rock from side to side. She was struggling for control of the situation against an unknown force. Then she primped her hair, gave Ophie her best barracuda smile and allowed herself to be guided gently but firmly away from the book nook.

Ophie tossed a triumphant smile my way, but I knew one way or another Jocelyn would settle the score. I picked up a copy of *The Long Quiche Goodbye* and in my most cheerful voice asked, "What did you think about Charlotte Bessette as the protagonist of this story?"

Sliding to the edge of their seats, the snowbirds seemed torn between wanting to run straight out the door and sitting tight in the hopes they'd hear more about the murdered book club member.

No one answered me. I held my breath for a heartbeat or two, and was about to ask the next question from my list, when Lisette bubbled cheerfully, "I liked her so much," and as she told us reasons why, we all followed her into the family-owned cheese shop with all its charm and mystery. Even the newbies relaxed, leaning back in their chairs.

Within a few minutes Jocelyn came out of the kitchen and walked straight out the door. I heaved a deep sigh of relief and began passing the cheese and cracker platter.

The café was quiet, as it usually was in midafternoon. Some swimmers, with hair towel dried and noses sun red, came in for a light snack, and folks stopped by for a takeout order or two. We'd reached the "choose the next book" part of the meeting when Aunt Ophie came out of the kitchen carrying a large tray with ramekins. She walked right into the middle of our circle and announced, "Chervil soufflé."

She nearly placed the tray on the bottom bookshelf, but Bridgy, who was right behind her with a pitcher of sweet tea and napkins, quickly steered her to Dashiell Hammett. And while the Potluck Book Club members crowded around eating soufflé and praising Ophie's talent in the kitchen, we settled on *Dinner: A Love Story* by Jenny Rosenstrach for our next meeting. I asked if anyone wanted me to call the library to put a hold on any copies they might have, but Lisette said she'd heard it's the kind of book she'd definitely want to own. The other clubbies agreed. The snowbirds bought the two copies I had on hand. I promised to order more and call when the books came in.

Ophie was in her glory, explaining how making soufflés in small portions cut the baking time so drastically that you could "whip 'em up" at a moment's notice for those occasions when guests arrived unexpectedly. She was sharing her culinary expertise, which included measurements like "somewhere around a cup and a half" and "if there's a little bit extra in the package, mix it on in."

She was up to "Don't forget to chop the chervil into specks. The more you chop, the more you release that wonderful licorice-like flavor" when the door opened.

Ryan and Lieutenant Anthony were gracious enough to stop at the counter and not barge into the middle of the ladies, for which I was immensely grateful. Ryan signaled me discreetly and I slipped away from the soufflé conversation.

"Don't look so fretful, Sassy. This time I have the best news."

My heart leapt. Please let the nightmare be over.

"You caught the killer?"

"I only wish." Ryan frowned, then brightened. "But we did bring you some measure of solace." He reached into his pocket.

Chapter Thirteen ||||||||||

Ryan handed me a tan envelope with a neatly typed white label. It said "Delia Batson."

"Go ahead, open it."

I pulled the flap, and a gold rectangle on a slim chain slid into my hand. Could it be? Delia's locket?

"Where did you find . . . ? How?"

Ryan was grinning like the Cheshire cat, and even the lieutenant flashed a broad smile, which showed off teeth so straight and even that I wondered if he had an orthodontist in the family.

"For a piece of pie, I'll tell all." Ryan snatched the chain out of my hand and headed to Dr. Seuss. Frank took a step back to let me go in front of him, murmuring, "Ladies first."

I brought two large slices of buttermilk pie and set a plate on the table in front of each deputy. Ophie sidled over from the book nook and waited to see their reactions to her pie. Ryan's mmm-mmm-mmm-ing was long, loud and not unexpected. Frank Anthony took a large bite of pie and began swooning in mock ecstasy. He demanded to meet the baker. The never-shy Ophie pranced forward with a beatific smile. Frank took her hand, raised it to his lips and said, "Please tell me you are not married so I can scheme to make you my own."

Ophie giggled and let her hand linger in Frank's for an extra moment or two, then before slipping through the kitchen door she looked over her shoulder at the lieutenant and with a kittenish wink, told him to stop by anytime, the pie would always be on the house. Ryan doubled over, and as upset as I was about all the chaos in our little world, I couldn't help laughing.

I walked the book club ladies to the door, and then I brought coffee to the table. Ryan ordered me to sit, waving the locket provocatively.

"I thought we had one last chance to find the locket. Suppose Miss Delia was wearing it when she . . ."

He let me fill in that blank.

"So the lieutenant called the Medical Examiner's Office and asked them to let us examine her personal effects. Her clothes were still in the dryer." At my perplexed look, he clarified, "Not that kind of dryer. Morgue dryer. It's special, er, different. Doesn't matter. Anyway, the tech mentioned that they were finished with her jewelry, prints, fluid tests and all. Turns out she had the locket pinned to her, er, unmentionables."

I smiled, remembering a time in high school when I had a college boy's frat pin. Since my parents didn't know about the "older man" in my life, I pinned it to my bra strap when my parents were around. I guess all women use the same hiding places, which begs the question, was Delia hiding the locket or keeping it close to her heart?

Ryan continued, "We took a ride over the bridge to Fort Myers and the ME's Office released the locket so we could return it to the family in time for the burial." He sat back with a broad, satisfied smile and handed me the locket and chain. "We thought you should be the one to give it to Augusta."

Although I hadn't known of its existence until a few hours ago, it felt oddly poignant to have the locket and the delicate gold chain in my hands.

"You're looking at the back. Turn it over." Ryan was eager to see my reaction.

I flipped the locket and there it was, one graceful swamp lily, with six thin petals arching from the center like swimmers diving in an elegant curve off the high board.

"How lovely." I stroked it ever so gently with my index finger. "It looks like the etching was done by hand."

"That's what I think, too." Frank's voice rose a notch. He was as energized as the rest of us. This was a more likable side of his personality. "I wonder why it's that particular flower."

Ryan didn't hesitate. "Easy peasy. The swamp lily blooms year round. Hopefully so does whatever this locket represented to Miss Delia."

Frank said, "Sassy, there's more to come. Open it."

My hands shook a little as I tried to work the delicate clasp. The locket was old and had been so precious to Miss Delia, I didn't want to break it now.

When it popped open, I guess I shouldn't have been as

surprised as I was to see an old black and white picture inside, so ancient that the person's features had all but faded away. An old-fashioned snap-brimmed fedora was still clearly defined.

"Who do you think? Maybe her father? Look at that hat. Men haven't worn hats like that since, oh, way before I was born." Ryan was clearly up for a guessing game.

I called Bridgy from the kitchen and of course Ophie tagged along. Bridgy was thrilled at the adventure of it all even as she pronounced the man unrecognizable.

Ophie wiped her hands on her apron and took the locket carefully. She moved to the window and gazed at the picture in the streaming sunlight. After a while she handed the locket back to me.

"For heaven's sake, that's not her father. It's her lover."

We gaped. She rendered every single one of us positively speechless.

Satisfied that she had us all agog, Ophie continued her thesis. "She might have kept pictures of both parents in her locket, but why only one parent? When a woman keeps a picture of a man for decades and decades, he was important. Someone she could never quite let go."

Then she waggled a finger between Ryan and Frank, saying, "You two rascals can only hope some pretty young filly will be carrying around your picture fifty or sixty years from now."

"You think the picture is that old?"

"Oh, easily. Soon after John F. Kennedy showed up for his presidential inauguration without a hat in 1961, men eased out of the habit of wearing them, and that was years after folks started using color film in their cameras. Between the black-and-white film and him wearing the fedora, I'd say this picture was taken mid-1950s or earlier."

"I suppose Miss Augusta will know who he is," Bridgy ventured. "But, do you think she'll tell us?"

Frank gave a one-shouldered shrug. "She's more likely to tell you than us. That's one reason we thought Sassy should bring her the locket."

"One reason?"

"Yes. The other is that the man in the picture could be our killer and we can't waste time grappling with Miss Augusta Maddox for information. You make a practical go-between."

Go-between! I swear that man is not happy unless he is tweaking my nose. Still, I smiled sweetly and said I'd be happy to help.

At that moment Ryan's shoulder radio began to squawk. He walked to the doorway, had a short conversation and when he turned back, his face was all business. Frank was already on his feet and they hustled out the door.

Bridgy looked at me. "Did you tell them about Bucket Hat and his threats?"

I got defensive. "I meant to, I swear I did, but they were in and out so quickly, and this is quite a distraction." I held the chain high in the air and the locket twirled slowly, the swamp lily dancing in the sun.

Bridgy huffed. "Honestly, Sassy. You could be in real danger. *We*"—she made arm circles wide enough to encompass every person on the island—"could be in real danger. And, what happened, you didn't think to tell the deputies, even though they were sitting right here eating our buttermilk pie?"

"My buttermilk pie," Ophie interjected.

I knew better and stayed absolutely silent waiting for the storm clouds to pass. Bridgy's temper was like a south Florida thunderstorm in August. Loud and threatening for about ten minutes, then the warmth of the sun burst through once again. In a few minutes it would be like there was no storm at all.

But the "no storm at all" part still seemed far off as Bridgy planted her hands in the dreaded elbows out, fists on her hips position. She was about to go back at Ophie and then she hesitated. Perhaps she was thinking of all the meals she'd have to cook until Miguel recovered if Ophie wasn't here. Bridgy dropped her hands and began clearing the pie plates. I reached for the coffee cups, and, hoping the storm had passed, I asked if she wanted to come with me to bring the locket to Augusta. Bridgy brightened immediately.

"Oh, I'd love to hear what she has to say about the picture. Let's get this place cleaned up."

We sent Ophie home on the trolley. Bridgy and I scrubbed and polished until every chore was done. Then we piled in the Heap-a-Jeep and drove a few blocks south to Miss Augusta's house. Augusta's Chevy was still in the driveway, probably exactly where I'd left it.

We climbed the porch steps and knocked on the door. No answer. Bridgy tried again, banging a little harder.

A stout woman wearing a broad-brimmed straw hat and carrying a garden trowel came around the hedge separating her house from Augusta's. She took off one thick red gardening glove and offered to shake hands.

"Afternoon. I'm Blondie Quinlin. I live over there." She pointed to the weather-beaten house on the other side of the hedges. "If you're looking for Augusta, she drove off with Pastor Kendall a while ago. Not back yet."

Bridgy and I exchanged looks, both thinking that Jocelyn must be irritated to no end.

Blondie wasn't done with us. "Lots of coming and going. I suppose it's about Delia?"

When we acknowledged it was, Blondie leaned in like she had a great secret to tell.

"You know, I play Mexican Train Dominoes. We rotate houses. Twice a month we play on Delia's block. I usually walk over. Exercise for the heart." She tapped her chest. "Anyway, that old man in the canoe. The one with the skull. He hangs out around there in the evenings. Used to see him all the time. Someone should ask him if he knows what happened the night Delia was . . . done in."

And she shuffled back to her own side of the hedge.

I scrolled through my cell phone to call Pastor John, but my call went immediately to voice mail.

"Do you think they're at the Rest in Beech?" Bridgy always giggled when she used the old-time islanders' colloquial name for the funeral home.

I shrugged. "They could be anywhere. Wait, I think I have Fern's cell from when we worked on the library book sale together."

Fern said Pastor John and Augusta had been there but she wasn't sure where they were going when they left. I told her we had a necklace that we knew Augusta would want to add to the burial outfit. Fern promised to tell Mr. Beech before he did, what she called, "the finishing touches."

We decided to sit on the porch swing and wait a bit, in case Pastor was driving Augusta home. The sleepy feeling induced by the gentle gliding of the swing was offset by the invigorating breeze coming in from the Gulf. I felt my mood shift from chaos to perfect harmony.

After a few minutes Bridgy asked, "What does Pastor's car look like? Do you remember? We could ride around and see if we can catch up with them. I really want to find out what Augusta has to say about the locket."

I vaguely remembered dark blue, but that was about it. Still Bridgy persisted, "The island's only so big. They can only be in one of a few places."

So we drove past the church and the florist. Then we rode aimlessly.

I was ready to give up, but Bridgy was still a bundle of energy, so I shouldn't have been surprised when she said, "Let's call off the search. I have a better idea. Drive on over to Bowditch."

Best idea ever. It was a beautiful afternoon, perfect for a shoreside stroll in the park, which curved around the northernmost tip of the island.

When we pulled into the parking lot, Bridgy pointed away from the side where we usually left our car. "Over there, park over there."

As I slid into the spot she indicated, Bridgy gave me a broad smile. "Gorgeous day, smooth water. Let's grab a double kayak and look for Skully."

Chapter Fourteen

"You're kidding, right?"

But she wasn't. To hear her tell it, our taking a kayak out into the bay and scouring the canals and inlets looking for Skully was a logical next step.

"First Jocelyn tells you that Skully has been hanging around Delia's house all the time. Now Blondie tells us the exact same thing. We know Skully. Decent guy. Wouldn't squash a spider. But he may have seen something and he didn't know he saw *something important*."

Her emphasis on those last two words included a sharp look that said only a fool would refuse to see the common sense appeal of her idea.

This caper was sure to make driving around the island stalking Pastor John's car seem reasonable by comparison; still, it was a lovely afternoon to be out on the water, no matter how crazy the reason.

We opened the back of the Heap-a-Jeep and I pulled out my ready-for-anything crate. When we first moved to the "land of sunshine," Bridgy and I learned a lot of local rules. Keeping a stash of "hurricane food" along with gallons of water and assorted-sized batteries is the law of the land, as is keeping a container or gym bag in the car trunk to hold all outdoor essentials. I use a green plastic crate I'd bought at the Dollar Tree. It's loaded with umbrellas, long- and short-sleeved sweatshirts and tee shirts, a worn pair of sneakers, assorted flip-flops, mismatched socks, sunscreen, bug spray, antibiotic ointment, binoculars, a bicycle horn and a half dozen hats and visors, some with long brims, some with short.

We slathered on the sunscreen and I stashed the bug spray and binoculars in my bag, along with the bicycle horn, which comes in handy whenever alligators swim too near low-slung watercraft or come up onshore to catch a few rays. Bridgy grabbed a long-sleeved tee and slipped it over her spaghetti strap top. We both snatched visors to wear front and back, to cover our faces and necks.

I couldn't resist a little dig. "Bridgy, do you remember the theme from *Cagney and Lacey*? How about we hum it as we paddle around the bay trying to 'detect' Skully?"

I didn't flinch when she whacked my butt with a handful of visors.

We walked over to the boat basin and were dazzled by the colorful array of canoes and kayaks hanging on boat racks and lying along the shore.

"Help you, ladies?"

A giant of a man with a perfectly waxed Hercule Poirot mustache, much grayer than Poirot would have ever allowed, was standing behind us, a clipboard in his hand. He was wearing a faded blue Fort Myers Beach tee shirt with "Boaters Do It on the Water" stenciled across his massive chest.

Bridgy must have flashed on Ryan's collection of "Deputies Do It Safely" shirts, because she asked in a soft undertone, "Do you think he knows Ryan?"

There was just enough of a breeze coming in off the water to carry her question farther than intended.

The man raised his eyebrows. "Ryan the Deputy or Ryan the Busker who sings in Times Square on Tuesdays? Know 'em both. You?"

Bridgy was all tongue-tied at being caught mid-whisper, so I answered, "We only know the deputy."

"Nice feller. Helpful, too. Gave me this shirt when I donated some prizes to a Christmas party for the children of fallen deputies. Good man. So am I, come to think of it. Name's Tony. What can I do for you gals?"

I told him we were looking to rent a kayak, and I casually pointed to a long two-seater.

"The green one looks like we could handle it."

Before he agreed to let us have the kayak, he grilled us, making sure we knew the differences between a kayak and a canoe. Then he asked when we'd last been out on the water, where we'd paddled and had we ever gone on our own without being part of a flotilla. We had to fudge our answer to the last question since our on-the-water experience was limited to group tours of Lovers Key and Bonita Beach. He seemed satisfied we were experienced enough to handle his craft safely, and showed us a couple of kayaks and talked about the differences.

"You looking for speed or stability?"

It didn't garner his confidence when Bridgy shouted, "Speed," while I landed firmly on the side of stability. He scratched his head and then muttered something about "women" under his breath before saying aloud, "Well, since you two don't agree, a sit-on-top model is out of the question."

He pointed to a silver kayak with no cockpit and a black seat and backrest much higher than I was used to riding. It looked far less secure than I'd like. Gentle though the bay was, I was afraid sitting high could lead to overturning in the wake of even the smallest speedboat. I'd be worried about balance the entire ride.

We settled on a fourteen-foot recreational boat, a compromise that sacrificed some of Bridgy's need for speed and gave in to my yen for stability. It was about five feet shorter than the green kayak, and the difference in length might slow us down but would give us a more secure ride. The two cockpits were wide and roomy for easy access getting in and out.

We rented the ubiquitous bright orange life jackets, loaded a couple of water bottles, a bag of chips and a pack of M&M's under the covered deck and pushed off, with Tony yelling after us, "Don't go too far, you two. I close at six sharp."

We balanced our double-bladed paddles and synchronized our movements until we had a smooth roll, barely moving the water's surface and gliding through the mangrove trees that spread out from the shoreline. I asked Bridgy exactly where we should look for Skully.

She laughed and lifted the right side of her paddle in the

air, while dragging the left in the water, throwing my careful rolling strokes off-kilter.

"Look around. Who cares where we go? We're in paradise. We work too hard and don't play enough. Paddle away. And keep your eyes peeled. Maybe we'll get lucky." And she dipped her blade back in the water, reducing my fear of capsizing.

We had nearly reached the end of the mangroves when Bridgy commanded, "Oops, paddles up. Duck crossing."

Kayak paddles barely disrupt the water, so kayakers could often get quite close to the bay's natural inhabitants.

"Darn. I don't have the nature book. Can't check the species."

Bridgy was quite forgiving. "Hey, we really aren't on a nature trip. We're looking for bigger game." And she laughed at her own silliness. We sat still watching a brown and white mama duck lead her ducklings from the shade of one black mangrove tree across the waterway to another. The mama swam a deliberate route, going far wide of the trees, to keep her babies from getting tangled in the maze of roots.

As soon as the ducks were safely out of our path, we swung out into Estero Bay. We'd entered the bay forty or fifty yards south of the northernmost tip of the island, Bowditch Point, where the salty water of the Gulf of Mexico started to become brackish as it flowed into the bay and met the inflow of freshwater creeks and rivers.

I have to confess that as much as I adore the beachy atmosphere of the Gulf side of the island, with its miles of pristine sand dotted with umbrellas, beach chairs, volleyball nets and the occasional outdoor bar, it can't compare to the freedom of skimming along on a kayak in the bay.

Bridgy suggested we paddle up to the bridge that connected Estero Island to San Carlos Island. Called Matanzas Pass, it was the narrowest waterway on the bay side of Estero Island, and once we were there, we could steal a quick look into canals and inlets, in the hopes of finding Skully or at least his canoe.

"Ryan told me the canoe was green with black buoyancy barrels held by rope on both sides. Should be easy to spot, right?"

"Only if he's here, Bridg, only if he's here. Didn't you hear Ryan explain to Rowena? Skully travels up and down the coast from island to island for no purpose I can determine, but it is his life and his work. Who's to say he's not halfway to the Keys by now?"

"Don't be such a Debbie Downer. It's a fabulous day. And looking for Skully gives us an excuse to hang out with the ducks and, oh look, is that the, what's it called, the poisonous stingray we learned about at the library seminar on 'what to stay away from in the water'?"

Naturally, she lifted her paddle so she could point, and I had to scramble for balance, not wanting to go splat on top of a poison fish. An extremely large diamond-shaped fish swam alongside our kayak. It was dark with light spots, and I remembered the slide presentation immediately. I could even see the name in the lower left corner of the picture of a brown fish with yellow-white spots.

"Spotted eagle ray. And it's dangerous if approached, but not aggressive, as I recall."

Bridgy turned and looked at me in alarm. We pulled

our paddles out of the water as quietly as we could and sat waiting until our new friend was well out of sight.

We crossed under the bridge and continued to paddle for another couple of hundred yards farther along the coast. It didn't take long for us to realize that we were getting tired, it was getting late and there was no sign of Skully or his canoe.

We stopped to admire a flock of great white herons high above our heads. If Skully was anywhere to be seen, the herons were high enough and circling wide enough to see him. But those of us in the kayak gliding along the water were plain out of luck. So we turned and headed back to Bowditch Point.

When we got to the basin we jumped out and pulled the kayak completely onto dry land, then we removed our gear and placed the paddles across the boat, the same way we'd found them.

"You're my kind of customers, coming back right before closing. Them folks think they can stay out on the water until they decide it's time to come in, well, I don't rent to them a second time. No siree. The annoyance ain't worth havin' their business."

Bridgy preened as though we'd gotten a gold star on a spelling paper in second grade. But while Tony was congratulating our promptness, I was staring at a green canoe with black buoyancy bumpers.

So I may have sounded a bit distracted when I told him how glad we were that he was pleased, when all the while, I was trying to figure out how to bring the green canoe into the conversation. I needn't have worried. Bridgy must have followed the direction of my pointed stare, because she screeched, sounding not unlike Jocelyn on the phone earlier.

115

"That canoe. Right there. Was it there all the time?"

Tony looked in the direction of Bridgy's outstretched hand.

"Oh, Tom Smallwood left that here. You know him? Another great guy."

I forced myself to speak in normal, measured tones. "We do know him. In fact we've been looking for him all day."

"I get it. Need some man's work done, huh? Tom's the best. Him and me built that deck. Ever see better craftsmanship? Not likely." And he stroked his mustache in a rough, very un-Poirot-like gesture.

Bridgy started, "Er, actually—"

But I jumped on top of her words. "Exactly! We need some work done and Skully came right to mind."

Tony laughed, a jolly thunderous sound. "So you heard about that? Then you know he's a mite peculiar for all that his work is near enough perfect.

"He come in right after you gals went out. I'm surprised you didn't see him. Though to tell the truth, I think when he don't want to be seen, he's damn near invisible. Anyway, he left the boat for the overnight. Does that once in a while when he has places to go, people to see. Guess this is one of those times. He'll be back tomorrow. Can I tell him where to find you?"

We gave Tony our information. As we walked back to the car, Bridgy was talking about our glorious time on the water while I was wondering how a man and a canoe could hide in plain sight.

Chapter Fifteen

We drove back to Augusta's house and saw Pastor John coming down the wooden steps from the porch. He kept walking toward his car until I hollered, "We have wonderful news."

That brought him to an abrupt stop.

"Have to hurry. Jocelyn has called twice in the past half hour." He tapped his wristwatch with his index finger. His face was flushed and he looked as harried as the White Rabbit in *Alice in Wonderland* who was "late for a very important date." Proof positive that Jocelyn could instill panic in even the kindest of souls.

I hurried to his side and whispered, "Ryan found the locket. I want to show it to Augusta before we bring it to Fern. Delia will be wearing it at the viewing."

"Viewing, oh my, no."

"She can't wear it? But Fern said . . ."

"Of course she can wear the locket." Pastor John was close to losing patience, although I was sure that had nothing to do with me. "But there will be no viewing."

Bridgy and I both looked at him blankly. No viewing?

"Augusta has decided." His voice was as unyielding as if Augusta were speaking. "The funeral service is tomorrow morning at the church. Ten A.M. sharp. Now I really must go. Have to put the finishing touches on my sermon. And coordinate with the organist. And the choirmaster. And find out why Jocelyn requires me to be home this very minute."

Clearly at the end of his tether, Pastor bid us a hasty good-bye and drove away.

"No viewing?" Bridgy raised her eyebrows.

"Don't look at me. This is the first I heard. Fortunate that he told us, though. This way we won't bring up the topic of a viewing and all will be serene."

We were on the porch about to knock on the screen door when we heard Augusta bellow, "You will not stay in Delia's house. You will not step one foot inside Delia's house. Go ahead, get a lawyer. What do they know, anyway? If you are coming tonight, rent a room. We got an island full of them." And we heard her slam the receiver of her telephone hard into the cradle.

I silently counted to ten and then tapped lightly.

"Miss Augusta? It's Sassy and Bridgy. May we come in?"

"Come on in. I'm just after talking to Delia's nephew, Josiah, who's 'bout as dumb as a sack of hammers. Don't want to drive up for the funeral in the morning. Too cheap to pay for a hotel room for him and his brother if they drive up and stay tonight. Wanted the key to Delia's house. Like I'd give him anything. Humph."

"No problem there. I think the sheriff still has the house sealed. Crime scene and all."

Bridgy gave me the elbow at the words "crime scene," but Augusta actually smiled. "Forgot about that. Should have let them go to Delia's and get themselves arrested for whatever the sheriff can think of."

"Disturbing the peace?" Bridgy was nothing if not helpful.

"Disturbin' my peace, that's for sure. Anyway, where's my manners? Come set down. Help yourself to a snack or a drink. People been right neighborly. My kitchen probably has more food in it than the Read 'Em and Eat."

My laugh wouldn't have been quite as forced if I didn't have an immediate vision of Aunt Ophie wildly tossing hundreds of pounds of recipe ingredients hither and yon.

Bridgy came back from the kitchen with a plate of cheese and crackers and a pitcher with orange slices floating in a cheerful-looking red liquid, and pointed out the white tape on the front labeled "nonalcoholic sangria."

"Clever, huh?"

"That's Blondie next door. Nice enough woman. Can't leave well enough alone in the kitchen, though. Always dropping an ingredient or adding something extra to tasty recipes been in the family for generations."

"Her family?"

"Anybody's family. Wish I had a nickel for every time she asked me for a recipe and then, a week or so later, brought over a sample to show me how she 'improved' it. Does it all the time. You better hope she don't come into the café. She'll beg you for recipes; then she'll be giving free samples of her 'fix up' of your food. Probably right from that little table in front of your door."

Augusta shook her head at the thought of our inevitable ruination.

I took the envelope out of my pocket and sat down on the couch next to her recliner.

"Ryan and Lieutenant Anthony found Miss Delia's locket."

Augusta's hand touched her chest, resting at the base of her throat as if to check that she was still breathing. Then she slowly extended her arm and I placed the locket securely in her palm.

She clutched it so tightly that I feared its corners would cut her skin. She shut her eyes. Then she relaxed her hand, opened her eyes and took a long look. As I had done a few hours before, she caressed the swamp lily etching with her index finger.

"Delia will be pleased as punch to wear this locket into the everlastin'. I owe Ryan a heap o' gratefulness. Where'd he find it? I'd almost given it up for gone."

"Miss Delia had it . . . among her clothes when she . . . died. It was in the Medical Examiner's Office." I tried to sound chirpy, as if, silly us, we should have realized where it would be.

"Hmm. Didn't know that was Delia's habit. Happy to have it, though. And in time for the funeral. Praise be. Guess I should let Mr. Beech know." And she started to reach for the phone.

"All taken care of. We called Fern and they are waiting for us to drop it by."

Augusta relaxed deep into the recliner. "Delia can go in peace dressed as she'd want to be."

Bridgy gave me the big eyes and her head nudged toward the locket. I'd forgotten about the picture.

"If you open it, there's a picture inside. We were wondering who the man might be."

Augusta looked startled. "Delia never showed me any picture. Could you open it? And let me get my cheaters on." She picked up a pair of Ben Franklin half glasses from the coffee table.

I leaned in and popped the clasp. Augusta pulled the locket close and stared at the picture.

"I can't believe it. In all these years, Delia never showed this to me or even hinted that the locket had a space for a picture. I never knew it opened. Who can this be?"

Augusta said we'd find a flashlight hanging on a hook by the front door and asked if one of us would bring it to her.

Shining the light directly on the photograph as she held the locket less than an inch from her nose, Augusta scrunched her eyes and peered through her glasses. Finally she flipped off the light.

"Nope," she said definitively. "Never seen him before."

Bridgy sighed. "I guess the mystery man will go with Delia to her grave."

I shot her a warning look, but rather than upset Augusta, Bridgy's romantic nonsense perked her right up.

"Dang it. You're a smart one. That's who he is—the mystery man."

Augusta looked at our blank stares and explained, "You wouldn't know the story. No one this far north of the Ten Thousand Islands would know. It was a long time ago, when we lived on farms near Everglades City. Things were different. Folks had obligations. Delia, especially. Her mother died when Delia was a young'un, and she did the cooking, the cleaning, the washing and all for her father and three brothers. It was her life and it suited her well, leastways that's what everyone thought.

"Not like today. You young girls own businesses, live away from your family and make decisions for yourselves. I don't approve or disapprove, just saying it's a different way of doing things."

"Now to tell the rest of Delia's story I'm relying on my memory of letters from my great aunt Sarah. Aunt to me on my mother's side and to Delia on her father's. It was the year I was away with a church group doing missionary work in the low country of the Carolinas." She stopped for a beat or two. "I'm a bit parched."

Bridgy reached for the pitcher of sangria, but I warded her off and went in search of the Buffalo Trace. I brought back a glass with a full two fingers and under Augusta's approving nod, sat down for the rest of the story.

"Delia was always a bit flighty. Unreliable-like. She'd be out hanging the laundry and the flutter of an orange sulphur butterfly would catch her eye and off she'd follow until a peregrine falcon caught her attention, then she'd follow him right along. Might be an hour or more before she'd get back to the laundry.

"Many a time her father and brothers complained that supper was late because she'd run off to pick a bunch of wild yellow sea daisies or that lavender lobelia she took a likin' to. Come back long after the men were home from the day's chores. The time came when Delia was missing more than she was home and her excuses were thinner."

Augusta took a deep swallow of her Buffalo Trace.

"Then he came knocking at the door. The mystery man. Said he met Delia at a church square dance and wanted to come courting all proper-like. 'Course her father turned the man away. Delia had responsibilities, like I said."

I'm sure that Bridgy was as horrified as I was. We needed to remember that this was another time, another place. We sat perfectly still, barely breathing, as Augusta continued.

"Next thing, Delia run off with him. Dang near to Miami. Her father and her brothers followed along, shotguns in hand, and found Delia before any damage was done, if you catch my meaning. She come home and no one ever mentioned the mystery man again. He up and left these parts. Or her brothers shot him dead. Hard to say which. Don't much matter. I'm guessing all that's left is this picture."

Augusta washed the end of her story down with a healthy sip of the Buffalo Trace and then turned the topic to another missing creature.

"Anyone found Delia's cat? That Bow is a sweet little kitten. Cats make me sneeze, but I'm sure Blondie next door would give her a safe home."

I told her Ryan was actively looking for Bow. But Augusta decided we needed a flier to help search for the missing cat, and Bridgy offered to help make one.

Augusta was looking through her photographs for a large, clear picture of Bow that could be centered on the flier, when the phone rang.

I reached for it, but August said, "No, I'll get it. Probably that pesky Josiah asked his cousin, Edgar, the one with the likable singin' voice, to try and sweet-talk me out of Delia's house key."

She said hello and was quiet for a few seconds. Then she exploded.

"You listen to me. Listen good. No one is buying any part of the Ten Thousand Islands. Not you. Not some resort company. Not for any amount. Show some respect to Delia and stop this tomfoolery."

With the old-fashioned metal telephones, the call can be disconnected with a really loud slam. The other person may only hear the usual click, but for the slammer the satisfaction doesn't fade. Well, Augusta cracked that receiver down with an explosion that could be heard on the mainland.

Then she took a long sip of Buffalo Trace, set the glass down and wiped her mouth with the back of her hand.

"That Rowena is a bothersome one. Why'd she think I had any of Delia's land to sell? And if I did, why'd she think it's any of her business?"

My cell phone rang in the middle of her rant.

It was Ryan calling to say that no one had seen so much as a whisker of Bow since Delia was found.

Looks like we'd be circulating those "Have you seen this cat?" fliers after all.

Chapter Sixteen ||||||||||||

A portly man in a dark suit with an appropriately subdued demeanor opened the door of the Michael J. Beech Funeral Home. He gave us a tight smile and pointed the way to Fern's office, even as he was plastering the somber mask back on his face and widening the door for an elderly couple who had come up the front walk a few steps behind us.

Fern jumped out of her chair-on-wheels and it bounced off the wall behind her, something that, judging by the scuffs on the paint, had happened dozens of times. She hustled out from behind what looked like a genuine oak desk and grabbed Bridgy and me for a group hug.

"I hate when we get clients who I know really well. Delia was such a sweetie. We're all going to miss her."

Then she stepped out of the hug and slid back into her professional self.

We were so used to seeing Fern around town in her

brightly colored tees and tanks spattered with flowers and chunky plastic jewelry that I marveled at how official she appeared in her work clothes, a dark gray skirt, black shell with matching sweater and low-heeled black pumps. I took a closer look and realized she did indeed have panty hose on, an item I'd not worn more than half a dozen times since we'd moved to Fort Myers Beach. Decorum or no decorum, I couldn't imagine having to wear them every day.

When I handed her the locket, she held it in her palm and examined it thoughtfully.

"I'm not sure I've ever seen Delia wear this, and you say Augusta wants it buried with her? That's odd."

"Not really. Augusta said Delia always wore it on special dress-up occasions. Delia kept it pinned to her bra on ordinary days, which even Augusta didn't know. The medical examiner found it." I pointed to the clasp. "Open it."

As soon as she saw the picture Fern smiled. "A long-lost love. I wonder who he is."

My eyebrows shot up to the ceiling. Bridgy laughed out loud. Fern was as sure as Ophie was that the man in the fedora had once been Delia's lover. Of course Augusta's tale of the mystery man had us inclined to believe they were right. Still, I asked, "Why a lover, why not her father or maybe a brother?"

Fern gave us a "don't question my wisdom on this" look, followed by a conciliatory smile. "We deal with bereavement all day, every day. However people spend their lives, they want to spend eternity with whatever they cherish most, be it a wedding ring, a favorite book, an algebra medal from sixty years ago, their childhood pet's favorite toy. You wouldn't believe the variety. But when it comes to pictures . . ."

Fern lowered her voice. We leaned across the desktop, anxious to hear her expert opinion.

"Speaking hypothetically, let's say someone dies."

She stopped. It took a minute for me to realize she needed us to accept that whatever she said was no more than a theory.

"Hypothetically, of course." I nodded in agreement.

Satisfied, Fern continued to whisper. "By all accounts the deceased has had a happy and fulfilling marriage for decades and decades. Yet after the family comes in to make the final arrangements, a longtime friend will show up with a picture of an old flame and beg us to place it in the coffin. Sometimes they even have a note from the deceased, expressing that wish."

Fern raised her voice back to a conversational tone.

"It used to bother me, fooling the family like that, but the older I get, the more I realize how complicated life is. Why should death be any less so?"

She snapped the locket shut and looked at the swamp lily etching. "A true barrier island memento. Well, that alone would make it worth burying with Delia. The old-time lover is a glorious bonus. I wonder why they never married. Do you think he died in a war?"

The story of Delia and the man pictured in the locket wasn't mine to tell, so I shrugged. "I guess we'll never know."

Fern signaled it was time for us to let her get back to work by standing up, her chair once again hitting the wall. In the midst of another group hug, we agreed that we'd all be at the service in Pastor John's church the next morning.

As she opened her office door, Fern said, "I imagine a lot of Delia's friends are upset that there isn't going to be a viewing. Even that scruffy looking handyman, you know the one with the skull in his bag, came in to check on viewing times. Wouldn't believe it when Roy at the door told him there wasn't any. I had to go out and tell him that it was quite true. Church service. Burial. That's it."

And she ushered us out.

We barely had our seat belts on when Bridgy said exactly what I had been thinking. "Is it me, or is all this moving along too fast? Delia's dead body was found yesterday morning, and by tomorrow she's gone for good."

I shook my head. "Not gone. Remember your catechism. We all reunite in heaven."

"I know. Why else would people want to bring pet toys with them? They're planning to play with the pet again in the afterlife. But what about pictures? What good is a picture?"

"I don't know. Perhaps if it's a picture that you've always used to help you remember the long-ago past, you want to make sure the memory doesn't fade in eternity."

"So, what would you take? In case I need to know someday."

Out of the corner of my eye I caught her impish grin. Turnabout is fair play.

"I'd take a copy of Aunt Ophie's buttermilk pie recipe. In case the angels want a sweet treat now and again."

Bridgy lightly punched my arm. "Hey, she's my aunt."

"I'm declaring that henceforth the recipe is the property of the Read 'Em and Eat. So there. Whoever goes first gets the buttermilk pie."

We were haggling playfully over custody of the recipe when I realized we had a more important question to consider. Why was Skully, who was undoubtedly the least sociable person I'd ever met, interested in attending Delia's viewing?

When I asked Bridgy what she thought, she deemed it a coincidence of geography.

"Delia and Augusta have lived on these islands their entire lives, and from what we heard Ryan say to Rowena, so has Skully. Probably their paths crossed a thousand times and he thought to pay his respects since she happened to die while he was here. If he was down on Big Pine Key or up on St. George Island, he wouldn't know she died and wouldn't be asking about the viewing and the service. Timing and location, that's all."

Somehow I wasn't so sure.

The next morning I was shifting hangers from side to side in my closet looking for an appropriate outfit for Delia's funeral service. I was mindful that Ophie would require us to pass well-mannered ladies inspection, so I avoided sleeveless tops, short skirts and pants of any length.

Shoved off to the left I found a black cotton man-tailored shirt with three-quarter sleeves. It had been on a hanger for so long that the front would need a quick touch with the iron, but I thought it would look classy if I wore a slim gold chain around my neck. I took out a gray knee-length A-line skirt but put it back, deciding that the color combo would look too much like I was Fern's clone. Two hangers past the gray skirt I found a long-forgotten olive pencil skirt. I moved to the window and held the skirt next to the blouse in the morning light. Perfect.

I stumbled to the kitchen in search of coffee and found

the table set with a pitcher of orange juice and a bowl of mixed berries for starters. Ophie was at the stove scrambling eggs with one hand and turning slices of bacon with the other.

"Good morning, honey chile. No matter you think your appetite is fit or poorly, you have to eat hearty to get through this most distressing day."

And she set a plate piled high with bacon and eggs in front of me, backing it up with a smaller plate of whole wheat toast.

It was a rare morning that Bridgy awoke later than I did, but I took one look at her stretching in the kitchen doorway and knew she hadn't been out of bed long.

Ophie placed a cup of coffee on the table and held off her cheerful "Good morning" until Bridgy sat down and took a sip or two.

With her elbow resting on the tabletop, and her chin supported firmly by the palm of her hand, Bridgy stifled a yawn.

"Worst night of sleep I've had in years. You'd think that would happen on the day we first found out . . ."

Ophie held a plate of bacon and eggs and set it down when Bridgy nodded. We ate in fret-filled silence until Ophie said, "Okay, enough of that feeling down in the dumps. We are going to put on our best clothes and go to church. We will sing. We will praise the Lord. We will celebrate Miss Delia's life. So you two put a smile on your faces. Well-mannered ladies know that a funeral provides us the opportunity to comfort the living. There'll be plenty of time to mourn the dead for years to come."

I laughed out loud. Bridgy looked at me as if I'd gone

mad, and perhaps she was right. On the other hand, Ophie gave me a wide smile of approval.

I smiled back. "Comfort the living! That's what I've been thinking since, well, since I saw how worn down Augusta has become over these last couple of days."

Ophie had begun to clear the table, but I put my hand on her arm and motioned her to sit.

"What is the one thing we could do that would provide the most comfort to Augusta?"

To Bridgy, most difficulties could be solved by attending an amusing party or meeting a new friend, so her answer was quick and sharp. "Find her a new BFF?"

"Bridget!" Ophie used her schoolmarm voice. "Would you go running out looking for a new best friend before Sassy was even in the ground? Where are your manners? Apologize at once."

Bridgy was genuinely startled. "Oh, Sassy, I didn't mean . . ."

I grinned when I saw the dismay in her eyes. Evidently I'd be missed.

My grin was contagious. We both started laughing, a low chuckle at first, and then we were holding our stomachs and wiping our eyes.

"Land sakes, I'll never understand you two." But Ophie's schoolmarm voice was gone, as was the tension in the air.

"I've been thinking that what Miss Augusta wants most right now is to find out who did this to Miss Delia. And I think we should try to make that happen."

"Shouldn't the sheriff . . . ?"

I cut Ophie off before she could finish the sentence.

"Oh, they should and they will, over time I suppose, but if the three of us work together, we can find out more than they can. We're in a café with folks coming in and out all day long. We hear what people say. They don't even realize we're listening. And we have friends in both the sheriff's office and on the newspaper."

"Aha!" Bridgy nearly knocked over her coffee cup. "I saw you being all flirty with Cady. You are one crafty investigator."

"Crafty means more than quiltin'."

We both turned to stare at Ophie, who shrugged. "I have no idea, but it's what my mama used to say whenever she thought one of us kids was trying to pull a fast one. She was mostly right."

And her glance drew our eyes to the clock on the microwave. We'd have to hurry to get to the church on time. I was happy that I got my idea out with no resistance. Once the funeral was over and our schedule was closer to normal, I was determined that Delia's killer would be caught and punished.

Chapter Seventeen

Ophie insisted we take Bridgy's sporty little Escort ZX2 because she deemed the Heap-a-Jeep too "scruffy" for a funeral. She refused to drive her roomy Town Car because she didn't know the roads. I mean, really, on an island less than eight miles long and not a mile wide at any given point, did she really think we'd automatically get lost because she was behind the wheel?

So there I was scrunched up in the backseat of Bridgy's perky red two-door response to her divorce. So much for ironing my skirt and blouse; by the time I unfolded out of this seat, I'd look like I'd taken a nap fully dressed.

As we pulled into the church parking lot, I was delighted that a large turnout was in the making. Delia, who'd never hurt another living being, not four legged, two legged or winged, deserved a royal send-off, and from the size of the crowd heading to the church, she was going to get one.

We parked at the far end of the lot in the spaces reserved for those going to the cemetery.

Aunt Ophie got out of the car, read the "reserved for cemetery vehicles" sign and started to bluster. "Why didn't y'all tell me we were going to the cemetery? In this car we look like a fire engine in the Fourth of July parade. You should have let me know. I would've driven."

I was still struggling out of the backseat. I'd decided butt-first was the easiest way to go, so I was giving Ophie a perfect view of my thoughts on the matter. Bridgy, who was remarkably patient with her aunt, even on this stressful morning, said, "Aunt Ophie, darlin', it would be too much for you to drive from here to the mainland and back, given the unfamiliar roads and all."

By the time I was out of the car and upright, Ophie was nodding in agreement as though she hadn't had her own words thrown back at her by her smiling niece.

I was smoothing the front of my skirt, trying to force the new wrinkles to lay flat, when Ophie saw Ryan crossing the parking lot. He was dressed in gray slacks and a white shirt with a blue and green striped tie, the one garment I would have sworn he didn't own.

"There is that nice deputy. Oh, I wonder if his handsome friend is here." And she began yoo-hooing Ryan, in a tone a bit louder than circumstances would dictate.

As Ryan headed our way, Ophie turned to me. "Should we tell him now? Tell him we'll help in any way we can?"

"Not the time. Certainly not the place." And I was happy to see her nod in agreement.

Ophie wasted no time in inquiring about Frank Anthony. "Where's your friend, the one who so liked my buttermilk pie?"

"Don't you worry your pretty little head, Miss Ophelia. He's here. Lots of deputies here. You can't be too sure who'll show up at a murder victim's funeral."

Murder victim—that still sent chills down my spine. I left Bridgy and Ophie chatting with Ryan and started to scout around the parking lot looking for an unexpected face, one that usually hides under a bucket hat. But no luck. I waved across the parking lot to Fern and was pleased to see Holly and Maggie walking into the church with Lisette. I spotted Rowena crossing the street deep in conversation with Judge Harcroft. Talk about an odd couple. Still, I was happy that the book clubs were well represented.

Bridgy came out of nowhere and grabbed my arm, steering me inside. We took seats on the center aisle, opposite an open window with a large fan spinning at top speed. Even this time of year, a crowded church could get uncomfortably warm. I noticed Ophie clutched a lace-trimmed hankie, ready to mop and sop as needed.

The pews filled quickly. The organist began to play a soft, but unfamiliar, tune. Dressed in his cassock, Pastor John came out on the dais from a side room, with two young acolytes at his heels. He fussed with some papers on the pulpit while one of his helpers straightened the numeral seven that had fallen askew on the hymn board. Then Pastor moved to the center of the dais and faced the rear of the church. The organist started the prelude to the entrance hymn, and we all stood as Pastor John walked to the doorway to greet the family and welcome Miss Delia into the church for the last time.

When the processional came down the center aisle, I was again struck by how shrunken and timeworn Miss Augusta had become. She didn't quite reach the shoulders of the two middle-aged men, one balding, the other with a paunch that completely hid his belt, who flanked her, and neither of them was any taller than average. I guessed they were Delia's nephews, although I didn't see a speck of family resemblance.

As I watched the family walk by, I noticed Frank Anthony sitting on the opposite side of the aisle a few rows farther back. He touched two fingers to his eyebrow and gave me a short salute and a broad wink. I was surprised that he and Ryan weren't sitting together, but then I realized deputies were probably scattered all around the church, watching for any sign of a killer who, perhaps, couldn't stay away.

Bridgy gave me an elbow to the ribs and when she had my attention, mouthed, *Skully*, and slid her eyes toward the outside aisle off to our left. Skully was sitting in the back row, keeping his distance from the other mourners. He seemed to have combed his hair for the occasion. He kept his eyes straight ahead as if determined to concentrate on the altar and not be distracted by folks jostling in various pews. After the service, I'd finally have the opportunity to ask if he'd seen any unusual activity around Delia's house, if not on the night she died, then anytime.

Pastor gave a strong and lively sermon about all God's gifts that surround us during our lifetime. He talked about the gifts of the sea, from the tiniest mollusk to dolphins and manatees. He told us about the gifts of the land, animals and flowers, bushes and trees. Then he reminded us Miss Delia was always respectful toward all God's gifts. He moved on to those she cherished the most, her friends and her family. And by the time he was finished awakening our memories of her gentle approach to every living thing, there wasn't a dry eye in the church.

Pastor introduced Josiah Batson, whom he described as Miss Delia's oldest nephew, and asked him to speak a few words about his "beloved aunt."

Josiah stood up, strode into the aisle and hoisted his potbelly before he struggled up the steps to the altar. He did a better job of climbing to the pulpit by grasping the ledge.

He cleared his throat, let his eyes wander around the church and, finally, spoke.

"My brother, Edgar, and I were tied by business to Everglades City, and you know how Aunt Delia was about traveling. Not something she liked to do. Still, as the oldest living member of our family, Edgar and I showed her the respect she deserved."

He looked around as though daring anyone to challenge him. Satisfied that we hung on his every word, he continued.

"We never missed a holiday that we didn't send thoughtful gifts and touching cards to our, er, beloved aunt."

Ophie's stage whisper was none too quiet. "It's like he read a description of what he should be saying and is throwing in the words he recalls but doesn't know quite where they fit. Thoughtful gifts, my aunt Fanny. If he has to call them thoughtful, he probably didn't think much about them."

Someone a row or two behind us shushed her, and we continued to listen to the insincere nephew.

"And didn't we have fun. My, er, beloved aunt Delia was such a jokester. Many a Sunday night we'd be on the phone telling stories and chuckling 'til all hours. Couldn't hardly keep her quiet."

A rustling reverberated throughout the church as row after row of funeral-goers looked at each other and considered what he was saying. *Is he talking about Miss Delia Batson?*

Pastor John had the advantage of sitting facing the pews, and he recognized trouble when he saw it. He rushed over to the pulpit and tugged on Josiah's sleeve, while booming loud enough for us all to hear, "Thank you. Thank you, Mr. Batson, for that tender eulogy to your aunt Delia."

As he led Josiah down the altar steps, Pastor signaled nephew number two to approach. The crowd was starting to settle down again. I'm sure we all hoped he knew his aunt better than Josiah did.

Pastor John clasped his hands and then spread his arms.

"You all know Miss Delia loved gospel music. Why, she often came to church on Wednesday nights to listen to the choir practice, and perhaps do a little toe tapping. Today her nephew Edgar will join our choir in singing 'I'll Fly Away,' a longtime favorite of Miss Delia's."

The balding nephew stepped over to the choir and moved behind a waiting microphone stand. The organist played the introduction and then replayed it. Not a peep from the nephew. At the third try, as if it was the one he'd been waiting for, Edgar belted out, "*Some glad morning . . .*" and signaled the choir to join in for the chorus.

Augusta was right. He had a strong, beautiful voice, a "Danny Boy" kind of tenor. By the time he reached the second stanza, we were all clapping or waving our arms. At song's end, the church was filled with people who would always remember Miss Delia's service as a warm and joyful event.

Pastor John shook hands with Edgar and then announced that Miss Augusta Maddox had arranged for a buffet in the parish hall immediately following the graveside ceremony at the Riverview Memorial Park in Cape Coral.

"For those not escorting Miss Delia to the cemetery"— here he gave a slight frown, indicating disapproval of those thoughtless folks—"my wife, Jocelyn, and the gracious ladies of the Food Pantry Committee will serve lemonade and cookies until it is time for the buffet. Now, let us pray . . ."

As I bowed my head in prayer, I took a quick look to the back of the church. Skully was still in the last pew, his hands prayerfully folded. Now that the service was nearly over, I was anxious to get to the parking lot so I could talk to him before we left for the cemetery. I glanced over my other shoulder, and Frank Anthony was still in his seat, looking every bit as attentive as one of Pastor John's acolytes. I decided it would be best if he didn't see me talking to Skully.

The choir sang "Shall We Gather at the River?" and Miss Delia Batson, who'd spent her entire life among the rivers, creeks and bays fronting the Gulf of Mexico, left her favorite church for the final time.

Once the recessional passed by I realized the folly of sitting on the center aisle. Pews were emptying in order, front to back, and it would be a while before we could leave. I turned toward the other end of the pew, hoping we could use the side aisle, but the row was full and my pew-mates were facing me, waiting to go out the center.

I was trapped. I looked at the spot where Skully was sitting, but his seat was empty. I scanned the throng moving slowly through the vestibule and thought I caught a glimpse of him. Perhaps he wasn't that far ahead.

Finally it was our turn. I moved into the aisle, but there was no way to push through the mourners without being extremely rude. I noticed that Frank Anthony was no longer in his seat. I wondered how he'd managed to beat the crowd. Flashed a badge? Probably not.

I pushed through the wide front doors and stood on the top of the church steps. I had an excellent view of the parking lot, but Skully was nowhere to be seen. Then I realized he didn't have a car. I hurried toward the curb, hoping to catch him walking away.

Chapter Eighteen ⅢⅢⅢⅢⅢ

I took a quick look in all directions. No sign of Skully. I rubbed the back of my neck to relieve the knot of dejection that was rapidly tightening and walked back to the parking lot. Cars were already lining up behind the hearse for the trip to the cemetery. I thought Bridgy would be standing beside the Escort tapping her toe and pointing to the time on her imaginary wristwatch, but she and Ophie were talking to Rowena, Judge Harcroft and an animated man wearing a dark suit and tie. He was very touchy-feely, first patting Ophie's arm and then putting a chummy hand on the judge's shoulder. His outfit made me think he was one of the ushers, but his attitude shouted "used-car dealer."

I circled the group until I was in Bridgy's line of vision, then I waved to get her attention. But when she and Ophie started to walk toward me, the stranger grabbed Bridgy's wrist and thrust a business card into her hand. He tried to give one to Ophie as well, but she shook her head and kept walking.

"Who's your new friend?"

Bridgy handed me the business card and unlocked the car. "Looks like they're ready to go."

Sure enough, the hearse had pulled out of the parking lot and, with headlights on, the cortege was inching its way toward Estero Boulevard. We were the last car in a long line, so I was still trying to get comfortable in the tiny backseat when the hearse started up the incline of the San Carlos Bridge.

Finally settled in, I looked at the thick cream-colored card. The logo showed a half-filled champagne glass, with a rose lying across its base. The card read: TIGHE KOSTOS, Vice President for Acquisitions, World of Luxury Spa Resorts.

"Is this the company that wants to buy Delia's island?"

"More likely the company that *will* buy Delia's island. At least according to the big shot in the suit."

"There they were, closing the deal, and Delia not even at the cemetery, much less in the ground." Bridgy adjusted her rearview mirror so she could look me in the eye. "Wouldn't surprise me if this Kostos guy would kill to get what he wants. You know how those corporate types are."

"Eyes on the road."

Didn't matter we were only going 5 MPH, Bridgy's driving always made me nervous. "He's probably showing off big-city bravado to the hayseed locals. I'm sure the nephews barely had time to unpack their overnight bags, much less consider a land deal."

"Well they had time to hire a lawyer," she shot back in her "can you top this?" voice.

"Lawyer? They just arrived. Where would they find a— not Judge Harcroft? How on earth? Rowena, that conniving . . . She found out about the nephews and probably had the judge blocking traffic at the foot of the San Carlos Bridge until the nephews crossed onto the island. He was a traffic court judge, you know."

I was only half kidding then, and only half kidding a few minutes later when I said, "Augusta will kill her for sure."

"Sassy, please!" Ophie made one of her well-mannered ladies speeches ordering us not to talk about killing in the middle of the funeral of a murder victim. I suppose I should have known there was a protocol. I mumbled an apology, but my mind was already looking for a way to thwart Rowena and her cronies. Delia wanted the land to stay undeveloped, and as far as I was concerned, that should have settled that.

We drove awhile longer then crossed over the Caloosa-hatchee River and made an immediate turn into the Memorial Park. Delia's plot was elevated high enough that I imagined she would enjoy watching the river flow ever westward into the Gulf.

After a brief graveside ceremony we mourners were back in our cars, left to find our way to the reception in the church hall.

We passed the turnoff for the Medical Center, and I felt a pang of guilt when I realized I hadn't yet visited Miguel. Definitely on my to-do list, and sooner rather than later.

There was a nice-sized crowd gathered in the parish hall. Four long tables and more than a dozen card tables were scattered about the room. Several women I recognized but couldn't name wore serviceable white bib aprons over their "church lady" dresses. Jocelyn signaled two of them who rounded up the others and they all marched into the kitchen.

The chatter around the room grew hushed as Miss Augusta came in through the main door looking frailer than when we stood at the graveside. Leaning on Pastor John's arm, she took slow, shuffling steps. The day and the circumstances were taking a toll. The nephews, looking extremely uncomfortable in such a communal setting, walked along behind her.

Pastor led Augusta to a table at the front of the room and eased her into a chair. Jocelyn came running out of the kitchen and began fluttering around until I thought Augusta would reach up and swat her away. Finally Jocelyn scurried back to the kitchen and returned with a cup and saucer. I didn't know what the beverage was, but I thought if it wasn't Buffalo Trace, it wouldn't do Augusta much good.

The crowd started to swarm in Augusta's direction, and the chatter grew louder once again. Left to their own devices, the nephews stood in the center of the room, looking for all the world like they wished they had anywhere else to be.

Holly, seeming all grown-up in a dark skirt and light blue V-neck blouse, and her mom called us over to a table. Since there were only two empty seats and three of us, Holly jumped up and offered her seat to Ophie, gaining a well-mannered ladies nod of approval. I signaled Holly to sit and swung an empty chair from the next table.

Bubbly as always, Holly bounced in her seat. She looked around to see who was nearby, and then she whispered as though we were coconspirators about to pull off a bank heist, "This was my first funeral service. I'm really glad it was for Miss Delia. She was slammin'."

I looked at Maggie, who translated, "Awesome."

"If we were at the Classic Book Club meeting together, she would always slip me a couple of hard candies. Butterscotch. My favorite. Once when I stopped by her house to drop off a book I borrowed, Miss Delia invited me in for cookies and she gave me this."

Holly held out her arm to display a bracelet with tiny shells threaded on delicately woven fishing line. While we were admiring it I stole a glance at Bridgy, who read my mind and nodded in agreement. The bracelet looked an awful lot like Skully's work.

One of the apron-wearing ladies invited us to the buffet sumptuously laid out on the long tables. As we stood up, I looked around. Augusta still had a crowd buzzing around her, each one wanting to give personal condolences. At first I didn't see the nephews, and then I did—off in the corner with Rowena, Judge Harcourt and the vice president from the resort. I was incensed. I thought about marching over and breaking up their "meeting," but out of respect for Miss Delia and especially Miss Augusta, I decided to ignore them.

Miss Augusta made a different decision. I didn't see her get up from her chair, but clearly her energy was renewed. By the time I noticed, she was marching, spine straight, shoulders back, directly toward the group that included the nephews. I jumped from my chair, hoping to head her off, but she didn't wait to get up close.

Still half a room away from them, she yelled, "Vultures. That's what you are, a thieving bunch of vultures."

The silence in the room was louder than a sonic boom. Pastor John and I, both on the move to head off Augusta, froze in our tracks.

Rowena took what I'm sure she thought was a conciliatory step toward Augusta, which only increased her rage.

"Stay away from me and mine you biggety troublemaker. I know what you're fixing to do. Talking those foolish boys into throwing away everything that was important to Delia. For shame."

Rowena opened her mouth but seemed to have thought better of getting in a battle with Augusta in front of half the town. She clamped her jaw shut and backed away, trying to slide behind Judge Harcroft.

Augusta shook her finger at the judge. "You're no better. In cahoots with the likes of her. Stealin' Delia's land for money. Honorable judge! Ha!"

Judge Harcroft's eyes nearly popped out of his head, but he, too, decided that only discretion would save his reputation, and he stayed silent. When I looked around, the resort vice president and Delia's nephews had completely disappeared.

Pastor put his arm around Augusta's fragile shoulders and led her back to her seat. Blondie Quinlin broke from the crowd of gray-haired ladies, moved closer, leaned over Augusta and whispered. Augusta nodded, a little smile playing on her lips, and she seemed to regain her composure. Deciding I wasn't needed at that exact moment, I turned back to my table.

" 'Biggety'! Miss Augusta called the Emporium lady 'biggety.' What does that mean?" Holly shrugged her shoulders and circled her hands from side to side, beside herself with excitement for having witnessed so much spectacle among the adults.

"Why, honey chile, biggety is southern for 'full of yourself,' possibly even 'overbearing'. And that pushy lilac-haired woman is nothing if not biggety." Ophie was always happy to provide language lessons along with her well-mannered ladies lectures and cooking advice. Her encyclopedic wisdom knew no bounds.

Maggie watched her daughter's face as she absorbed the meaning. "See, Holly, you and your friends have a language all your own and sometimes so do your elders."

"Biggety!" Holly was gleeful. "I know a lot of kids who are biggety! Can't wait to intro the word on Twitter." She pulled out her cell phone and began tapping the keyboard.

Cady came over, pulled up a chair and asked what the kerfuffle was all about. When Bridgy and I explained the resort company expressed an interest in an island Delia supposedly owned, Cady said it all made sense.

"The newspaper received a letter from some company asking for any biographic information we had on residents who were at least third- or fourth-generation Floridians. They were primarily interested in 'family land.' I bet it was the same company.

"The request for land information struck my publisher as odd, so he responded that we don't have anything like that available. I guess they had other resources."

Blondie stopped by and I introduced Cady. After hellos all around I asked what she had said to Miss Augusta that helped her regain her self-control so quickly.

"I told her that Willie Harcroft wet his pants in the schoolyard during recess in third grade. I know it for a fact because I was there when it happened. And now when Augusta looks at him, she'll see a little boy wearing enormous black spectacles and sodden dungarees who spent the rest of his grammar school years known as Wee-wee Willie." Blondie's high-pitched voice trailed behind her as she moved on to spread the story.

Our entire group exploded with laughter, which snapped Holly's attention away from her keyboard. "What?"

Ophie patted Holly's hand. "Never you mind. We're being silly is all."

The crowd thinned out and Augusta held her own in a social sense, shaking hands and thanking everyone for their kindness. The nephews never came back to take up their share of the responsibilities, so Bridgy and I decided to ask Miss Augusta if she needed us to help.

Her smile was soft and gentle.

"Delia is buried with her locket thanks to you gals. Past few days have been easier for me with all you done. If I could ask one more favor, please see if you can find Bow. Delia loved that cat. We need to find her a home where she can roam free but still have a place to get her neck ribbon changed and get a taste of vittles."

It was the last gift Augusta could give Delia. Bridgy and I were determined to make it happen.

I left Bridgy talking to some of our café regulars and went off to wash my hands. Rowena waylaid me as soon as I stepped out from the women's room. "Sassy, you must help me."

Before I could answer, she glanced all around.

"Not here, but soon. It's a matter of life and death." And she hurried out the side door into the parking lot.

Chapter Nineteen ‖‖‖‖‖‖

I took my seat next to Bridgy, who said, "Don't you look mystified. Are you pondering the meaning of life?"

"Almost. I met Rowena in the hallway and she wants to talk to me about a matter of life and death. What can she possibly mean? And why me of all people?"

Bridgy's response was brittle. "Cold hard cash is the only thing important to Rowena. She says 'life and death' but she means 'help me make money.' Maybe she wants us to do some consignments for her."

As soon as she said it I knew she was right. Bridgy's acute understanding of people's faults and weaknesses never ceased to amaze me. Here I was thinking Rowena feared for her safety, but more likely, she was worried about her cash register. The tragedy of Delia's death had me thinking drama, drama, drama.

Ophie came back from the dessert table with two paper

plates each piled with homemade brownies. Cady and Holly were both reaching before Ophie sat down but leaned back in their chairs as soon as she cleared her throat.

"That's better." Ophie nodded her approval. "Excellent table manners all around. Now"—she pointed to the plate on the left—"these have walnuts. The others are plain."

We all chose from one plate or the other, and I was smart enough to say, "These are all right, but something's missing. Not quite as yummy as yours."

Ophie beamed. "Why thank you, darlin'. Let me have a taste." She nibbled, pronounced the brownie to be short on cocoa and then proceeded to polish it off. As she wiped a crumb from her lip, she glanced around the hall.

"This space isn't much bigger than the Read 'Em and Eat. Yet it seems roomier. Hmmm. I bet if you got rid of those ugly old bookshelves, you would have a wide-open dining area just like this. More comfortable for the customers. Easier for the servers to move around. Yesterday I bumped my hip, not once but two different times, squeezing between tables." And she smoothed her skirt from waist to thigh as if she had Miss America–sized hips, which hadn't been true for decades.

"Are . . . ?" Before I could finish asking if Ophie was crazy, Bridgy clamped her hand on my wrist, signaling immediate silence.

"Aunt Ophie, that is quite a suggestion. Isn't it, Sassy?" Everyone at the table, except apparently Ophie, knew that the bookshelves were the heart and soul of the café for me. With all eyes pointed in my direction, I managed to echo, "Quite a suggestion."

Ophie nodded, satisfied that the matter was settled. I

could only pray she wouldn't arrange for carpenters to start tearing the café apart at sunrise.

Working harder to distract me, Bridgy announced that she and I were going to visit Miguel and asked Maggie if she would mind giving Ophie a ride home.

Oblivious to Bridgy's motive to keep us apart until I calmed down, Ophie said, "Why, I wouldn't mind visiting Miguel myself," even as Maggie agreed to drive her back to the turret.

Bridgy signaled "no" by fluttering her hand a little too close to Ophie's face, which might have started a well-mannered ladies lecture, but Ophie was distracted by Cady, who chose that exact moment to ask if Ophie would be willing to be interviewed for a public interest piece for the Sunday edition of the newspaper.

She was so busy nodding and batting her eyelashes that she barely noticed when Bridgy and I stood, mouthed a silent thank-you to Maggie and left the table.

We spent a few moments assuring Augusta that we would be available for any help she might need, and as we left her in the comfort of a circle of women from the church, she boomed, "Sassy, don't forget your promise."

I stopped dead still, turned and gave her a solid thumbs-up. She smiled and returned the salute. We were coconspirators until Delia's killer was found.

Bridgy raised a questioning eyebrow, but I shushed her and nodded toward the heavy oak front door. She read that correctly as "I'll tell you outside."

The door to the parking lot opened. The sunshine was so blinding, I didn't recognize the two men coming through the doorway.

Bridgy leaned in. "Now's your chance. Tell them about Skully." And she stepped farther back into the vestibule, determined to avoid a difficult conversation in the blazing sunshine. It was then that I recognized Ryan Mantoni and Frank Anthony, both still dressed in street clothes.

I wavered. I didn't mind talking to Ryan, but Frank Anthony was bound to be trouble. He'd get all uppity, accuse me of hiding evidence or some such. Still, there was probably no way I could avoid it. We were all crowded in the vestibule, and Bridgy was never going to let me walk through to the parking lot without talking about Skully.

Ryan asked how Miss Augusta was managing, and that gave me a chance to describe the scene between Augusta and the nephews. In the interest of delay, I was toying with the idea of sharing Judge Harcroft's third grade misadventure, when Bridgy, totally out of patience, said, "For goodness' sake, Sassy, tell them about Skully."

Was it my imagination or did their ears twitch? I took a deep breath and then charged forward with a jumble of words crossing the stories from both Jocelyn and Blondie.

An older couple walked into the vestibule from the reception but hesitated when I suddenly stopped talking. Ryan, always the gentleman, opened the door to the parking lot and made a "come right this way" gesture. The man took the door handle from Ryan with a nod of thanks, and they left us to our conversation.

Frank Anthony decided that we were in the worst possible spot and told Ryan to find us a better one. We stood mutely until Ryan came back with Pastor John, who shook Frank's hand.

"Lieutenant Anthony, so nice to finally meet you. Why

not use the parsonage? Jocelyn and I will be busy here for at least another hour. The side door is unlocked."

Jocelyn! After all her oohing and aahing about the handsome new "sheriff," I was amused at the thought of her coming home to find him sitting in her own house, albeit with guests. Well, I could always hope that this interview, as the sheriff's deputies liked to call it, would be quick.

The side door was indeed unlocked, and we sat in a cozy den adjacent to the kitchen. I wondered if everyone else was as uncomfortable as I was at being in Pastor and Jocelyn's home without them present. Remembering my foraging through Miss Delia's house with Ryan, I decided that the deputies were probably used to going wherever their jobs took them.

And of course there was no host or hostess to offer a glass of sweet tea, or even a sip of water.

Following the same routine I noticed when they interviewed Miss Augusta, Ryan looked to Frank, who gave a slight nod. Then Ryan asked me to tell them what I had heard about Skully and reminded me to start from the beginning and include what I told them before we were interrupted in the vestibule.

I had finished recounting my first and second conversations with Jocelyn and was about to say that Blondie told us basically the same thing, when my phone pinged. I glanced down in my lap involuntarily, and when I saw a text message from Maggie I opened it without thinking. Of course I stopped talking as I did so. We were together when we met Blondie, so Bridgy started to fill in, but the lieutenant wasn't having any of it.

He shushed her with a curt "We'll get to you soon enough."

Two can play that game. I deliberately leaned over to show Bridgy the text.

OPHIE HOME WE R 2 CYA

Bridgy, never one to take being silenced lightly, said, "Great news," and grinned as if she'd won the Florida State Lottery.

"Can we please get back to Skully?"

Ryan's pleading outranked Frank Anthony's impatience, so I politely repeated what Blondie had told me, including the rotation of her regular Mexican Domino game, which was the reason she frequented Delia's street.

And with no discernible signal, Ryan and the lieutenant shifted roles. Frank became the questioner and Ryan the observer. Frank got out of his chair and stood with legs akimbo and arms crossed. By now I knew he liked the height advantage as an interrogation technique, but he looked for all the world like Yul Brynner in *The King and I*, a movie Bridgy and I watched a gazillion times during our junior year in high school when Bridgy played the role of Lady Thiang, the King's head wife, in the school drama club. I kept expecting Frank to burst into song. "Shall We Dance?" or, more likely, "A Puzzlement."

That would have had entertainment value, but instead I had to sit there and listen to Frank hammer away at the fact that I had my first conversation with Jocelyn before he interviewed me and I neglected to tell him.

Then he had me painstakingly outline a timeframe connecting my second conversation with Jocelyn, my conversation with Blondie and the visit he and Ryan made to the café to bring me the locket.

In his mind, I'd been withholding information again. Still, he was civil until Bridgy told him we'd kayaked out in the bay hoping to find Skully so we could ask if he saw any unusual people around Delia's house. Then he hit the roof.

He threw his hands up in the air and turned to Ryan. "You call these women your friends. How do they not understand that murder is serious business?"

Frank ran his fingers through his hair, but unlike Cady, who used it as a smoothing mechanism, Frank ruffled his hair until it looked like a rooster comb.

By the look on Ryan's face, if he could have shriveled up and blown away like a fallen needle from a sand pine tree, he would have done so and gladly.

The ordeal ended with a clearly frustrated Frank Anthony telling us to "cease and desist." Yep, he actually said those exact words, ordering us to stop interfering with an official murder investigation. As if we were interfering. We couldn't even find Skully no matter how hard we tried. Glad to be out from under the repetitive blast of questions, Bridgy and I strode across the parking lot to her sporty Escort, anxious to get on with our afternoon. As she hit the clicker that flashed the lights and unlocked the door, I clapped my hands and shouted, "Freedom!" much to the surprise of the few mourners walking from the parish hall to their cars.

I jumped into the passenger seat.

Bridgy flipped on the air conditioner. "Freedom? Really? We were only being questioned. We weren't in jail."

I dismissed the deputies with a back flip of my hand.

"Oh, not that. Freedom from a backseat that was clearly designed to carry a couple of grocery bags or a tennis racket, not a full-grown person no matter how I twisted and bent."

Bridgy slid her iPod in the car dock and hit "Scramble." We hummed along to the Black Eyed Peas and then I played air guitar accompanying Brad Paisley. When "Love on Top" by Beyoncé popped out of the speakers, we sang along, hit "Repeat" and sang again until we crossed onto the mainland. I was luxuriating in the space the front seat gave me to wiggle and bounce in time to the music. I kept an eye on Bridgy. Dancing while driving was as dangerous as texting while driving, but she seemed content to sing along, tapping her fingers on the steering wheel.

Just as Bridgy turned into the Medical Center parking lot, I realized we didn't have a get-well gift.

We decided she'd drop me off so I could run into the gift shop while she parked the car. It was a great plan until I stepped out of the car. As I turned to close the door, Bridgy held up her hand, "wait a minute" style. I leaned down to hear whatever she'd forgotten to tell me and was instantly sorry.

"Why don't we ask Miguel what he thinks about expanding the café floor space? I mean, can he comfortably cook for a greater number of customers with only us to help out in the busy times? That's definitely part of the equation."

She laughed as she said it, but that didn't make it any easier to take. Too stunned to answer, I slammed the car door, hoping it rattled her molars. Did she seriously think I'd consider turning the Read 'Em and Eat into a café without books?

Chapter Twenty

Bridgy found me in the gift shop paying for three gaudy get-well balloons, a box of crème-filled chocolates and a white ceramic bud vase filled with yellow gerbera daisies.

"Epic choices. Miguel loves chocolates. Flowers are cheery, and . . . what does the blue and green balloon say? *¡Qué te mejores!* Is that 'get well' in Spanish?"

"Well at least that's what the sign on the counter says. And don't pronounce the 'j' like that."

In the elevator Bridgy cautioned me not to expect much from Miguel. When she visited yesterday, he was loopy on pain meds, extremely sleepy and didn't make much sense. We tiptoed into his hospital room only to find Miguel, left leg propped up and in a cast from hip to ankle, spinning around in a wheelchair. A harried-looking middle-aged woman dressed in yellow scrubs was trying desperately to stop him.

"You will get hurt, I promise you, with all this spinning and fooling around. Now pay attention to what you're doing," she demanded, but Miguel wasn't having any.

On the next spin, he saw us in the doorway and came to such an abrupt stop that he nearly fell out of the chair. He grabbed the edge of the bed rail to steady himself and ignored the therapist's triumphant "I told you so."

"Hola, chicas. ¿Qué pasa?"

He wasn't at all the sleepy patient Bridgy described, although loopy might still apply. I felt compelled to screech, "Miguel, careful!"

His grin was mischievous. "I conquered the chair no problem. The crutches are the real torture. And Esther runs the torture chamber."

Rather than be offended, the lady in yellow smiled and extended her hand. "Esther Johnson. I run the physical therapy section, and believe me, I've had worse patients. Miguel will be fine on his own when the doctor sends him home. Well, I'll leave you to visit. Please don't let him spin."

And with a shake of her finger toward Miguel, she was gone.

"Lucky I moved from my old second-floor apartment near Times Square to the bungalow. Only two steps. I can manage *sin mucho problema*. Say, what are you doing here so early in the day? Who's running the café? Is Ophie in my kitchen? I warn you, she's very sloppy."

I laughed out loud. Sloppy doesn't begin to describe Ophie's methods. Still, I wasn't ready to tell Miguel about Delia, so instead of answering, I thrust the balloons and chocolate at him.

Bridgy held up the vase and set it on the windowsill.

While he was opening the box of candy, Miguel asked us to tie the Spanish language balloon to the handle of his wheelchair and the other two to the foot rail of his bed.

"Tie the red balloon a little lower. Now can you raise the orange and yellow one to the same height? *Gracias*."

As soon as we had all three balloons anchored to his exact specifications, Miguel handed me the chocolates, shouted, "Balloon fight!" and rolled into the narrow space at the foot of the bed. The *¡Qué te mejores!* balloon bounced against each of the balloons tied to the bed rail. Then he spun and lined the chair up, preparing for another run.

Miguel totally ignored our protests. He cheered when the wheelchair balloon knocked the first bed rail balloon smack into the second. Waving his arms in victory, he asked for another chocolate to celebrate his righteous win.

"So nice you came to see me. My sister Elena and my aunt are at the Edison Mall looking for men's big and tall clothing. While I am neither, my cast takes up a lot of room. I am going to need pajamas, shorts and, you know, other clothes that are wide in the leg so I can take them on and off."

The stray though that a leg cast would make skirts come in handy passed through my mind. I subconsciously smoothed my olive green skirt, and the motion caught Miguel's eye.

"You two look fancy for an ordinary day. What's going on? You looking for a bank loan? We moving to a bigger place? I warn you, too many customers at one time and I will need an assistant chef. Figure that into your calculations."

That caught me off guard. First Ophie, then Bridgy and now Miguel talking about a larger space. Was I the last to know? For the moment I set it aside.

"Nothing like that. We closed for a funeral. You know Miss Delia? Comes in with Miss Augusta? Always sits at Emily Dickinson?"

"*Sí.* The quiet one, *no*? *¡Dios mío!* A sweet lady. We used to talk about Miami. Tell me what happened. Does Miss Augusta have her cat?"

"Bow? You know Bow?" I was floored.

"My bungalow is one street behind Miss Delia's house. I'm at the other end, closer to the bay. All the time Bow would turn up in my yard. Each day a different color ribbon around her neck. You know Miss Delia found her at the water's edge in Bowditch Park, right? That is how she came to be called Bow. The ribbons were a sign."

Bridgy and I looked at Miguel in astonishment, but he seemed not to notice and continued.

"Bow is a house cat, sort of, but she needs a lot of freedom. I got the feeling that I was only one of her stops. So, where is she? And what happened to Miss Delia?"

We told him what little we knew about Delia's death and ended by saying that since no one turned Bow in to Animal Rescue, we were all on the hunt, including Ryan.

When Esther came back into the room and said she hoped we had a nice visit, we knew she was signaling that we should leave.

As soon as we got in the car, Bridgy said, "Cheering up Miguel depressed me, especially talking about Delia, and with Bow missing . . . There's only one place to go. Times Square for ice cream."

"You read my mind."

Traffic heading back to the island moved at a slow crawl. But the day was cloudless, and as we crept along, the view of herons and egrets flying and diving for dinner in Estero Bay was relaxing. We were rewarded for our patience by an open parking spot right off the square.

As ex–New Yorkers we always got a kick out of Times Square, Fort Myers Beach style. Set right on the edge of the beach, it's a delightful plaza of shops leading up to the long and elegant pier that juts far out into the Gulf of Mexico. The square is dotted with benches as well as tables and chairs. Plenty of room to sit and relax. The centerpiece of the plaza is a freestanding pedestal topped by a hefty square encasing round clock faces fronting in all four directions. The clock stands about fifteen feet high and can be seen from the street and the beach. Hence the name Times Square, but the area could have been named "the heart of downtown," because that's what it is.

We were walking past a man sitting at a round metal table who seemed to be talking to himself. Bridgy grabbed my arm and whispered, "It's the resort guy. Should we say hello?"

As we came up behind him, we heard a harsh voice blast from the speaker of his iPhone sitting on the table.

"I don't care if you have to marry the old cousin. You get me that island. You won't have a job if you come back without the deed to that land."

Bridgy and I exchanged glances. Perhaps this wasn't the best time to speak to Mr. Kostos, but before we could make our escape, he slid his chair back, ramming me in the leg. He muttered, "Sorry," but barely looked up as he stood. His rudeness annoyed me, so I felt obligated to annoy him back.

"Mr. Kostos, how nice of you to attend Miss Delia's funeral, although it would have been nicer if you waited until she was buried before trying to negotiate the purchase of part of her estate."

He looked at me as though I was from Mars until he recognized Bridgy. He remembered his manners long enough to say, "Nice to see you again." But he was clearly flustered, probably wondering how long we'd been there; how much we'd heard. He opted for impeccable civility.

"Please sit down. May I buy you an iced coffee? Ice cream, perhaps?" He looked around as if searching for a server in the midst of this self-serve plaza.

He seemed relieved when we declined but still felt the need to explain his actions. Once again he pulled out his business cards.

"As you can see I work for a highly reputable company. We've been in the industry for more than fifty years." He looked at Bridgy. "Didn't you say you work at that café up the boulevard? I can drop off some brochures. Show you the quality of our resort designs. World of Luxury Spa Resorts is a company of international esteem." He made a big show of staring at his expensive-looking wristwatch, plotting his escape.

"With all due respect, Mr. Kostos, we're not interested in the quality of your company's work. We're interested in why you used our friend's funeral as a place to try to cut a business deal. Passing out business cards at the church. Trying to negotiate a sale at the reception. It's hard to believe that a company that conducts business in such a way could be well regarded by anyone."

He turned beet red, pursed his lips and shook his head. "I told Ms. Gustavsen . . . But she's, well, a bit overeager."

Was that the best response he could come up with? Blame Rowena?

"Rest assured we're Miss Delia's friends, and we are going to let it be known far and wide that she didn't want that land sold ever, to anyone." I delighted in giving him a verbal smack down. And we turned to leave.

Kostos growled, "Like anyone is going to care what a couple of waitresses say. You environmentalist freaks don't understand business."

"Oh, we understand business, buddy. We own the Read 'Em and Eat. Decent companies don't destroy nature; they work hard to coexist."

Walking away, I flung over my shoulder, "You have a lot to learn about doing business here on the Gulf Coast."

The next morning was hectic at the café, with patrons at every table and more than a half dozen boaters lined up at the counter waiting for box lunches for their group trip to Mound Key. We were all pressured by the hustle-bustle. While I was filling thermoses and she was bagging the take-out orders, Ophie joked, "Did Miguel say when he was coming back to work?"

The boaters left, promising that for their next day trip they'd call in their orders ahead of time. The early crowd began to thin, and the late risers straggled in for their breakfast. A few of the regulars asked how Miss Augusta was managing, which reminded me that we should check on her later in the day.

I was walking among the tables, refilling coffee cups,

when Ryan came in. He stopped at the counter and signaled. Without so much as "hello," he told me to get Bridgy and come outside.

I was remembering when Cady made me come outside to learn the awful news about Miss Delia. Ryan must have seen the dread on my face, and brushed away the worry, saying he had a happy surprise. Then he gave it away by asking us to bring out a saucer of milk.

Bow.

Bridgy told Ophie to watch the front and picked up a container of milk. I already had a saucer in hand.

A pet carrier with Fort Myers Beach Animal Rescue League stenciled on its side was sitting on the bench outside our door. Bow was wearing a ratty-looking green ribbon that had long since come undone, and her fur was dirty and matted, especially the long hair on her stomach and britches. We put some milk in the saucer, but when I reached to open the carrier, Ryan cautioned me.

"She was kind of feisty when we found her. Actually scratched the first guy on the scene."

I unlatched the carrier door carefully and slid the saucer inside. Bow gave me a suspicious look and turned up her nose. So I turned up my nose and added, "Humph." Two could play this game. I closed the carrier door thinking that once I moved out of sight she'd start to drink. I took a few steps away, and soon enough I heard Bow lapping up the milk.

"Ryan, I never thought Bow would be found. We were all so worried. Even Miguel loved her. He was so upset when we told him she was missing. Where did you find her?"

"Bowditch Point."

"And we were there yesterday." I was irked. "We should have looked for her. Isn't that where Miss Delia found her years ago? I guess after witnessing the murder, she headed for the last place she felt safe, poor kitty."

"That's quite a trip for a cat to make on foot, especially with all the extra people and cars here for the season. How do you think she managed without getting hurt?" Bridgy wondered aloud.

"The thing is," Ryan faltered, "Bow wasn't alone. We found her with Skully."

Chapter Twenty-one

Bridgy and I both started talking at once.

"Bow was with Skully?"

"Why did Skully have her?"

Ryan shook his head.

"No idea. An early-morning jogger found Skully, bloody and unconscious, next to his canoe at the tip of the Point in Bowditch. Looked to be that way for hours. Bow was sitting right next to his shoulder. When the jogger tried to render aid, Bow scratched and clawed at him, so he stopped trying and called 911. Dispatch sent us and called the Animal Rescue League as backup. We weren't much help. Bow fought to keep our guys away from Skully. Nobody wanted to hurt her, but we had to get him looked at. Animal Rescue showed up, and one of their ace handlers coaxed the little spitfire into the carrier. To stop her pitiful crying, Animal Rescue set the carrier right next to Skully until the EMTs took him away. I talked Animal Rescue into letting me bring her to you. Before I can turn her over, you have to promise to bring her for a checkup right away. Never know what she's been through the past few days. The Animal Rescue folks want an update after a vet takes a look at her."

"And Skully, what happened to him?" Bridgy was biting her lower lip.

Ryan grimaced. "We don't know. He was at water's edge. Looks like he was pulling his boat in or pushing it out when he slipped and hit his head. He was mega lucky. He was unconscious and his nose was inches from the high tide watermark. He could have been swept into the Gulf, a goner for sure."

My mind was whirling like a dervish. I couldn't see this as an accident. Skully was a boatman, rowing up and down the Gulf of Mexico his entire life. Delia was attacked and now Skully. It was all too much of a coincidence for me to accept.

Bridgy asked, "Will he make it?"

"Too soon to tell." Ryan was as emotionless as his job warranted. Still, he showed a kind heart. "So, can I leave the cat with you? It's you or Animal Rescue. You'll take her to be checked?"

I didn't hesitate. "Absolutely. And, please, we definitely want to know as soon as there is any change in Skully's condition."

"Ten-four. I have to get back. Busy day. Thanks for taking care of the cat. I'd give her a farewell pet, but the mood she's in, she'd probably bite off my finger."

Ryan half jogged over to his department car and peeled out of the parking lot.

Bridgy picked up the milk container and said, "I better get this inside before it sours. And then we should get Bow cleaned up and checked. I want to go with you to drop her off at Miss Augusta's. I'm sure Bow will be a measure of comfort."

"Augusta's allergic. She can't take Bow."

I looked at Bridgy, who was biting her lip again. I knew she was thinking what I was about to say out loud.

"Poor Bow. Do you think a sweet kitty who loves to roam free will be happy living in the turret with us?"

Bridgy shook her head. "First things first. Let's find a vet, make sure Bow's healthy and get her cleaned up. And we need to pick up a new ribbon. Do you think we can find one the color of Delia's special dress?"

Bridgy's sense of fashion never failed.

We hid Bow, still in her carrier, in our little office behind the kitchen and prayed the health inspector wouldn't be making his rounds today. I put another plate with some bits of tuna next to her milk and went back to work. When I checked her a half hour later, she was curled up fast asleep.

Finally the morning hustle died down. Bridgy and I were sweeping and scrubbing in anticipation of the lunch crowd. Just as a retired couple from Kentucky visiting for the season walked out the door hand in hand, Cady walked in.

"I heard Delia's cat showed up. I bet Miss Augusta will be happy. What did she say?"

I automatically picked up the coffeepot and nudged him in the direction of Robert Frost. He started to decline, but I said, "Fresh. Made ten minutes ago. And Ophie just took some corn bread out of the oven."

Bridgy went into the kitchen and came back with a

couple of slices of corn bread with a healthy dollop of honey butter on the side. She set it down in front of Cady, and then she and I sat on either side of him.

Cady groaned as his eyes slid back and forth between us. He picked up the butter knife and set it down again.

"Okay, let's have it. Get all your questions out of the way, and then I can enjoy my corn bread and coffee."

"Questions?" I was all wide-eyed innocence but could see that he wasn't buying my act.

"Questions. You know by now I've spoken to the sheriffs and the Medical Center about Skully and you want me to tell you the absolute latest information."

I feigned indignation.

"You came here specifically to ask us about Bow. We didn't ask you anything."

"Bow?"

"Miss Delia's cat."

"True, but I can see now that wasn't my best idea. You two have curiosity written all over you."

"Are you trying to tell me that you don't care about Bow? She's merely another part of your story?" My indignation was rapidly becoming real.

Cady's face told all.

"Aha! Hoist on your own petard."

Always the grammarian, he responded, "Actually, the line is 'hoist *with* his own petard.' *Hamlet*, you know. It means . . ."

"I *know* what it means. Now stop dithering and tell us what you can."

Cady's shoulders slumped momentarily, and then he decided to make the most of being the center of attention.

He took a sip of coffee, broke the corner off a slice of corn bread and slathered it with honey butter.

He took a bite and chewed for what seemed like forever. It was bread, for goodness' sake, not an overcooked steak. He knew I wasn't a patient woman, and yet he chewed on.

Cady swallowed, took another sip of coffee and said, "Tell me about the cat."

I wasn't used to him trying my patience, but I went along with this information "trade."

"She was hungry and bedraggled. Ryan said they found her next to Skully. She clawed and spit at anyone who came near until someone from Animal Rescue lured her into a carrier."

Bridgy jumped in. "She needs a checkup and we promised to take her to a vet. Do you know one we can use?"

"Sure. Cynthia Mays, a block past John's church, right before the drugstore."

Bridgy nodded at me to keep prodding Cady while she went to call the vet's office.

As soon as she moved away, Cady looked me directly in the eye.

"I'm not sure why you think I'm totally gullible, but before I tell you even one word, you have to promise me that this whole idea of you and Miss Augusta 'looking into' Miss Delia's murder is a farce you are playing to keep Augusta happy."

I folded my hands on the tabletop and tried to look like a prim and proper schoolgirl.

"Honestly. All I'm trying to do is make sure that Miss Augusta is in the loop, so to speak, so that she doesn't wind up hearing bad-to-worse news about Delia from some deputy's aunt, or, God forbid, see an update on WINK news. It wouldn't be good for her heart."

Cady looked concerned. "I didn't know she had a heart condition."

Now I was stuck. Far as I knew she was healthy as a horse.

"Well, she is nearly eighty. Can't be too careful."

When he nodded in agreement, I felt less like a liar.

Bridgy came back and thanked Cady profusely.

"That vet's staff is super nice. As soon as I explained the circumstances, the lady checked with the doctor and said we should bring Bow by as soon as we close up shop. She'll not only give Bow the once-over, but she'll send a report to Animal Rescue for us."

Cady's version of what happened was much the same as Ryan's. Cady was certain that an outsized high tide wave caught Skully off balance, knocked him down, and he whacked his head on the side of the rowboat.

"Happens at high tide all the time." He looked at his watch. "I've got to run. Tell Ophelia that her corn bread is outstanding." And he made that hair-smoothing gesture as he hurried out the door.

Bridgy looked at me.

"So? Accident?"

"Not a chance. What was Skully doing at the Point when we know he was always welcome at Tony's boatyard? And didn't we see his canoe at Tony's night before last with our own eyes?" I shook my head. "There's a lot more to this."

The door opened and hungry folks looking for lunch started to pile in.

Business was booming as more and more snowbirds

flocked to the island. Each day the number of customers increased. Creative as Ophie was in the kitchen, I missed our highly organized and never overwrought Miguel. After Ophie insisted, not once but twice, that a real cheeseburger could only be made with American cheddar, Bridgy got testy.

"The customer asked for Swiss."

"That's the second time in half an hour. Y'all know the customer's not always right, in spite of that old saying. If they want Swiss, let 'em vacation in the Alps. Why are they here at the beach?"

Each time, Bridgy took over the stove and fixed the *Swiss Family Robinson* Cheeseburger, biting her tongue and not telling Ophie we offer Swiss cheeseburgers and we intended to serve them. I like to think that's what I would have told her; then again, maybe not.

Still, during a particularly busy half hour, as we exchanged dishes at the pass-through, I had to giggle when Bridgy whispered, "I know the budget is tight, but do you think we could offer Miguel a raise when he comes back to work?"

Just as the café was quieting down, Rowena came in for a takeout of sweet tea and Miss Marple Scones. While I packed up her order, she browsed the bookshelves and came back with a hardcover of *We Have Always Lived in the Castle* by Shirley Jackson.

"Says here she wrote 'The Lottery.' That was required reading in my high school. Chilling." She shivered involuntarily. "This the same kind of story?"

I told her I supposed that it was a different kind of chilling, but chilling all the same. "Give it a try. If you don't like it, the library is always looking for these classic books. You can give it to Sally as a donation. She'll put the Emporium on a bookplate."

Head librarian Sally Caldera was a savvy fund-raiser. If you donated a usable book to the library, she'd put a "dedicated by" sticker on the inside cover. If you owned a business, Sally would put the name of your business on the bookplate. And since she, and she alone, judged which books were acceptable, I found local merchants often asked me if this book or that would meet Sally's criteria.

Sure enough Rowena decided to try the Jackson book. I took her payment and went to offer a high chair to a couple coming in the door with an active toddler. The mother accepted gratefully.

A few minutes later Bridgy was standing behind the register waving a book in hand. "Are we holding this for someone?"

Rowena had forgotten her book. I told Bridgy to put it under the counter and if Rowena didn't come back for it by closing, we'd drop it off on our way to the vet.

Later that afternoon, I was sitting in the Heap-a-Jeep and I didn't mind that Bridgy was in Rowena's longer than I thought she should be, because Bow was purring softly in the carrier. I fancied she was getting used to me. When Bridgy came out of the Emporium, she was waving a length of blue ribbon exactly the color of Delia's special dress.

"Look what I found."

I grabbed the ribbon from her hand.

"I love it! Bow, look what Auntie Bridgy found for you. When Doctor Mays gets you cleaned up, you'll be such a pretty girl."

Of course I made the mistake of holding the ribbon in

front of the carrier, and Bow took a swat at it, hitting the carrier doors and yowling her discontent.

Bridgy ignored the cat. She was focused on Rowena.

"You know what's odd? Rowena was redoing her display of Skully's shell jewelry. Besides the wire designs, she had a lot of his fishing line jewelry. I had no idea he'd sold her that, too."

"Lucky for her she arranged the consignment while Skully was still healthy enough to sign it. Now who knows?"

But the mere mention of Skully jiggled loose the question I thought of earlier. Why was Skully mooring his boat at the Point, when he mostly used Tony's landing, less than forty yards away?

We turned north out of the parking lot, ready for Doctor Mays to give Bow her examination and spruce-up, so we could tie her new ribbon around her neck and let Augusta know she was fine and dandy. Of course, where Bow would live was another problem entirely.

Chapter Twenty-two

The Island Veterinary Center was a melon-colored stucco building that fronted Estero Boulevard. Bright yellow shutters with cutouts of kittens and puppies added a warm and welcoming look. As soon as we got out of the car Bow perked up. She started to meow and tapped the carrier door as opposed to the forceful swatting she'd been doing from time to time.

The waiting room was empty except for a grandmotherly type sitting behind the counter. She looked up from her computer monitor and gave us a friendly smile. I guess she pressed a button somewhere on her desk, because the door behind her opened and a tall African American woman came through. A black and gray striped blouse tucked into a bright red skirt peeked out from under her crisp white medical coat. She gave us a generous smile but, intent on her patient, bent to the carrier immediately.

"Bow, honey. I'm so sorry for what happened to Miss Delia and I apologize for being thoughtless. I expected you were with family, safe and sound. Poor kitty."

When she stood straight the doctor shook our hands. "I'm Cynthia Mays. Bow's been my patient since Miss Delia rescued her. Tragedy, isn't it?" She shook her head and then morphed back to veterinarian rather than potential friend.

"Let's get Bow into the examining room."

I handed her the carrier, and when we didn't move, she motioned. "Come along."

Once inside, the doctor placed the carrier on a table, snapped on plastic gloves and opened the door slowly. She didn't have to entice Bow, who walked right out and began sniffing the paper table covering.

Doctor Mays said, "She's looking for her treat. On wellness visits every patient gets a treat first thing. So when they have to come back, they remember the treat before they remember the prodding and poking."

Then she picked the cat up tenderly. "No treat yet, Miss Bow. Not until we're sure it's safe for you to eat."

I blushed, knowing we never thought it might not be safe when we gave Bow milk and bits of tuna back at the café. Still, she seemed none the worse for it, so we stood quietly by, amazed at how cooperative Bow was.

We heard the doctor say, "Uh-oh." Then she looked closer at Bow's right flank and reached for a scissor. She snipped a chunk of hair and sealed it in a plastic baggie, writing a notation on the outside.

Finally Doctor Mays opened a drawer, took out a cat treat and hand-fed it to Bow. I marveled. I'd be afraid she'd nip me. But then I'm not a veterinarian.

"Bow seems okay physically. The only indication of possible trauma was some blood matted in her hair, but she has no injury so it's not her blood. I bagged, signed and dated it for the sheriff's office. Given what happened to Miss Delia . . .

"Bow's emotional well-being is another matter entirely."

Bridgy and I nodded mutely.

"We'll get her cleaned up and fed and then I'd like to keep her overnight as a precaution, and then, we'll see. Have you given any thought as to where Bow will be living now that Miss Delia is . . . gone?"

Bridgy and I exchanged a telling glance.

"What?"

I shrugged helplessly. "Miss Delia's cousin, Miss Augusta Maddox, is allergic and can't take Bow, but she's looking for a friend or neighbor who can."

"I was wondering if either of you would be interested in giving Bow a home."

"We'd love to, but we live in an apartment," I confessed mournfully.

The doctor hit the foot pedal on the sink and put an ounce or so of water in a bowl for Bow. Then she slid the cat and the bowl in the carrier.

"You stay right here, my sweetheart. Inga will be right in to get you cleaned and fed."

Doctor Mays ushered us out the door and into her office, where she explained what we already suspected. Bow was so used to the freedom of living in a house where she could come and go, wander through backyards and track fish among the mangroves, living in an apartment would be unsuitable.

"Dangerous, even. Who knows what lengths she'd go to trying to get her freedom? We need another solution. Let me keep her a day or two while you scout out the perfect home. Otherwise, we'll see if Animal Rescue has anyone on their list who lives in the right kind of house and is willing to love her." The doctor emphasized the most important criteria.

Before we left, we gave Doctor Mays our contact information along with the teal blue ribbon Bridgy bought at the Emporium. The doctor bade us good night and promised that Bow would be gorgeous the next time we saw her.

On the way to Augusta's house Bridgy and I worked out a plan. The way news spread around the island, Augusta may well have heard about Skully. We would tell her the happy news about Bow. If she mentioned Skully, we'd admit that Bow was with him. If she didn't question, we wouldn't say a word.

A haggard-looking Augusta was already in her pajamas no matter that it was still daylight. Happy as she was that Bow was found and safe, she couldn't shake the faded look of someone whose life had been irretrievably changed.

"That Doctor Mays, she loves her animals. Just seeing her will do Bow a world of curing. But we got to find Bow a home." She looked at us and raised an eyebrow. "I don't suppose . . . ?"

I shook my head. "Apartment dwellers."

"Won't work then. Apartment'll kill her for sure. Watching a bird fly by the window, out she'll try to go. I'm sure you'll do your best to get someone to give her a happy home."

Doctor Mays, Augusta, everyone was holding us accountable for Bow's safety and happiness.

"Speaking of getting, you find them wreckers yet?"

The past few days I'd barely had time to comb my hair, and I absolutely did not want Miss Augusta to know about my run-ins with Bucket Hat, so I smiled brightly and promised that my next stop was to scout out the research desk at the library, hoping to find anyone who's showing interest in sunken galleons and the like.

She leaned back and her shoulders relaxed. "Okay, then, I'll hear from you shortly."

When we got in the Heap-a-Jeep, Bridgy checked the time on her phone.

"We could rush over to the library with about twenty minutes to spare before closing time. We're not likely to be able find out much in those few minutes. I say we visit Miguel." As a practical matter she added, "The hospital stays open for visitors far later than the library."

It made sense. How much could I really find out in a few minutes, and besides, I was wondering if Miguel was still full of sparkle, or if his broken leg was starting to wear him down.

We made a quick stop in the gift shop again and were surprised to find Miguel in bed instead of tearing around the room in his wheelchair or on crutches. Our balloons were still flying high, although now the three were a colorful bouquet, all tied to a cup hook someone had screwed into the wall several paint jobs ago.

"¿*Qué pasa?* How is my kitchen?" His smile was less manic than yesterday, so I suspected the dosage of his pain meds had been reduced.

Instead of answering, I dropped a fluffy toy cat right on the edge of his bed. It wasn't quite as coal colored as Bow, but with a red ribbon tied cheerily around its neck, it was a sweet imitation. "Bow is fine. Sheriff's deputies found her at the Point and she's at the veterinarian right now."

Miguel's head drooped and I noticed he pushed the cat off to the side.

"What? I thought you'd be happy. Are you okay? Is something wrong?"

"Nothing wrong. I am pleased that Bow is safe. I wonder how you are managing in the kitchen. Ophie is an okay cook, but . . ."

He didn't need to worry about that right now. I swallowed the urge to tell him Ophie was driving us crazy. We both reassured him that the café was humming along, and we passed on greetings from some of the regulars.

"Sally Caldera stopped in to ask if you wanted her to reserve any specific books to keep you entertained during your recovery. She's so thoughtful. Any books you can think of?"

Miguel stared out the window for a couple of minutes, ignoring us completely. He turned back to us, flapping his hand dismissively.

"I'm tired. I need to rest." And he closed his eyes, expecting, I suppose, that we would disappear before he opened them again. Finally, we did.

In the elevator, I asked Bridgy what we'd done or said to upset him.

"I don't know. He's probably starting to realize the long road ahead before his life is back to normal. Visiting hours won't end for a while. I'd love to see Skully, if only we knew his real name." She took out her phone. "I'll call Ryan."

"We know his name. He told Rowena, remember? Thomas Smallwood. Ryan said Skully was unconscious. If he still is, we could leave a gift at his bedside. Probably won't get many visitors." We got off the elevator and I led the way to the glass-walled gift shop.

Instinctively I steered away from balloons and plush animals, knowing they wouldn't have much appeal. On a shelf toward the back I found a wooden canoe filled with hard candies and wrapped in blue cellophane. Just the right touch.

The receptionist directed us to a room on the second floor. A nurse was feeding an elderly man on one side of the white curtain partially drawn between two beds. Skully was lying in the other bed with his eyes closed. Coma? Sleep? We had no idea.

I tiptoed across the room to his night table and began shifting things around so I could put the canoe where he could reach it. I was moving his tissue box when Skully opened his eyes.

"Who?" His eyes swung from me to Bridgy and back again. "Oh, you two. From the café." An almost-smile crossed his lips. I couldn't be sure whether he was glad to see us, or pleased he was able to recognize us.

I held out the canoe and he took it with the hand that wasn't attached to tubes and wires. "Thank ye kindly. Nice of you to visit. Could you set it on the table?"

Bridgy's curiosity got the best of her, so she skipped all the niceties and went straight to what bothered her most. "You're such an experienced sailor, how could you wind up unconscious on the beach inches from the water's edge?"

"Damned if I know."

He caught the puzzled look on our faces. "I don't remember a dang thing after I went for supplies and loaded up the canoe in Tony's boatyard."

Bridgy went all owly eyed. I opened my mouth and

closed it again. I'm sure we both had the same thought. If Skully's boat started out at Tony's dock, how did it wind up beached at the Point? It was quicker and easier to walk from Tony's to the Point than to row.

I decided to try again. "You don't remember anything?"

"Nope. Wish I did. Reminds me, I got to ask them sheriff fellas where my boat is, and my supplies, come to think of it." He rubbed his forehead and winced. "Head still hurts."

"Mr. Smallwood . . ."

"Call me Tom, or Skully. I don't mind either one."

"Thank you, Tom." I decided to steer the conversation away from what happened before I asked about Miss Delia. "Bridgy saw Rowena's display of your jewelry at the Emporium. She says it's magnificent. We didn't realize that Rowena consigned fishing line pieces. We thought the wire jewelry was what caught her interest."

"Couple of fishing lines, is all. She said it might catch the eye of folks who liked to fish."

We chatted for a few minutes, asking questions about the shells found up and down the Gulf. Skully was an expert and Bridgy had an interest, so I stayed silent waiting for my opening. Finally the shell talk petered out.

"It was so nice of you to come to Delia Batson's funeral yesterday. A neighbor mentioned they'd seen you around her house now and again. Were you two close friends?"

"Name ain't Delia Batson. According to the preacher and the papers we got, her name is Mrs. Thomas Smallwood. Been her name for more than half a century."

I was stunned into complete silence. Behind me, Bridgy gulped loudly.

Skully sagged against his pillows, visibly relieved he could finally talk about his lifelong secret. In stops and starts, he told us the story we'd heard from Augusta when she recollected Delia's mystery man.

Skully's eyes brightened as he told us how they met, fell in love, and when her father objected to their romance, the two young lovers ran away and got married. His face clouded with anger when he talked about Delia's father and brothers tracking them down and then dragging her back to the Everglades.

"I wanted to fight for her right then and there in that boardinghouse over to Homestead, but Delia was a gentle soul. She patted my cheek, told me not to fret. Said she'd go home for a while and someday . . ." He looked past us, staring without focus, perhaps at the clock on the wall, perhaps at memories from decades ago.

"By the time her pappy died and her brothers cut her loose to make room for their wives, we was both too set in our ways for much changing. Still, I'd stop by of an evening whenever I was on the island. Have some supper. Fix whatever needed fixing. Kept an eye on her, I did."

"And no one knew you were married?"

"Nobody's business, 'cept ourn."

I couldn't argue with that.

"And," I hesitated, "the night she died, were you, er, on the island?"

He flinched as though I'd smacked him, and smacked him hard. Bridgy looped her hand around my wrist and gave a quick tug as if trying to pull my words back into my mouth.

Skully's shoulders slumped, and that faraway look recaptured his eyes. Finally he whispered as if only he could hear, "First time I saw her. Pretty slip of a girl, bright blue ribbon in her hair, chasing butterflies through a field, mile or so from town. I kept my eye out. When I got up the gumption to speak to her at a church social, well, I was took by her sweetness. But her family wasn't havin' it. All these years, I still see the girl with the ribbon in her hair."

He heaved a shallow sigh and then dragged his mind back to the present. "Lord spare me, I truly wish I was on island that night, but I was over to Matlacha costing out a dock rebuild."

My heart broke for his sadness. I reached out with the only words of comfort I had. "She wore the locket close to her heart until the day she died."

"Little gold locket? I etched a swamp lily on the front. We went shopping for a wedding ring, but she saw that locket and nothing else would do. Said a ring would only get in the way of washing and cleaning. So I bought her the locket. She carried a picture of me hid in her purse. She took it out and had the shopkeeper put it in the locket right then and there."

He closed his eyes and I thought perhaps he was drifting off to sleep, but I guess he was viewing his memories, because he said, "Delia was a fine woman. I was honored to know her."

"How did Bow wind up with you on the Point?"

"That I do know. After I got word about Delia, I wanted to take a look at the house one last time. Bow was sitting in the sea grapes down along the bay side at the end of the street. Crying pitifully she was. 'Course she knows me, so she come to me right away. I took her, put her in my sack."

"She's going to be fine. She's at the vet. I'm sure Doctor Mays would be happy to hold her until you are released—"

"Cat can't live in a canoe like a man can. I only meant to find her a home."

A nurse came to change his intravenous medication, and we wished him happy dreams.

People were streaming through the lobby, most leaving but some were hurrying upstairs to catch a few minutes with a loved one before the end of visiting hours. Bridgy and I never said a word until we were in the car. I took a sharp right turn out of the parking lot and the words burst from me like an unexpected swell catching a surfer off guard.

"You know what this means? Skully is Delia's heir. If she owned islands, he owns them now."

Bridgy sniggered, "That'll set Tighe Kostos on his heels."

"Um-hm. Him, Rowena, Judge Harcroft, even the nephews. They're all in for a surprise." My mind was racing. "You know what? I don't think we should tell them. Not up to us. Let them tilt at windmills."

On the drive home, we took turns guessing how they would all react when they finally heard the news. Bridgy couldn't decide whether Judge Harcroft would sentence everyone involved to a lifetime of listening to him pun Dashiell Hammett's name in a repetitive soundtrack of "I must *Dash*, I must *Dash*." Or perhaps wrapped in the ignominy of it all, he'd give up his lawyerly persona and one grand and glorious morning we'd find him wandering Times Square dressed in cutoffs and a low-cut tank, his tangled gray chest hair overflowing.

I voted for the cutoffs and chest hair. I'd heard "I must *Dash*" enough times to last me until my nursing home years.

During the breakfast rush I had a lot of trouble pushing Miguel to the back of my mind. Every time I went to pick up a meal at the pass-through, I thought about how unresponsive he'd been, how depressed he looked. Miguel was one of the most cheerful, energetic people I knew. It was painful to see the accident have this effect on him. I made a mental note to call our insurance agent to check on our workers' compensation policy. I couldn't remember, with all the papers we signed, how that was handled in Florida, or how long Miguel would have to be out of work before it took effect.

Our small business health care plan would help with his medical bills, but it had a deductible, plus he was going to need car service, home care, physical therapy—I was sure they weren't covered. Bridgy and I already agreed to pay his salary at least until his first workers' comp check came. We were blessed by having free help in the kitchen via Ophie, so the pressure was off for the moment. Although we flippantly lamented that we might have the added expense of a cleaning service to follow her around.

With all the money and recovery worries, no wonder Miguel was feeling down; he had a lot to mull over. I was determined to talk things out with him, alleviate his concerns as soon as I had the chance. I hustled through the dining area serving, bussing tables, and when I had a free moment, I refilled the coffeepots and the iced tea pitcher we kept behind the counter.

When I saw Rowena open the door, I grabbed my order pad. She was always in a hurry. As if to prove it, she slapped her hand on the counter, demanding attention, no matter I was a mere two feet away.

Annoying as I found her behavior, I pasted a smile on my face and asked what I could bring her.

"I have a new client coming in and I'd like three, no make it four, of those muffins I had the other day."

"Lemon with poppy seeds?"

"The very ones"—she lowered her voice—"and I need a few minutes of your time."

Not clear whether buying the muffins or taking up some of my limited time was her highest priority, I stood there waiting for her to snap at me to hurry with the muffins, or to yammer at me, likely telling me how I could solve the "life or death problem" she mentioned at Miss Delia's funeral reception.

"Sassy, I'm desolate, absolutely desolate." She stopped to see if her choice of words and quivering tone had the desired effect, so I tried to look interested, concerned, even.

When she decided I passed muster, her tone swung from quivering to highly confidential.

"I need your help. You must speak to Augusta on my behalf."

"Listen, Rowena. I know Miss Augusta was fired up at the reception, but I don't think it'll soothe her one bit if I do your apologizing for you—"

"Apologize? Why would I apologize? If anyone should be asking for forgiveness, it's Augusta. She caused a scene. That's the entire problem in a nutshell."

I rubbed my temples. Why was it always so difficult to follow Rowena's train of thought?

"There's no way I can make Augusta apologize to you."

Rowena looked to heaven, her eyes filled with disbelief. She pushed the idea away with a flap of her hand.

"Don't be ridiculous. Augusta wouldn't say she was sorry to the Lord himself, never mind that she'd just stepped on His big toe. No. I want you to make her stop panicking the boys."

"Boys?"

"Delia's nephews." Now her tone moved to impatient. "They got all squirmy after Augusta's ridiculous outburst at the church hall. I'm afraid they're going to back out on the real estate deal I've been negotiating with Tighe Kostos. I'm telling you, Sassy, I need this commission. It's life or death for me. And Augusta has frightened those boys half out of whatever limited wits they may have. Augusta has them paralyzed by indecision, afraid of what she'll do to them if they sell the island to the resort company."

I chuckled to myself, knowing the nephews were out of the inheritance picture. Still, I played along. "What makes you think Miss Augusta would listen to me on a matter of such personal significance?"

"Oh, everyone knows Augusta has a soft spot for you and Bridgy, just like Delia did. You two are a younger version of them. Heck, you'll *be* them in forty, fifty years."

Much as I loved Miss Delia and Miss Augusta, I blanched at the thought of them as role models. Replicating their waning years wasn't a life goal for me. Still, I let that all slide.

"Rowena, take my advice. Give Miss Augusta a few days to recover. Miss Delia's death was sudden and tragic. Takes some getting used to. You might find Augusta more agreeable a few weeks from now."

"Weeks? We barely have days." She leaned closer, practically whispering in my ear. "Kostos told me his job is in jeopardy. If he doesn't close this deal, good-bye high six-figure salary for him and a hefty commission for me."

I was starting to feel the kind of power that comes with knowing more than the other players in the game. Before it went to my head, I tried changing the topic, as an easier way to resist Rowena's pressure to help her betray Delia's wishes.

"Bridgy and I went to the hospital to visit Miguel. Afterward, we stopped to see Mr. Smallwood."

Her chin dropped, but I hurried on, pretending not to see how surprised she was. "Poor man is really foggy brained. He doesn't remember his accident at all. Seeing him reminded me that Bridgy said you have quite a bit of his fishing line jewelry in the Emporium. I'm thinking of buying a few pieces for my mom."

Always the salesperson, Rowena said, "You won't believe the selection I have. You could send shell jewelry to your mother for any occasion or no occasion at all for years to come. Do you want to walk back with me and take a look?"

By changing the topic, I'd carelessly trapped myself. The dining room was nearly empty and the lunch crowd wouldn't be in for a while. I had no excuse. I set Rowena's box of muffins in front of her, and while she searched for money in her gargantuan purse, I took off my apron and told Bridgy I'd be AWOL for a couple of minutes.

During the short walk across the parking lot, Rowena asked about Miguel and then segued to Skully.

"I heard he was in a coma. Pretty much at death's door. You say you spoke to him? And he answered?"

"It's really sad. He has no idea what happened to him at the Point, although the rest of his memory appears quite intact. He recognized Bridgy and me, remembered the café." I shrugged. "It's so hard to predict what a head injury will do. He might never remember what happened."

As magnificent as Skully's wire jewelry was, I was enamored by the down-home charm of the fishing line pieces. Rowena had a fairly large quantity of both. Although I intended to look, not buy, I found a necklace my mom would love. A calico scallop shell pendant shaded from light pink to a darker mauve hung from fishing line that Skully had woven with a macramé-like touch. Its aura was delicate and strong all at the same time, just like mom.

I asked Rowena to set it aside for me, saying I'd come in tomorrow to pay. Always pushy about every dollar, she asked me to come back after work, and she pouted when I said I had an appointment at the library to do some research right after the café closed.

"You're going snooping, aren't you? Trying to find out what happened to Delia? You think I don't know? The entire island knows that Augusta recruited you to help her look into the murder. Well you listen here. With a killer running all over the island, only a fool would keep on snooping. I didn't think you were that kind of fool."

Chapter Twenty-four

When I returned to the café Bridgy was straightening tables and chairs. She looked at me with one eyebrow raised in a definite question, which I answered immediately.

"It was easier to go over to the Emporium and buy a gift for my mother than to waste my breath trying to tell Rowena that I refuse to intervene between Augusta and the nephews. You were right," I added, "Rowena's life and death issue is all about money—her commission when the nephews sell the island to the company Tighe Kostos represents."

Then I started laughing.

"OMG! You didn't tell her, right?" Bridgy was jumping around like a flea. "We agreed we wouldn't tell anyone."

"Oh, calm down. Rowena's the last person I'd tell. She deserves to get skunked when the truth comes out. Skully's a quiet man. If he wants the world to know he's Delia's widower and heir, he can grant Cady an interview and have the story printed for the world to read. My lips are zipped." I closed my mouth tight and ran my index finger and thumb across my lips as if locking a plastic sandwich bag.

We got louder and louder until finally Ophie poked her head all the way out the pass-through.

"You two are worse than a couple of tweens stopping in for a shake after school." And she ducked back into the kitchen, which only set us laughing harder until the front door opened. The new snowbird members of the Potluck Book Club came in, accompanied by two men, recently sunburned, whom I took to be their husbands.

"We could hear you gals giggling all the way across the parking lot," said the one whose name I remembered as Iris, "and I said to Ed—this here is my husband, Ed—'I told you this is the happiest place in town.' Is the chef around? I need her to give me the chervil recipe again. I lost it between here and home. And Connie here never wrote it down at all."

She stopped speaking long enough to look sideways at her negligent friend, but as Bridgy and I so often do, Connie simply ignored her.

I sat the group at Dr. Seuss, placing menus and water in front of each of them. Ed began spouting the quotes on the table. "*The more that you read, the more things you will know.*" He followed that up with "*I meant what I said and I said what I meant.*"

I stood a few feet away until they called me over.

"So with all these great quotes stuck in between pictures of *The Cat in the Hat*, *The Lorax* and who all else"— he picked up his menu—"I suppose I'll find *Green Eggs and Ham* on the list of choices?" And he gave a broad wink to his tablemates.

When he opened the menu, I pointed to the eponymous item, subtitled "Mexican vegetable omelet with *salsa verde* and grilled thick-sliced ham."

Both men ordered *Green Eggs and Ham*, chuckling as they did so, while their wives settled on Agatha Christie Soft-Boiled Eggs with Miss Marple Scones. Two coffees, a decaf, one tea.

Later, when I came around with the refill coffeepots, Connie asked for more tea. I brought a fresh cup and she nudged her husband in the side.

"Go ahead, smart guy, ask her."

He fidgeted with his napkin, twisting and untwisting, before he said, "Just some gossip is all. We were invited to play at the golf club down toward Lovers Key. We were having drinks in the clubhouse and overheard a man, showy type wearing one of those fancy blue-faced TAG Heuer watches, complaining into his mobile phone. He was accusing the person on the other end of the call of not realizing all the chaos 'since the old lady died.' That's a direct quote. Then he mentioned treasure scavengers or some such, looking for an island to use as a base, and well, the price was going to go up.

"The other guy didn't like it much; we could hear that right through the phone. When the call ended Mr. TAG Heuer sat slumped for a minute, then he straightened up, ordered a shot of Macallan's 18, polished it off and headed to the showers."

Connie's husband sat back in his chair, satisfied that he'd done his duty. I was still waiting for the question.

"For goodness' sake, Alfie, ask her."

"Oh. We were wondering if he was talking about the woman who was murdered, and what are treasure scavengers anyway?" Alfie pointed to Connie. "She said you'd know, being the woman was a book club member and all."

I knew I disappointed them with my lie that I had no idea who the man was or if the women he mentioned was Miss Delia. Still, they cheered a bit when I told them that treasure scavengers, locally called wreckers, search the bottom of the sea for sunken ships. They were surprised to learn that there are hundreds of treasure-laden Spanish galleons resting on the bottom of waters surrounding Florida.

Ed asked how so many ships came to be sunk, and they were thrilled that, although some were dropped by hurricanes, others were sunk by pirates. I told the tale of the *San José*, destroyed by a hurricane on the far side of Tavernier Key in the early 1700s. The part where some of the treasure was recovered as recently as the 1960s had them mesmerized. They heaved a collective sigh when I summed up by saying the galleon shifted and was once again unreachable.

They were so excited at the thought of gold and silver coins, jewelry and plates that I suggested they stop by Tony's boatyard, rent a metal detector and walk it along the shore any morning after a stormy night. That would make them genuine treasure scavengers and they could keep whatever they found. Iris's husband began checking the weather forecast on his iPhone, ready to plan an outing. They all began talking at once.

Alfie's story about Tighe Kostos in the golf club bar gave me a lot to think about, but the café was humming and I had no time to focus, so I continued to smile, serve and clean.

At long last my only customers were two middle-aged ladies sitting at Barbara Cartland, who took turns looking at the bookshelves and commenting on titles one or the other of them might enjoy. They knew each other's tastes quite well and would likely be browsing for a while. I poured myself a glass of sweet tea, grabbed a blueberry muffin and sat at Emily Dickinson for a short break before cleanup.

Bridgy finished serving a takeaway order and joined me.

"Whew, busy afternoon. Season is moving into high gear."

"And thank heavens for that. The snowbirds go a long way toward paying our bills." I sat back in my chair, took a long sip of tea. "I heard something interesting today. Tighe Kostos and some group of wreckers are in competition for Delia's island."

I told her what Alfie overheard. She looked to heaven.

"Poor Skully. He doesn't even know what he has and folks are plotting to take it away from him."

I disagreed. "Poor them if they come up against him." I amended with an idea that just occurred to me. "Unless he wants to sell. Lots of money involved, according to Rowena."

"Nah. If he knows Delia's wishes, he'll honor them, money or not. Where'd you hear this anyway?"

I told her about my conversation with the Canadians and the description of Kostos in the club bar. "As soon as they said the watch face was blue I knew it was him. Remember when we saw him in Times Square, he made a show of looking at it twice to make sure we'd see it?

According to Connie's husband that brand of watch is super pricey."

"I guess he thinks it goes well with his Saint Laurent suit."

I gave her a look filled with question marks.

"I love when you look at me like that. Makes me feel so smart. Anyway, I forgot you weren't with us in the church parking lot when Rowena introduced us to Kostos. Ophie, fashionista that she is, admired his suit and asked if it was a Kenzo. He blanched at the thought and opened his jacket to show her what he called the 'extraordinarily fine stitching' and managed to display the Saint Laurent label."

I shrugged. "You lost me at Kenzo. I can't imagine what's going to happen to his fancy clothes and watches when his boss dumps him and he's living on the beach collecting shells."

"He'd probably be happier," Bridgy observed.

"That's how we see it. Him? Not so much. Listen, as soon as we close I'm going over to the library to do some research on sunken ships and then I'm going to find out if wreckers are really after Delia's island."

Bridgy hesitated. "Sassy, you do realize that we don't know if there *is* an island."

"Oh, there's an island, maybe more than one. What we don't know is whether or not Delia has legal ownership or only a collection of ancient family papers." I started ticking questions off on my fingers. "Where is Delia's island? Did she really own it? Was she murdered by someone over possession of the island? And the most important question"—I added my pinky to the three straight up fingers—"who killed her?

"I have an appointment with Sally at the library research room. She said she'd help me find the latest on any current or future salvage operations. Who knows, maybe I'll be able to track down Bucket Hat and have it out with him once and for all." I hoped I sounded braver than I felt.

"No you don't. If you get a glimmer of where he might be, don't run off. Call me, I'll go with you." Bridgy started nibbling on her lower lip, a clear sign she was fretting.

Sally Caldera pushed her eyeglasses to the top of her head, bunching her long russet curls into a crown-like mass. She was patiently explaining to a crotchety man that, no matter what his reason, books in the reference collection cannot leave the library. He continued to say "but" and she continued to explain. Finally he stormed off in a huff, but not before assuring Sally, and everyone else in the building, that he'd have her job.

Without so much as a grumble, Sally said, "Next?"

Then she looked up. "Oh, Sassy. Nice to see you. How can we help you today?"

"Well, for starters you can guarantee me that grouch"—I pointed a hitchhiker's thumb in the direction of the departing loudmouth—"will never come to the Read 'Em and Eat for lunch."

"He's disappointed. You'd be surprised how many people think that there are exceptions to the rule about reference material. Why just the other day . . ." Her curls formed a halo as she gave her head two strong shakes. "Never mind. How can I help you? On the phone you mentioned wreckers."

"Not exactly—well, maybe—but first I'd like to see

whatever you have on the Ten Thousand Islands, books, maps, historic documents."

Sally came round from behind the desk and motioned me to follow her to a corner in the back of the room.

"We have a ton of information, much of it from NOAA and the Fish and Wildlife Service. And of course we have books filled with the history and geology of the area. Some are quite scholarly, some are more diary-like." She pointed to a row of waist-high flat files. "We have topographical maps, climate maps, nautical charts . . . nearly any map you can imagine, including copies of hand-drawn maps from centuries ago."

She picked up a book chained to the side of the flat file and flipped it open to a page half filled with signatures. "You'd have to sign in for the maps and then, as with all the material, you have to stay in this area." She indicated the tables and chairs between where we were standing and her desk.

I nodded without really listening. My eye caught two familiar names in the sign-in book and intermittently another name, unfamiliar to me, popped up.

Rowena's scrawl was barely legible, but I knew it well. She often paid for her book purchases by check. The two times that Tighe Kostos visited the map collection, he signed with a grandiose signature that included his title and company.

But Ellis Selkirk had an extraordinary interest in the flat maps, and when I flipped to the previous page, he'd signed in there a few times as well. I turned my attention back to Sally.

"This Ellis Selkirk has been here a lot. Did you ever notice him wearing mirrored sunglasses and a bucket hat?"

Chapter Twenty-five ꟷꟷꟷꟷ

"Oh, I know who he is. He's focused on a few precise areas and researches them intently." Sally leaned down, opened a drawer in the flat file and carefully removed what looked like a nautical map. "He always wears a faded green bucket hat. The aviator glasses usually hang from the neck of his shirt." She lowered her voice. "And he swears under his breath when he leans over a map and the glasses clatter to the tabletop.

"This is one of his favorites. It's a copy of a 1922 hand-drawn map of the Gulf extending south from Cape Romano along the Ten Thousand Islands."

She spread the map on a table and we both stared at it. I asked a question that often popped in and out of my mind since we moved to the Gulf Coast.

"You know, I've always wondered how many islands there are. I mean, really, we took a boat ride down to Key

West last year, and I know we went past a lot of islands along the coast, but . . ."

The librarian in Sally was always happiest when she could answer a patron's inquiry. I watched her consider, striving to be exact. "Well, no one's ever counted them, of course. There are so many types of landmasses down there." She dropped her index finger to a spot on the map. "Right here on the south bank of the Chatham River, Possum Key is a large island, while on the north bank is a smaller body, originally a shell mound, which provided fertile farmland for the likes of Edgar Watson and other settlers arriving either side of 1900. Many of the tiniest islands are actually tangles of mangrove trees growing out of the water, their roots trapping soil."

"Edgar Watson? Isn't he the one who was murdered? Every hurricane season people talk about that killing like it happened last week."

"Yes. Shot on Chokoloskee by a crowd of neighbors, right after the Hurricane of 1910. Peter Matthiessen wrote several fascinating books about the time and the place, describing the Ten Thousand Islands as the last American frontier, full of outlaws and renegades forced to leave other states before the law caught up with them. I'll get you one of Matthiessen's books. I recommend *Shadow Country*. It's eight hundred pages, but once you read it, you'll know exactly what it was like to live in the Ten Thousand Islands a century ago."

I nodded absently, my curiosity wrapped around Bucket Hat's interest in the area, not a hundred-year-old murder. I asked Sally what she thought lured Bucket Hat to the library.

"The NOAA maps. He'd bring his own copies of NOAA maps and try to match them to the landmasses on our maps, which are, as you can see, ancient and may not be as accurate as today's maps. The oldies have other gifts, like colloquial names, or markings of creeks or long-ago islands that don't exist today."

"You mentioned Noah before. What exactly . . . ?"

"Sorry, its shorthand for the National Oceanic and Atmospheric Administration, NOAA. You know, the hurricane guys."

"Do they have maps indicating sunken ships?"

"Do they ever." Sally bent over the map on the table, tucking a stray lock of hair under the arm of her eyeglasses. "All along here"—her hand fluttered up and down the Gulf west of the islands—"in fact, all around the coast of Florida, there are hundreds of sunken ships."

I grinned. "A few hours ago I was telling some snowbirds about the pirates, the hurricanes and all the treasure ships. It wouldn't surprise me to find them walking metal detectors on the beach after the next stormy day."

"Mr. Selkirk isn't interested in a few gold coins buried in the sand." Sally brushed aside the metal detectors and brought us back to the maps. "He's fascinated by the idea of finding a three- or four-hundred-year-old ship that's bursting with gold and silver."

She caught my eye to make sure she had my undivided attention. "The NOAA maps he brings with him are all from the wreck and obstruction system—you know, maps that indicate where wrecks and obstacles are situated on the Gulf floor. Could be any type. Maybe a decommissioned ship sunk to become an artificial reef. Maybe a ship that ran aground on a sandbar, or"—and here her eyes twinkled with delight—"maybe a treasure-laden Spanish galleon sunk by hurricanes or pirates." She deepened her voice to a growl. "Aye, matey. Pirates."

The adrenaline that rushed through me pushed my giggle shriller than it needed to be. But I was psyched. To me, his concentration on overlays of maps said Bucket Hat was playing for high stakes. And that could be dangerous for anyone in his way. My mind was reeling. Suppose there was an offshore shipwreck he wanted to explore and he was looking for a home base? If he suspected that Delia had clear title to islands in an area where the surrounding land is government owned and protected, how far would he go to get hold of her land?

While I signed the book so I could look at the maps, Sally scrambled through the drawers to find some modern print maps and copies of a few more hand-drawn studies, all charted in one decade or another during the last century. When I spread them on the table, I could see the nuance of difference in topography, especially the insignificant islands, some of which seemed to appear, disappear and then appear once again.

By the time Sally came back with *Shadow Country* and *Killing Mister Watson*, both written by Matthiessen, my head was about to explode with theories, most of which convicted Bucket Hat of murder. No jury, no trial, just me.

I piled my library books in the Heap-a-Jeep and headed to the turret, anxious to share my new information with Bridgy.

I was already talking as I rushed into the apartment, only to have Bridgy shush me into silence and point to the phone at her ear.

She was smiling and gushing into her cell. "No. No problem at all. Of course. We'll take care of it. No. It's definitely not an inconvenience. See you later."

"Sas, I have such great news. Grab a bottle of water. Do you want me to drive?" And she marched past me. She had her hand on the doorknob before she realized that I stood rooted to the spot. Clearly this was one of those frequent times when Bridgy was overjoyed and I had not even a hint as to what was going on.

"Come on." Her insistence was all the more annoying because my head was filled with Ellis Selkirk and the Ten Thousand Islands.

"Wait a minute. I picked up news at the library that you're going to want to hear."

Bridgy looked at the books still resting in the crook of my arm. "You can show me the books later."

Frustrated, I dropped my books on the hall table. "Okay. What's so important?'

"Miguel is home. And if that is not important enough for you, he's going to adopt Bow. So we have to go to Doctor Mays's office, get Bow and deliver her to Miguel." Bridgy glanced at the clock on her phone. "It's getting late. Let's hustle."

She had trumped me once again. As manic as I was about finding Bucket Hat, he'd have to get in line behind Miguel and Bow. Having been home for less than five minutes, I turned and followed Bridgy out the door.

We zipped along the boulevard. Traffic was light because most islanders were home having dinner. I always marveled how quiet the town got by five o'clock only to liven up again an hour or so later.

I thought Miguel would be in the hospital for weeks, but when I asked Bridgy why he was being released so quickly, she pointed out that hospitals don't want people taking up bed space and trading germs with other patients.

Miguel's sister Elena explained to Bridgy that Miguel badgered the doctor until he got permission to go home provided he had live-in help. Fortunately, Elena and his aunt Caridad agreed to stay at his house. Esther, the long-suffering therapist I'd met on my first visit, was arranging for home therapy until Miguel was able to go to the physical rehabilitation center.

As someone who'd never had more than a head cold, the caretaking arrangements alone would be enough to frazzle me. I had a flickering thought of being trapped in the turret with Bridgy and Ophie running my life. For good measure, my well-meaning but chronically disorganized mother would show up with herbs she grew in her basement garden in the Brooklyn brownstone where she raised me on organic milk and mung bean hummus. She'd waltz in, stroke my brow, then force me to drink some potion made with dandelion, elderberry and Lord knows what else.

I was thankful that my being healthy kept my mother's cures at bay. Of course, she'd say that the reason I'm healthy is because of all the concoctions she fed me through the years.

Doctor Mays told us that Bow was in fine fettle and ready to venture out in the world.

"I sent a full report to Animal Rescue. Please give them a call and tell them about Bow's new home so they can register the owner and close out her case. Come on back to the examining room. Wait until you see how well she is doing."

Bow was lying in her carrier on the exam table where

we'd first left her yesterday. Doctor Mays put two treats on the table and opened the carrier door.

Bow pranced out, her black coat all clean and shiny with her new blue ribbon tied gaily around her neck. She ignored us all, but we knew she was content because she held her tail high. She sniffed her treats and then chewed them daintily. Doctor Mays rubbed gently behind her ears, and Bow purred in response.

The difference between the bedraggled, angry cat Ryan brought to the café and this gorgeous, happy creature was amazing and I said so.

Doctor Mays had an infectious, full-throated laugh. "She only needed a bath and familiar hands treating her tenderly. You say she's going to live with a friend?"

When she heard that Miguel's house was a regular stop during Bow's daily jaunts around the neighborhood, the doctor nodded. "That is an ideal choice. Of course she'll be mewing around Miss Delia's house for a while, but as long as your friend knows to look for her there . . ."

The doctor coaxed Bow back into her carrier and then latched the door.

"Since you are only going a few blocks, the safest place for the carrier is on the floor in the backseat, where it can't bounce or roll. If the carrier doesn't fit, then you'll have to level the car seat with blankets or a pillow and belt the carrier to prevent it from falling."

Doctor Mays handed us a gift bag decorated with faces of puppies and kittens. Her business card was stapled to the handle. "Please give this to Bow's new friend. Some treats, a can of food and a pet first-aid kit."

We must have looked surprised because she continued,

"You'd be amazed how often little mishaps need attention, especially for a cat that runs free part of the day."

Walking across the parking lot, I asked Bridgy, "You didn't tell me. How did Miguel decide to take Bow, especially now, with his leg and all?"

"Elena said it was Caridad's idea. Miguel told them about Delia and how Bow visited his house all the time. Caridad said she thought Miguel and Bow could each use a little company. Apparently she didn't have to say it twice."

We were nearly at Miguel's house when Bridgy finally remembered that I'd come home all bubbly and full of news. Turning off the boulevard she asked me what I'd learned at the library that had me so excited.

"I know who Bucket Hat is. His name is Ellis Selkirk. He's investigating sunken treasure ships off the coast of the Ten Thousand Islands. I intend to find him and confront him about Miss Delia."

Bridgy was silent for a moment, then, "And have you thought about what you are going to do when he says, 'I killed her because I don't like troublesome old ladies, and if you don't shut up, I'll kill you, too'?"

And she pulled the car next to the sea grape shrubs that lined the front of Miguel's house.

It was really exhilarating to be part of Miguel and Bow's reunion. When I lifted the cat carrier out of the car, Bow instantly sensed a familiar place and tried to stick her nose through the carrier door. She turned her head this way and that and began sniffing enthusiastically. We were so near the edge of Estero Bay, I'm sure Bow had the sensation of home.

We could hear voices from the patio. We called out rather than walking in unannounced. Elena came around the side of the house and invited us back. Miguel and his entourage were sitting on the patio. Miguel's leg was elevated on a pile of cushions. He and his cousin Rey were talking about soccer. Rey seemed to think Brazil had the greatest team in the world, while Miguel argued strongly for Argentina. Caridad was pouring a thick and creamy drink into tall glasses.

She gave us a wide, toothy grin. "Ay, just in time. I am

making *batidos*. The milk will help Miguel's leg bone grow strong. Sit down. You have one, please."

"That looks delicious. What flavors?"

"Papaya. Mango. A little banana." Caridad placed a glass, overflowing with the fruity milkshake, in front of Rey. Then she put one a few inches out of Miguel's reach. "What's the matter with you? Greet your guests."

Miguel was reluctant to look directly at us. I knew he must be tired and overwrought since the accident, but I'd never seen him so depressed. If being home hadn't cheered him yet, maybe seeing Bow would do the trick. I set the carrier on the table right in front of him.

"We brought your new roomie."

Bow's face was still pressed against the carrier grate. Miguel inclined his head until they were nose to nose. He made kissing noises and Bow responded with a quiet meow. Then Miguel unlatched the carrier door.

Rey picked up his glass and leaned back from the table. "Are you sure . . . ?"

Miguel shushed Rey and then began whispering to Bow as he lifted her from the carrier. "*Hola, chica*, you look very pretty today."

He held the cat to his chest and she snuggled in. Then just as we were all oohing and aahing at such a cute scene, Bow made her escape. She jumped out of Miguel's arms and scampered behind a rattan end table.

I started to go after her, but Miguel held up his hands.

"No worries, she is looking for her water dish. Elena, you put it where I told you, *sí*?"

"Yes. Yes, Mr. Fussy." Elena looked at us and shrugged. "He has done nothing but give orders since he decided the cat was going to come here to live. We have enough supplies—"

"And we brought more." I handed her the bag from Doctor Mays. She set it in front of Miguel, who looked at the card.

"Doctor Mays. Wonderful woman. I would have no one else take care of my Bow."

I was surprised. "You know Doctor Mays?"

"Oh, *sí*. She and I are on the Hurricane Committee. Our subcommittee is in charge of seeing that all the domestic animals on the island are cared for should there be an evacuation. Pets must be allowed in shelters. You weren't here for Hurricane Charley . . ."

Miguel continued to chatter away, his usual happy self once again in evidence.

When Bow finished lapping up some water, she took a casual stroll around the patio and then darted into the cluster of sand pines that stood between Miguel's house and the mangroves edging Estero Bay. She meandered back to the patio and scooted behind a clay planter that was home to an overgrown bush of some type, and she didn't come out.

"Nap time," Miguel announced, and everyone jumped to help him inside.

"Not me. Bow. Behind the planter is her favorite spot for a nap." Bow was falling rapidly back into her old routine, which brought a glow of satisfaction to Miguel's face.

That was the moment I finally relaxed. Miguel was home surrounded by family and friends, and was all the happier for it. Bow had a loving new home. Bridgy was deep in conversation with Caridad, cooking terms and ingredients flying back and forth. I gave her the high sign. She answered with a thumbs-up. Our little world was returning to normal.

Except . . .

I thought of Miss Delia and my promise to Miss Augusta. That stirred the restlessness inside of me, and I knew we had to get going.

I touched Miguel on the shoulder. "It is so good to have you home and happy. We'll stop by again soon."

I was surprised by a spark of irritability that flitted across Miguel's face, but gentleman that he was, he said, "*Gracias.*"

Elena walked out to the car with us. "Thank you for being such loyal friends to my brother. It is hard for our family to have him so far away. The rest of us live in either Miami-Dade or near Orlando. We have each other. He lives on this island all alone."

"He's not alone," I assured her. "He has us. And many other friends."

Bridgy added, "Please, please call if we can help. Really, anything you need."

Elena's smile turned frosty. "The Guerra family will take care of him. We always take care of family."

Bridgy's face reddened. "Of course you do. That goes without saying. But one of us can always sneak away from the café to help with shopping or to drive Miguel to the doctor."

"Ah yes, the café." Elena's tone was as cryptic as if the café was a crucial piece in a puzzle she had nearly solved.

Bridgy pulled away from the curb, both of us smiling and waving to Elena and to Caridad, who'd come up behind her.

As soon as we were down the block, Bridgy let go of her smile and fretted. "What is going on here? Do you think Miguel blames us for the accident? Maybe the whole family blames us."

I thought about it. "No, there's more to it. Miguel loves us. He loves the café. He loves creating new recipes, he loves our regulars, he loves—"

"I get it. I get it," Bridgy cut me off. "But you do agree that something doesn't feel right? Miguel is withdrawn. That day in the hospital I thought he was tired and in pain, but now he's home, surrounded by family, has adopted Bow and still . . ."

She shook her head as if she was the one tired and in pain. She stopped the car when we reached Estero Boulevard.

"We going home, or . . . ?"

"Home. Definitely home."

Ophie was sitting on the terrace watching a sunset cruise glide along the Gulf.

"Come look at how gorgeous this scene is. If I were an artist, I'd sit here and paint seascapes all day long." She turned away from the window. "Didn't know how long you'd be so I made a cold chicken salad and corn bread. That way, dinner is always ready. If you want to wash up, I'll set out the food."

With grapes to add sweetness and water chestnuts for crunch, Ophie's chicken salad was over-the-top delicious.

Bridgy wondered aloud where the tangy came from.

Ophie played mysterious for a minute and then confessed that her secret ingredient was a mixture of white pepper and onion powder.

"Extremely important that you mix them together before you add them to the dressing," she emphasized, proud as a peacock that her salad was a hit.

Bridgy thought the dish would make a nice addition to the menu at the café, and we went back and forth about quantity and how long we could reasonably leave chicken salad in the fridge before it would have to be thrown out.

Finally we decided that we'd do a trial, a one-day special of two dozen servings. If it sold well, we could make it a weekly item and expand the serving numbers.

"I'd be available to eat the leftovers." Bridgy was always happy when we had a new dish for our customers to try. Then she glanced at Ophie and said hastily, "Not that we'll have any."

I was beginning to squirm. I really wanted to talk to Bridgy about Bucket Hat, but it never seemed to be the right time. So I plunged in, trying to create an end to the chicken salad conversation.

"How about Wednesday? Could we make Ophie's chicken salad the special of the day for the next few Wednesdays?"

Bridgy nodded, but Ophie asked what we were going to name the dish.

"Aunt Ophie's Chicken Salad, of course." Bridgy patted her aunt's hand, satisfied that the issue was resolved.

Ophie, normally not one to hesitate, looked uncomfortable.

"Darlin', I'd be pleased as all get-out to have the salad named after me, still I wonder if y'all could come up with a book title, make it entertaining. With all the cats and turtles and fish Dr. Seuss wrote about, surely there's a chicken book there someplace."

"Not that I know of. The only fun story with a chicken title that comes to mind is 'Chicken Little.' You know, 'The sky is falling!'"

Ophie gave her head a vigorous shake and then patted her hair to make sure that not one strand fell out of place. "Sassy, you're the book person. Surely you can be more original than that." She stood up and began to clear the table. "You have until Wednesday to decide on a suitable name."

Bridgy looked at me with big round eyes and then looked down at the tabletop before Ophie noticed. We both knew I was in deep weeds.

I moved to the patio and opened the windows. A soft breeze ruffled my hair, and the salty fragrance of the Gulf, as always, calmed me. Carrying a plate of oatmeal cookies and a pitcher of sweet tea, Bridgy sat down and commented on how peaceful the evening was. I nibbled on a cookie, drank in the loveliness of the Gulf and watched the sun slide leisurely below the horizon.

While drying her hands on her apron, Ophie stuck her head through the doorway to ask if we wanted anything else before she closed the kitchen. Bridgy and I exchanged looks. Behind Ophie's back, we always hooted at the image of Ophie putting massive iron chains across the kitchen door and holding them fast with a humongous padlock that couldn't be opened until reveille. Sure, we knew she meant the kitchen was all tidied up and she was turning out the light. But we still liked to poke fun, only not to her face. We said we were content, and Ophie headed back to the kitchen, untying her apron as she walked.

Bridgy leaned over and whispered, "Out comes the padlock."

We were still smiling when Ophie came back, carrying my library books. "I found these on the hall table. Are they for a book club meeting?" She held up *Shadow Country*. "This one is awfully heavy to the hand. Is it a heavy read as well?"

"I don't know. Our local librarian, Sally Caldera, recommended it. It's a fictionalized account about a murder in the Ten Thousand Islands a hundred years ago."

"Well, I hope you enjoy it." She bounced the hefty book in her hand a time or two. "Feels like too much reading for me."

She set the books on the table and asked what I'd learned at the library.

"Well, I started out wanting to learn more about the Ten Thousand Islands and where Delia's land might be. And then I stumbled across the name of that man with the Bucket Hat. Ellis Selkirk. I'm sure he's staying on the island, because he signs in at the library's research and map center at least two or three times a week. Now all I have to do is find him."

Ophie stood up, walked into the hall and came back with the telephone book. "You mean all *we* have to do is find him."

She pulled out a chair and sat. "Far as Delia's land goes, don't you think Augusta would know exactly which island Delia owned?"

Chapter Twenty-seven

I had no idea what she thought we'd find in the phone book.

"He wouldn't be listed there. I doubt Selkirk is a resident. He's only here to organize his expedition."

Bridgy snorted. "You make him sound like Ponce de León—'organize his expedition.'"

"Don't be a brat. I have no idea why he selected Fort Myers Beach. He could have pulled together his wrecker crew in lots of places. Marco Island. Everglades City. Even some of the Keys, like Marathon or Big Pine. Any of those are closer to the Ten Thousand Islands, if that's the geography that interests him."

Ophie tut-tutted. "Honey chile, if y'all are going to pursue a conniver, you have to learn to think like one."

Bridgy got it right away. "Squee! He wants to be far enough from his target so that anyone interested in the sunken treasure ships offshore of the Ten Thousand Islands won't know what he's planning."

I was a step or two behind her, but it made perfect sense. If Bucket Hat had a specific ship in mind, he wouldn't want the entire wrecker community to know about it until he had his team and equipment lined up and his permits in order.

"It's at least—what?—fifty, a hundred miles from here to Cape Romano, and that's only the northern tip of the Ten Thousand Islands. If he stayed in a place that was closer, someone might notice. Here, no one would have paid him any attention if he hadn't been mean to me."

I exhaled a "that will teach him" humph.

Ophie picked up the phone book. "He has to be resting his head on a pillow somewhere. Do you want to start with the hotels or the B and Bs?"

She flipped pages back and forth, ripping out any that might help us find a temporary resident.

"If we don't find him as a guest at any of these places"— Ophie held up the thin papers covered with excruciatingly tiny print—"we can call the Realtors during our downtime at the café tomorrow and see if anyone with that name arranged a rental."

I had to admit, Ophie seemed to have a knack for finding someone, whether he wanted to be found or not. I wondered if she had some wild stories about people she'd hunted down in the past.

We each took a page from the phone book and sat in different rooms so that our background noise wouldn't sound like a busy call center.

After hearing "I'm sorry, we have no guest by that

name" from about ten apologetic desk clerks, I was starting to think our efforts were futile. I plugged my phone in the charger and wondered if Bridgy and Ophie were doing any better.

Bridgy was on the patio crossing a name off her list with a felt-tipped pen.

"Darn, I've been using the point and not pressing down, but I blotted out half the numbers for the Mid-Island Motel. Now I'll have to look it up."

I slid a ball-point pen across the table to her. "Keep this with your list for tomorrow. I think we've had it for tonight. Where's Ophie?"

"Kitchen. She's putting together a cheese and fruit platter. Says we need to keep up our strength 'til the job is done."

Ophie came in carrying a plate of grapes, pineapple chunks and Swiss cheese cubes stabbed with colorful toothpicks, the ones with cellophane curly tops. I wanted to make a joke about Swiss cheese apparently being fine to serve with fruit but not with burgers, but since Ophie turned out to be a crackerjack member of our investigative team, I decided prudence should win the day.

Chatting about nothing in particular, we munched away. After a few minutes, Ophie stood and stretched, saying she needed to get back on the phone. When I told her that it was late, we'd call again tomorrow, she arched an eyebrow.

"Honey chile, it's never too late to call hotels and such. They're open all night. Why once, at a hotel in Atlanta, I had such a stitch in my side I thought it was appendicitis for sure. Doubled over in pain at two in the morning, I called the desk and don't you know that darlin' young lady sent me an Alka-Seltzer and I was right as rain the next morning. That's why they answer the phone at night. For emergencies."

She was so resolute that Bridgy and I couldn't help but giggle, which moved Ophie straight to vexed.

"I'm just explaining to y'all."

"Aunt Ophie, Sassy didn't mean it's too late to call the hotels. She meant it's too late for us to sit up calling. We need our beauty sleep. And we have a busy day tomorrow, don't we?"

Bridgy looked to me for confirmation and I realized that she was right.

"As a matter of fact tomorrow is the Classic Book Club, which means it's our longest day of the month. The club started out as a YA—young adult—Club so we scheduled it for four o'clock because the kids would need time to get home from high school on the mainland. It didn't quite work. For three months in a row the only one who showed up was Holly—you remember, Maggie's daughter."

Ophie spent a few minutes describing Holly and Maggie as well-mannered ladies, lest we thought she forgot.

"Anyway, by the third month I'd decided to cancel the YA Club, but as it happened, Sally Caldera from the library had stopped in for lunch. When I was whining about my lack of success, she offered to come back.

"That month's book was *Dracula* by Bram Stoker. Holly impressed Sally when she offhandedly mentioned that Stoker's real first name was Abraham. By the time the meeting was over, Sally suggested that since the kids didn't seem interested in showing up, we change the name to Classic Book Club and open it up to everyone. It's become quite popular."

Bridgy chimed in, "Ophie, you might want to drive your own car to the café in the morning so you can leave at the normal closing time. I usually stay for the meeting in case customers wander in."

Ophie thought about that for a minute, her chin resting in her palm. Then she smiled. "Great idea. I can use the free time to track down the elusive Mr. Bucket Hat."

And on that cheerful note, we said good night.

When the afternoon rush ended, I took some time to review my well-worn copy of *The Turn of the Screw* by Henry James, a masterpiece of gothic psychological drama. I checked my notes and crib questions carefully and then circled the chairs in the book nook. I wondered how many readers would show up. Usually I remind the members as I see them. Occasionally I send out cheery emails or notes. But with all the chaos that surrounded us since Miguel's accident, I hadn't had time to draw a breath, let alone do any outreach.

Bridgy asked if I wanted to serve sweet tea or iced decaf coffee. We had plenty of each so I decided on both.

Maggie and Holly were deep in an animated conversation when they walked through the door. They headed straight for the book nook. Their chatter sounded like mother-and-daughter Sturm und Drang, with Holly wheedling and Maggie using the no-nonsense mom voice.

Lisette Ortiz came in carrying a bunch of mixed flowers. "I thought we should brighten up the book nook since we are discussing such a dark story."

I thanked her and brought the flowers into the kitchen.

Ophie offered to arrange them, and when I walked into the dining room, Judge Harcroft and Jocelyn had joined the group sitting in the corner.

I looked at the wall clock, put on my brightest smile and took my seat. I was pleased at the turnout. I started by asking if anyone had to struggle to accept the fundamental theme that James was striving to reveal.

Holly giggled. "You mean the whole 'corruption of innocence' thing? With the kids? I think that was way more horrifying in the dark ages when he wrote the book than it is today."

Lisette hesitated and then jumped in. "I wasn't sure if we were supposed to believe that these events were actually happening in the lives of the governess and her charges or if the governess herself had some mental stress that made her imagine these ghosts and tragedies. After all, we were getting the entire story from a narrator who communicated with her by letter at the time."

Ophie placed a vase overflowing with Lisette's bouquet on Dashiell Hammett. Judge Harcroft sat straighter and started to object. Then he must have realized that he doesn't own the table but only uses it for meals.

Wishing us a satisfying meeting, Ophie fluttered her fingertips and gave me a meaningful glance. "I have an assignment, so I can't stay. In a bit Bridgy will be bringing out a treat I whipped up for y'all. Enjoy."

Jocelyn, who'd been quiet a tad longer than I'd come to expect, took over the conversation with a lengthy harangue. Lisette was absolutely wrong. James did not intend us to doubt the governess's sanity. Yada, yada, yada.

I found myself wishing Rowena had shown up. When

she and Jocelyn battled with each other, at least they left the rest of us alone.

Maggie, who is the sweetest, most polite person, decided to take on Jocelyn.

"Well, let's remember that the governess was awfully young, perhaps too young to be left in charge of such a forbidding household. The children's uncle put too much on her shoulders. Of course being so young, she thought she was capable of more than she actually was. Time equals maturity."

From the look on Holly's face, I could see that Maggie's comment, with its emphasis on youth, was a double-edged sword. The discussion continued until Bridgy brought out a tray of mini cream cheese tarts. I started to ask, but she headed me off. "Ophie made them during the morning lull."

As usual, the sight of food brought the conversation to a grinding halt, so I suggested we decide on our next book.

Holly jumped and picked up the plate of mini tarts, offering to serve. Judge Harcroft graced us with one of his louder "clearing of the throat" noises, before suggesting we consider *The Three Musketeers* by Alexandre Dumas. He assured us that we would find the adventures of D'Artagnan and friends to be uplifting and filled with adventure, a sharp contrast to the Henry James book, which the judge declared to be tedious.

We all looked at one another nodding in agreement. I was rummaging through the bookshelves in my mind's eye when Jocelyn snapped, "*The Three Musketeers*. That's rich. Who are they? You and Delia Batson's two mealy-mouthed nephews, all colluding to steal everything that woman loved most. You should be ashamed."

Bridgy was at the counter. She lifted two pitchers, one of sweet tea and one of iced decaf. She put them right down again and glared at me as if I were the troublemaker. Clearly we would be denied our drinks until I stopped the coming battle.

"I think *The Three Musketeers* is a great choice. Does anyone else have an opinion?"

Holly, who was passing out paper plates, each with three mini tarts, handed one to Lisette and held the plate in her other hand just out of Jocelyn's reach. "I think that's a great idea. I saw the movie with Orlando Bloom when I was a kid. I'd love to read the book."

Then she slowly handed the plate to Jocelyn, who said, "Thank you," and pushed a tart between her lips, which I sincerely hoped would keep her mouth shut.

As if I, rather than Holly, had been the victor, Bridgy gave me an "atta girl" smile and brought over the pitchers. I stood to help her serve the drinks and glanced at the classics shelf. I was grateful to see three copies of Dumas's book. I would hate to have to decide between giving one to the judge and one to Jocelyn. Now I had enough books for them and Lisette. I could catch up with Holly and Maggie later in the week.

The front door banged open and Ophie roared in like a hurricane.

"Thank the Lord y'all are up to the snacking part of your meeting. I need Sassy and Bridgy in the kitchen right away."

Ophie disappeared into the kitchen while Bridgy and I exchanged "what now?" looks.

I smiled at the book club members, suggested they help themselves to drinks and followed Bridgy to the kitchen. We barely got through the doorway when Ophie puffed out her chest triumphantly.

"I found him. I found Ellis Selkirk."

Chapter Twenty-eight

Bridgy and I stopped in our tracks, absolutely bug-eyed. Whatever we were expecting Ophie to say, that wasn't it.

"How—?"

Ophie reached over her shoulder and gave herself a pat on the back.

"It takes a lot of cunning and womanly wiles to track down a cheating husband. And this fella is a different slice of the same pie. I sat outside the café, whipped out my cell and started calling, hoping to find this Bucket Hat by the end of your book club meeting, and darned if I didn't.

"Here's his address." Ophie handed me a piece of paper, one edge all jagged as if she snatched it hard from a pad. She'd scribbled notes and phone numbers and then methodically crossed them out, but one phone number had an address written underneath it. Ophie had circled the address with multiple rings pressing the pen harder with each go-round, as if savoring her success.

I still wanted an answer.

"How did you find Ellis Selkirk's address?"

"I told you last night. If we couldn't find him in a hotel or B and B, he must have rented a house or a condo. If he has those young fellas you were talking about staying with him, the whole group would be far less noticeable in a house. So I looked on my pages from the phone book and started with any Realtors whose ads suggested houses rather than apartments. Found him on the sixth call."

She stopped, plainly waiting for applause, which we dutifully gave her.

"I spoke to Charmaine at Mid-Beach Realty, who was eager to help me resolve the dilemma I was using as my cover. Isn't that what they call it on television? A cover? Sounds so much better than 'a lie,' don't y'all think? By the by, I invited Charmaine to stop at the café for lunch on the house any old time. I'd love her to come on a Wednesday so she can enjoy my chicken salad." Ophie looked at me directly. "Have you found me a spectacular chicken name yet? Wednesday is right around the corner."

"You wait. Sassy'll come up with a humdinger of a name." Bridgy jumped in and shifted focus. "I'm dying to know about the 'cover' you used."

"Why, I told her that Mr. Selkirk had ordered catering platters for a business gathering he's hosting and that, silly me, I lost the work order that included his address. Here we are with the food all prepared and no idea where to deliver it."

Bridgy gave Ophie a big ole bear hug, while I chortled,

banged my hands on the counter and declared her to be brilliant.

Blushing with pride, Ophie pointed to the paper in my hand. "I've done my part. What's our next step?"

I took a good look at the address.

"Bucket Hat lives only two blocks from Miss Delia's house. When I first met him, he told me he'd seen Miss Augusta and Miss Delia leave here and drive off in Augusta's car. That beat-up Chevy isn't hard to spot. He could have followed them around town anytime."

"But why would he go after Delia and not Augusta?" Bridgy had a valid point.

I had no concrete answer.

"Maybe Miss Delia was more convenient. He might have found her by chance. Perhaps he saw her sitting on her porch one day and decided to talk to her alone rather than tackling Augusta and Delia together. Divide and conquer."

Lisette knocked on the kitchen door. "We're leaving."

OMG, I'd abandoned my clubbies. Awful. I hurried back into the dining room. Jocelyn was gone. I offered copies of *The Three Musketeers* to Lisette, Holly and the judge, who surprised me by saying the book is so long, he'd rather download it to his e-reader. Who would have guessed that Mr. Lives-in-the-first-half-of-the-twentieth-century would own an e-reader and actually use it?

Maggie said she and Holly usually shared the books they read book club but by sharing they'd never both be able to finish *The Three Musketeers* before the next meeting, so she bought two copies. I gave her a whopping discount and hurried all the clubbies out of the café. By the time I locked the door, Bridgy and Ophie were straightening the chairs in the book nook. Bridgy asked what our next step was going to be and popped the last of the mini tarts in her mouth right as I was going to grab it.

I poured a half glass of iced decaf and sat at Dashiell Hammett, thinking about how to approach Ellis Selkirk. My brain was in gear but it was a sluggish gear. I was dithering with any number of alternatives.

As I sipped slowly, the primary choice became more obvious. I had to walk up to his house, knock on his door and speak to him directly.

Once I said it aloud, I knew it was what I needed to do.

Bridgy and Ophie disagreed.

Bridgy used her schoolyard voice to remind me that Bucket Hat threatened not only me but all my friends.

Ophie was calmer and politely suggested that we get "one of those handsome young men" from the sheriff's office to go in my place.

"No. I have to take care of this myself."

Bridgy screeched for a minute or two and used words like "crazy" and "irresponsible." I sat patiently until she ended her tirade with, "If you insist on going to his house, I suppose I should go with you. Let's get this place cleaned up and do the deed."

Ophie threw up her hands. Bridgy and I scrubbed and straightened in peaceful silence. Ophie hummed tunelessly as she jangled cutlery and moved condiments from here to there without actually cleaning a thing. Still, we were done quicker than I thought we'd be.

We locked up the café, and I was relieved that Ophie didn't offer to come along. I was apprehensive enough without having to listen to her remind me that I'd get more flies with honey or some other well-mannered ladies riff on how to deal with a potential murderer who, I was sure, was capable of carrying out the threats he made to me.

Bridgy suggested that we call Cady to meet us, and since I was driving, I handed her my phone.

"Speed-dial eight."

She was leaving a long, convoluted message. I told her there was no need, he'd call back in a few minutes, but by the time I parked the Heap-a-Jeep in front of Ellis Selkirk's house, we hadn't heard from Cady.

There were two cars in the driveway, so I was sure we'd find someone at home. I hoped it would be Bucket Hat himself.

"Ready?"

Bridgy nodded.

I knocked on the front door more forcefully than necessary, but I wanted to sound strong—at least to myself.

Without his hat and sunglasses, Ellis Selkirk looked like any retiree wintering at the beach. But his eyes turned to hard steel when he recognized me.

"You have some nerve coming to my house. Haven't you caused me enough trouble?" He gave Bridgy the once-over. "Who's she? Tell me why I shouldn't throw both of you right off my porch."

Next to me, Bridgy shrank back just enough to force me to have courage for the both of us.

"Mr. Selkirk, there's no need to bully us. You came into the café and asked me about our friends, who they were and where you could find them. One of those women was murdered a few hours later. Makes me wonder if you found her."

"You're not only nosy, you're stupid." And he started to close the door.

I couldn't believe I had the brass to stick my foot between the door and the threshold.

Selkirk looked down, and I could see him contemplating whether to crush my foot or answer my question. He released the pressure on the door.

"I'm going to tell you what I told them sheriff's boys. Then you go away and don't bother me or my crew. Deal?"

I nodded.

"Worth the talk just to get rid of you."

My head reared up like a startled hawk, which was enough to make him tell me to calm down.

"Thanks to the young guys who run their mouths, you already know we're wreckers. I had no interest in any land the old ladies owned or didn't own. The kids were afraid that the old ladies could actually stop our project so they came running to me. I wanted to placate them all until we got our State permits and then it's off to work we go."

I half expected him to sing "heigh-ho, heigh-ho." Instead he narrowed his eyes, peering to see if we were buying his story. I held my face in neutral and didn't dare look at Bridgy.

"Okay, let's end your little *Encyclopedia Brown* routine right now. There's been too many stories floating around the wrecker circuit about the discovery of treasure from the 1715 flotilla over on the Atlantic coast. You know, a trinket here, a plate there. Few thousand bucks at most. The young ones were becoming anxious, talking about moving over to the east coast.

"Like I told those two from the sheriff's department,

the night the lady was done in, me and the boys sailed down to the Dry Tortugas. We dropped anchor and I regaled them with beer, grilled fresh fish and stories about the *Atocha* and its multimillion-dollar treasure. Needed to let them know there was plenty of good wrecking in the Gulf. I couldn't afford to lose a crew I worked so hard to recruit and train.

"Now go away." He started to push the door closed. I hastily removed my foot.

Back in the car, I checked my phone. Cady hadn't returned Bridgy's call. I tried again.

When Cady didn't answer his phone, I left a message asking him to meet us in Times Square for ice cream in an hour.

Bridgy liked the idea. "Any opportunity for an ice cream break. Why an hour?"

"I thought we'd want to talk between the two of us. I mean, if what Bucket Hat says is true—remind me to ask Ryan if that is what he told them—we can eliminate him as a suspect. Those young wreckers might behave like something out of *The Goonies*, but they'll hold up as an alibi.

"And I want to do a little shopping on Old San Carlos. Get some Fort Myers Beach flip-flops, shirts, visors for Miguel's family. You know, fun gear. If they hadn't come and stayed, we'd be doing his caretaking, which would make running the café that much harder."

We finished our shopping and were walking to Times Square when I realized that Cady never called back. Bridgy doesn't pay attention to people's particular habits and was inclined to think he'd gotten her message and would show up.

"That's so not Cady. He answers every call within

minutes and, annoying though it may be, he expects the people he calls to do the same."

I picked up my phone and hit speed dial eight. Cady answered on the second ring.

"Where have you been? I've been calling."

Bridgy's hands were flapping up and down in our "tone it down" signal.

I softened my scolding. "I was beginning to worry. Come on over to Times Square, I'll buy you an ice cream." I listened for a moment. "See you then."

"His car charger broke. He didn't even realize. His cell is always plugged in. Work, car, home. Phone died in mid-interview. He's back at the office, using his landline to finish his calls. We'll see him in a few."

I decided on a double scoop of chocolate marshmallow in a cup, while Bridgy opted for peach ice cream in a sugar cone, topped with cookie bits. We sat at a table not far from the pier and savored our ice cream while watching a dozen or so swimmers splashing in the Gulf. Cady sneaked up on us.

"Started without me, I see."

I would have apologized, but my mouth was filled with cool and delicious, so I smiled while Bridgy offered him a lick of her cone. When Cady went inside to buy himself a treat, Bridgy asked if I was going to tell him about Bucket Hat.

Before I could answer, he was back carrying a banana split with butter pecan ice cream and a mountain of toppings.

"Tell me what?"

"Remember the man who was threatening me in front

of the café and you rescued me? Bucket Hat? Well, he didn't kill Delia."

Cady sat between us and started scooping chocolate syrup over the whipped cream in his cup. He stopped with his overflowing spoon right in front of his mouth and said, "I never thought he did."

Then he put the spoon in his mouth. I swear the ice cream was an excuse not to say another word.

Chapter Twenty-nine

The way Cady was eating his banana split ever so slowly reminded me how he'd played with his corn bread and honey butter while Bridgy and I waited not so patiently for information about Skully. Using food to create suspense. So irritating. He must have sensed I was having trouble controlling my desire to knock his banana split into his lap and call it a great big "oops," because he put down the spoon and sat back in his chair.

Involuntarily, I leaned forward.

"Your guy Bucket Hat has invested loads of time and money into a venture that could reap him hundreds of millions of dollars long term, so why would he care about some little island?"

"Not just any island. Privately owned land in the Everglades. Has to be worth a fortune."

"Not a fortune equal to a Spanish galleon loaded with

treasure. There are fortunes and there are fortunes." Cady went back to eating his ice cream.

"Well then"—I was determined to have the last word—"we've eliminated one suspect."

Bridgy, who'd been concentrating on her ice cream cone and pretending she wasn't listening to us, pushed her chair back.

"More napkins. Anyone need anything from inside?"

She hurried into the ice cream parlor without waiting for us to answer. She knew and I knew that Cady was about to lay down the law. Again.

"You know I worked in Jacksonville before I came here. I hung out with a great bunch of reporters, stringers, editors, photographers, even a couple of television news anchors. We frequented a pub owned by a retired offset printer nicknamed Inky. We worked hard and played hard, and when a story was hot, chasing it was no-holds-barred."

I nibbled on my ice cream, waiting for the lecture part of this story.

"Right after I moved down here, there was a grisly murder up there. The body of a middle-aged man was found in Jennings State Forest. His fingers and teeth were missing. Every reporter I knew wanted to break the story. To be honest, I was a little sorry I'd moved away.

"County and state law enforcement worked in tandem, but progress was slow. The press was running out of headlines. How many ways can you say 'the investigation continues'? Dilly Harris—"

"Dilly?"

"I know. He really lost at the name game. Parents named him Dilbert after a rich uncle and then the cartoon came out. He could only take so many jokes. His byline reads Bert but we all call him Dilly. Anyway, he picked up a hot tip and followed it on his own, hoping for a Pulitzer. Instead someone shot him in the leg when he stepped into the men's room of a roadhouse off I-10. Four years later Dilly uses a cane and the murderer has yet to be caught."

He gave me a stare that was as hard-edged as Bucket Hat's.

"You have to stop playing with this. Murder isn't a game."

Bridgy came back and tossed a few napkins in front of each of us.

"Eat up, you two. Ice cream is melting."

I telegraphed a promise to Cady with my eyes, and he nodded in return. Satisfied that would keep him off my case for a while, I finished my ice cream before it turned to soup.

We showed Cady all the touristy presents we bought for Miguel's family. He offered to have a free subscription of the *News* delivered to Miguel's house for a few months.

"Must be tough being housebound all the time."

He picked up his phone but it was dead again. "I can't believe my car charger died. I do most of my work on my phone."

"We do most of our work on our feet." Normally I wouldn't push to remind him that he had it easy compared to folks in other lines of work, but I wasn't going to let that lecture go without retaliation.

I gave him Miguel's address and he borrowed Bridgy's phone to call in the subscription. He was always doing kindnesses for other people, which made him really likable.

What made him not so likable was when he tried to tell me what to do. That's why I didn't mention our next stop was Augusta's house. What would we do if he wanted to join us?

We sat in the plaza until Cady left for work. Then I told Bridgy I wanted to visit Augusta.

"We know for sure that it wasn't Bucket Hat who killed Delia. Augusta needs to know that. And Ophie is right. If anyone knows about Delia's island, Augusta would be the one. I don't know why I never thought to ask."

"Because she pushed you in the direction of the wreckers so that's where you went. Not your fault. You were trying to help a friend."

I loved that I could count on Bridgy to tell me I was aiming for right, even when I went all wrong.

When we pulled up, Augusta was on her front porch booming at Blondie Quinlin, who was standing on the sidewalk with a cloth grocery bag in her hand.

"No need. No need for you to cook. I still know my way around the kitchen. If it's Sunday dinner you want, I'll roast a chicken."

Augusta rolled over Blondie's objections and cut the conversation short. Her words started a thought percolating. I hoped I would remember to flesh it out at home.

"Looks like I got company. Come in, girls, and tell me what you know."

We exchanged pleasantries with Blondie, who strolled along toward her own house. We climbed the porch steps and tried to give Augusta the tiniest of hugs, but she was more interested in rushing us inside for a talk.

"Come on in and take a seat. You know where the kitchen is, help yourself. Plenty of snacks and cold drinks."

Augusta's refrigerator was packed with casseroles and platters of hors d'oeuvres. Her kitchen counter was covered with assorted plates and bowls, sparkly clean and neatly labeled with the owner's name. I'd have to remember to save Augusta the trouble of delivering the dishes to their rightful owners. Bridgy and I could take care of it easily.

I scattered some strawberries and green grapes among a few pieces of flatbread covered with garlic cheese and put a handful of mixed nuts in the middle. Bridgy took glasses out of the cabinet and started pouring sweet tea.

"Fine for me. Better check with Augusta. See what she wants."

Augusta requested ice water and lemon, which was a better idea than the Buffalo Trace I thought she might want.

We settled around the coffee table. After all that ice cream, I really didn't want to eat, but I did want to delay telling Augusta the bad news.

I was reaching for a few nuts when Augusta said, "Plenty of time to eat after you tell me what you found out about them wreckers. Did they kill Delia?"

I stopped in mid-reach and told her what we'd learned about Bucket Hat and his crew. I emphasized that Ophie, Bridgy and I had worked hard but the answers we were finding didn't point to the wreckers.

When I was done, I took a long time sipping sweet tea and waited for Augusta's disappointment to rain down on me.

Augusta leaned her head against the back of her recliner and closed her eyes. Bridgy and I sat stone still.

When Augusta opened her eyes, she leaned forward.

"You gals have stood up for Delia and that's a kindly thing. You found her locket, her kitty, and you proved to me that those wreckers weren't her killers. Not much more you can ask of friends, but I'm inclined to want one more favor."

I had tears in my eyes. "Miss Augusta, you name it. We'll do it."

"I need you to take a close look at Josiah and Edgar. Would they have killed their aunt for a bit of inheritance?"

Bridgy looked frantic, and I signaled "calm yourself" with the palm of my hand. If what Skully told us was true, there was no inheritance for the nephews, but they didn't know it. I decided this wasn't the time to tell Augusta about Delia's husband.

"We'll take a look. In fact, we'll start tomorrow."

Bridgy picked up a flatbread and promptly dropped it cheese-side-down on the coffee table. By the time we cleaned the mess, she was less flustered.

"What would help us to look into the nephews' intent is to know for sure if Delia holds one or more deeds down in the Ten Thousand Islands. They might be valuable enough to lead someone to commit . . . a crime."

Augusta leaned her head back and closed her eyes again. She stayed that way for so long that I feared she'd fallen asleep. Finally she looked at us.

"Sorry. I was remembering . . . the old days. Me and Delia were born in the Ten Thousand Islands. So was my mother and both of Delia's parents. The family that connects us comes from all around Chevelier Bay. Delia's mama was born down on Lostman's River and she had family livin' here and there all the way north to Rabbit Key. Them islands was a hard place to live. Between the skeeters and the gators, there was hardly room left for people. That's how my mama used to tell it. Wasn't far wrong.

"But it was good farming land. A family could grow limes, sugar, anything needed a lot of water. Mostly, if you loved the animals, the birds and the fish, it was a happy place to grow up 'cept for the storms and floods. And the poverty.

"The old ones always talked about how Florida had its own money crash a few years before the big one in 1929. Took its toll on families. Before he come to the islands to marry mama, my father's family had three generations on the mainland around Punta Rassa working the cattle ranches. When times got hard, my older brothers went back there looking for any kind of work. Lots of folks moved to Miami, others as far north as Jacksonville."

Her face clouded at the memory of families scattering.

"Some sold their property, some up and left. Then the government come, talking about making the Everglades a national park. World War Two was in the way for a while, but right after, the park come into being. Some folks took a bit of money for whatever land deeds they held.

"But even before the war most families had moved inland. My family and Delia's lasted longer. We left and settled around Everglades City in the early 1940s, along with some other aunts and uncles. We had deeds to the islands. Just didn't live there no more.

"About twenty years after the national park come to be, my brothers and I decided to sign the land over. I kept the deed to one island for a souvenir-like, never intended to live on it. That's what I was telling those wreckers. Young folks, new to the coast, don't know who owns what, is all I was saying."

A couple of birds were croaking back and forth outside

the window. I looked at Bridgy, who knew birds nearly as well as she knew shells.

"Egrets, I think."

Augusta agreed. "Couple of egret nests down by the bay. They gossip back and forth, not as loud as the hawks, so I don't pay them any attention.

"As to islands the Batson family owned, I don't know what they did. Delia being a woman the men treated like a servant, I'm not sure her brothers would've even told her if they done anything at all. If she has papers, I guess they'd be in her house. One reason I wouldn't give the nephews her keys. Didn't want them noseying around."

We sat awhile longer, ate some fruit and then took our leave, promising to see what we could find out about the nephews.

I was in the middle of making the U-turn to head home when Bridgy asked the bombshell question.

"If, close as they were, Miss Augusta doesn't know whether or not Delia still had any land in Ten Thousand Islands, can you tell me why Tighe Kostos is so sure that Delia owned an island large enough to build a resort?"

I was tired, ready to call it a day.

"To quote the legendary philosopher Scarlett O'Hara, 'I'll think about that tomorrow.' "

Chapter Thirty

Judge Harcroft came in for breakfast slightly later than usual. I'd been steering folks away from Dashiell Hammett because I wanted the judge in a contented mood. He opened the *Fort Myers Beach News* and sipped his orange juice. I served his Hammett Ham 'n Eggs over hard, and then kept my eye on him.

When he finished eating, I approached.

"Excuse me, Judge, are you representing Josiah and Edgar Batson, or is that merely a rumor?"

"Attorney-client privilege."

He rattled his broadsheet as if shooing me away. That pushed my buttons.

"I have no interest in your privilege or in the Batsons', for that matter. I want to speak with the resort guy you were talking to at the funeral reception for Miss Delia."

I struck a nerve. He dropped the newspaper and slid his

index finger back and forth in the collar of his spotless white shirt.

"That was terribly awkward. Still, my clients . . ."

So much for attorney-client privilege.

"I'd like to speak with him on an unrelated matter. Do you know where he's staying?"

I stood by the judge's side, holding the refill coffeepot over his cup, but didn't pour until he answered.

"I believe he has accommodations at the Tower View. You should be able to leave a message for him there."

I said a polite thank you and poured his coffee. There was no reason to mention that I had Kostos's business card with his cell number printed right on the front. I wasn't planning to talk to him on the phone.

As the time of day became more suited to brunch than breakfast, only three tables were occupied. I used the break to browse the shelves in the children's section and found the book that came to mind when we were at Augusta's house. I thumbed through a few pages. It was as perfect as I recalled.

The man sitting at Alex Haley used his index finger to air-draw the universal sign for "check, please." He paid his bill with a nice tip and wished me a great day. I topped off the coffee cups at both occupied tables. No one objected, so I figured they'd be there for a while.

I pushed through the kitchen door. The "Ophie is in the house" cooking rubble was becoming so familiar that I barely noticed.

Bridgy was pleading with Ophie to tell her which of the ingredients on the counter could be put away. Ophie ignored her and they both ignored me. When I didn't place an order for a customer, they finally looked up from their chores.

I flashed a triumphant grin and held the book high over my head.

"I found it. It's not yet Wednesday and I found it."

Ophie was rolling a ball of some kind of dough. Hands covered in flour, she rushed from the counter and made a grab for the book.

"Watch the flour. I promise it's a fabulous children's book. Get cleaned up. You can read it and tell me what you think."

"At least let me see the cover."

I held the book in front of her face.

"*Chicken Sunday*? How will that work for a Wednesday special?"

Totally exasperated that I'd interrupted when she was trying to get Ophie to tidy up the clutter, Bridgy chimed in, "Aunt Ophie, you're due for a break. Why don't you wash up, sit in the dining room and read the book. I'll bring you some berries and you can call us if someone needs help."

She turned and glared at me like she was the Wicked Stepmother and I was Cinderella.

"You can help me wash down the kitchen."

Not even a thank-you for trying to make her aunt happy by finding a book name for her chicken salad. Just "get to work." Humph.

While I toiled, I thought of how Bridgy made me crazy a few short days ago. The more I thought, the harder I scrubbed the stove top. Soon I was boiling inside as if all six jets were blazing. I marched to the counter and confronted Bridgy toe-to-toe.

"So, what do you want to do with the books, donate them to the library or throw them away like so much trash?"

"What? What are you talking about?"

"In the church hall Ophie talked about getting rid of the books to make more table space. Then when we visited Miguel, you wanted to ask him if he could handle cooking for a bigger crowd."

"I was joking."

"Joking? When you say 'let's get rid of your beloved books,' that's no joke."

"I know you were already outside the car, but didn't you hear me laugh? I thought if we pretended we were considering a change and asked Miguel's opinion, show how indispensable he is to us, it would cheer him up. As it turned out he was in such high spirits I forgot about the whole idea."

I stayed quiet, which threw her into a tizzy.

"You really believe I'd consider getting rid of the books, the book club meetings, everything? They're what make the Read 'Em and Eat unique, not just another restaurant at the beach. The books give our customers a connection to one another and to the café. You think I don't know that?"

"It was a joke? You're sure?"

"Yes, I'm sure. Don't look so long-suffering. I hate when you do long-suffering. I promise there will always be books and book club meetings and clubbies hanging around. You think I'd want to miss the semi-monthly Rowena-Jocelyn battles?"

That started me giggling. As soon as she was sure I wasn't angry, Bridgy joined in, and I guess we were too loud, because Ophie stuck her head in the pass-through.

"Shush, right now. New customers came in and we can hear you all over the dining room. Well-mannered ladies—"

"We're sorry." I pulled my order pad from my pocket. "I'll get right to it."

Bridgy leaned in for a tentative hug. "Are we okay?"

"As Holly would say, we're slammin'." And I gave her a quick hug.

I could have used roller skates to serve the lunch crowd. Bridgy put two pitchers of ice water and paper cups on the table outside for the customers sitting in the sunshine waiting to be seated. She came back inside wiping her brow.

"We need an umbrella out there. Or better yet, an awning."

"Sure. Order some sailcloth. You sew. I'll hang." I chuckled, more because we both knew we'd weathered another friendship storm than because my words were amusing.

When the café was down to a few post-meal coffee drinkers, I was feeling like a used floor mop and looking for an excuse to rest for a minute, when Ophie came out of the kitchen, holding *Chicken Sunday* in her freshly washed hands.

"I don't understand how you could name Wednesday's special *Chicken Sunday*."

"We'll call the salad '*Chicken Sunday* on Wednesday.' We write the specials on the chalkboard, and for this one we'll put two copies of the book on the ledge. When people ask about the specials, we'll talk about the book, play up the grandma role."

"Sell salad and books as a package deal?"

"Exactly!" I pretended I'd been planning that all along. "How about we take a dollar off the price of the book when bought with a salad? Think the grandmothers will go for it?"

"Once they taste my chicken salad, all I can say is, you better order more books." Ophie did that spin on spike heels thing she does and went back to the kitchen.

Keeping an eye on the few remaining customers, I peeled an orange and leaned against the counter eating it section by section as I planned my next move. I was determined to discover whether or not Delia owned an island.

If I called and scheduled a meeting with Tighe Kostos, he'd prepare some elaborate version of "none of your business" and that would be that. My best plan of attack would be to catch him off guard at his hotel. He'd never expect to see me in such an upmarket place as the Tower View, and I'd have a better shot at getting the truth out of him.

I called Bridgy out of the kitchen and confided my plan. She offered to go with me and started biting her lower lip when I told her I wanted to go alone.

"Is this because you're still mad about the book misunderstanding?"

"No, silly. I think Kostos will feel less threatened if he only has to talk to one person. Remember how defensive he was at Times Square?"

"Oh yeah, he was that. Listen, check the tables and then meet me in the kitchen."

My plan was in motion. I did another round of "can I get you anything else?" and then ducked into the kitchen. Bridgy came out of the office, holding some black material and a pair of turquoise-studded sandals.

"I knew we had clothes in that little alcove behind the computer. If you are going to stroll the Tower View, you have to look the part. Here's a wrap skirt and shoes. Couldn't find a top that would work, though."

247

As soon as she heard the word "clothes," Ophie, Queen of Fashion, pushed away the pie plate she was lining with dough. She peeled off her plastic pie-lining gloves and asked where I was going. Bridgy got no further than "fancy hotel" and Ophie whipped off her apron, revealing a teal dress cinched by a wide silver belt. The buckle had an ornate Celtic design rimmed in black.

She undid the clasp and tossed the belt to me. "The skirt and shoes will do. But that dreary white shirt you're wearing . . . Go inside and put on the skirt and sandals."

When I came out looking, I thought, fairly chic in white tank top, black skirt, fancy belt and snappy sandals, Ophie sighed loud enough to be heard in Brooklyn.

She circled me a time or two and then ordered me to take off my bra.

"Wait a minute."

"No, honey chile, you wait a minute. The only reason on God's green earth to wear a shirt that large is because you're letting the girls run free. Take off the bra.

"Where did I put my purse? A little war paint will cover far too many hours in the sun, at least at your age."

Bridgy fled, muttering she'd serve the remaining customers, leaving me to deal with Ophie entirely on my own.

Much against my will I reached back, unclasped my hooks, dropped the straps down my arms and pulled the whole bra through the neck of my shirt like a magician working a glamorous trick.

"That's better. Now blouse the top at your waist and tighten the belt."

I stopped myself from covering my chest. It didn't feel right to go braless in the café. Ophie opened her bottomless purse that weighed a thousand pounds and pulled out every type of makeup known to womankind. With a heavy hand she applied turquoise eye shadow to my eyelids and a warm-toned pink blush to my cheeks. She leaned back and nodded in approval.

"These colors are gorgeous with your auburn hair."

I unconsciously folded my arms across my chest.

"Stop that. Don't wrinkle the shirt. She pulled a plastic bag out of her purse and untangled two long silver chains, the longer one thick with scattered black beads, the shorter one thin and delicate. "Here, put these around your neck. Oh Lordy, today is our lucky day."

She pulled a long silver barrette from the bag, took a chunk of my hair and clipped it high behind my left ear.

"Now walk over there and come back to me like I'm seeing y'all for the first time."

As I did so, Ophie smiled. "I am truly an artist." She patted my shoulder. "Of course you gave me a lovely canvas to work on."

Bridgy opened the kitchen door, took one look at me in my hastily fashioned outfit and went all giddy.

"Tighe Kostos won't know what hit him."

Chapter Thirty-one ||||||||||

I pulled the Heap-a-Jeep into the exquisitely landscaped parking lot of the Tower View Hotel. It wasn't until I parked that I started to wonder if I'd gone through all this for no result. There were a thousand things Kostos could be doing, business things. Why would I expect him to be sitting poolside, waiting for me?

The hotel patio surrounding the pool sits on the first floor and serves as an observation deck for the beach and the Gulf. I'd planned to hunch my shoulders to prevent my braless-ness from being obvious, but as I walked around the pool, there were so many bikini bodies, I started to feel overdressed.

Most of the men lounging at poolside wore hats and sunglasses, many with zinc oxide–painted noses. So, while appearing casual, I had to peer as closely as I could to be sure I didn't pass by Tighe Kostos without noticing.

Lots of hustle-bustle in the lobby, including about a dozen people with "Pruitt Family Reunion" tee shirts arranging and rearranging themselves for group pictures. I was wondering why they were taking indoor pictures on such a fabulously sunny day when a lady I pegged to be Grandma Pruitt said, "Okay, now let's take some by the pool." She stepped out on the patio and the entire clan followed along.

Although the two or three men reading newspapers in the lobby reminded me of Judge Harcroft, none of them resembled Tighe Kostos in the least. I hung out at the elevator bank for a few minutes but no luck. I was about to continue searching the hotel public spaces when two Florida business types—golf shirts and well-pressed khakis—came toward the elevators. One suggested they get a drink, and they walked off to the left.

Remembering what I'd heard about his fondness for expensive scotch, I decided to look for Tighe Kostos in the bar.

A floor-to-ceiling window framed a stunning seascape of the Gulf. I stood inside the doorway and looked around as though I was meeting someone. One of the businessmen I'd seen by the elevator bank gave me an appreciative glance as I walked through the bar. I smiled inwardly. Ophie had done quite the job dressing me.

Sure enough, Kostos was sitting at the end of the bar looking like the view was the last thing on his mind. I took the seat next to him, and when I ordered a Top Shelf Long Island Iced Tea, the bartender asked if I wanted Cîroc vodka.

"Unless you have Stoli Elit."

He cocked one eyebrow to signal "as if" and turned to the back bar to make my drink. As I had hoped, Tighe

Kostos knew his expensive vodkas as well as expensive scotches. He made a quarter turn so he was facing me.

"Hometown drink?"

"No. I'm a Brooklyn girl."

"Close enough."

Not to me, but I let it slide. I thought he'd recognize me, but he didn't. He kept glancing at his phone, which was lying on the bar, then at his watch and back and forth.

I wouldn't ask my questions if he was waiting for an "any minute now" phone call. I didn't want him to have an excuse to break away from me before I got answers.

He pushed the phone to one side, signaled the bartender and tapped his glass for a refill. Then he held his glass up in the air, looked at me and said, "Cheers."

The glass was halfway to his mouth when he put it down and looked at me closely.

"Don't I know you? That's not a line. I think we met once before. At the golf club? The Costellos' cocktail party?"

I was surely working my outfit if he thought I moved in those circles. *Well*, I thought, *here goes*.

"We met the other day in Times Square."

He drew a blank and then he knew. His expression transformed from comprehension to distaste.

"No. You were one of those obnoxious women? Delia Batson's friends?"

"Yep. I'm Sassy Cabot." I reached out to shake hands but he cringed.

"You and that other one. Nothing but trouble."

This wasn't going nearly as well as I had planned. I decided the direct approach was my only chance.

"Please, Mr. Kostos. Answer one question and I promise you'll never hear from me again."

He might hear from Deputy Mantoni and Lieutenant Anthony but, I could safely promise, not from me.

He stood up, chugged the rest of his drink and reached for his phone. I touched his arm and looked up as soulfully as I could.

"Please?"

"Oh all right. What's your question?"

"What makes you so sure Delia Batson owned property in the Ten Thousand Islands?"

He snorted, clearly surprised by my question. "That's it?"

He pulled a business card out of his pocket and tossed it on the bar.

"You see that logo? World of Luxury Spa Resorts is the biggest company of its type on the planet. If our research department says that she owns property that we want, then . . . she owns it." He slammed his hand on the bar with finality.

I sat there, my eyes getting rounder, my eyebrows reaching for the sky, until he realized that such a vague answer wouldn't make me go away.

"Okay, look, there's not much more I can tell you, but for what it's worth . . . The company has folks who follow recreation and vacation trends among the financial top 10 percent. Right now environmental trips are growing by 200 to 300 percent a year. But most folks don't want to sleep in a tent or make their own breakfast. Kind of an oxymoron."

He looked to see if I got it, which I did.

"Anyway, the Everglades National Park is a stellar

attraction, but there's no five-star hotel catering to the tastes of those, ah, higher-income folks. So the researchers started going over the land records, plot by plot. They followed the history of every inch and found that a number of pieces of parkland are still, at least technically, in private hands." He seemed to think he was finished explaining.

"And Miss Delia's land?"

"Well, the researchers sent engineering teams down to look at the privately owned plots. Right off, they liked the Gulf access of the Ten Thousand Islands. I was surprised how many bits and pieces there were. Ultimately, they determined that the land that suited our purposes was owned by Miss Delia Batson, resident of Fort Myers Beach. The lawyers looked at it for a while and thought they could make a case for privatization. All I had to do was get Miss Batson to sell. She was a stubborn old bird. At least the nephews are turning out to be more practical." He looked at his watch and turned toward the door. "Remember, I never want to see you again."

Yeah, like he was going to be on my Christmas card list any decade soon. Still, there is an island. And now it belongs to Skully.

I hurried to get back to the café, and while I changed out of my glam outfit I told Bridgy and Ophie what Kostos explained to me about the way his company investigates the ownership of properties. It did tie in rather neatly with Augusta's history of the Ten Thousand Islands.

I was sweeping the dining room floor when the door opened and Holly came dancing in, swinging a bulky plastic bag in her hand. She stopped in front of me, did a graceful pirouette and stuck out a foot shod in a black leather pump.

"Look at me. Kitten heels. I've been begging for months, but mom says"—and here she mimicked Maggie's voice—"heels can damage your spinal alignment and your feet." Back as herself she continued, "There's going to be a teen dance at the church, and I can't wear flip-flops or sneakers, so I said, 'Mom, chillax, time for grown-up shoes for this girl.' Mom tried for some wedge kind of heel, but when I saw these . . . hard-core, right?"

I fussed over the height and the graceful curve of the heel. At an inch and a half or so, Holly could probably dance all night without doing much damage to her feet.

Bridgy came out of the kitchen and, when she saw the new pumps, so perfect for a teenager, decreed Holly should have a chocolate float to celebrate. She went behind the counter, whipped one right up and set it in front of Holly, who was sitting at Emily Dickinson switching her elegant shoes for the old pair of Dockers slides that she was carrying in the bag.

"Wear them around the house for an hour every day for a week before the dance; otherwise you could wind up like Sassy in our freshman year of high school, walking home along the streets of Brooklyn in an elegant emerald green satin dress and Laurence D'Ambrio's sweaty socks."

Bridgy and I exchanged giggly looks at the memory. After the first few dances I was in such pain I kicked off my new spike heels and left them under my chair. Hours later I could barely get them on my feet, and when I finally did, I couldn't stand, much less walk.

"You wore some man's socks? Did you start a trend back in the day? Like the mismatched socks we wear?" Holly was in awe of my daring fashion statement.

"Laurence was a boy a grade ahead of us. He did offer his shoes, but they were so big, I kept tripping. The socks were a compromise."

"And Sassy gave him a sweet ole smooch as thanks." Bridgy was having too much fun telling the story.

Holly nearly choked on her float. "You kissed a boy for lending you his socks? The ones he wore all night? That's beyond gross."

It was a side splitter all the way around. When we finally stopped laughing and wiping our eyes, I felt better than I had in days.

Bridgy took Holly's empty glass to the kitchen where she, hopefully with Ophie's help, was finishing our closing ritual. I walked Holly to the door and locked it behind her. I'd just turned away when she banged on the glass, waving a piece of paper.

"This was on the ship's bell. Has your name on it."

I took the paper and stuffed it in my pocket so I could relock the door. Just as I flipped the lock, I heard a crash in the kitchen. Remembering Miguel, I ran in, but this time nothing was broken but a tray full of china. I raised my eyes to heaven in a silent prayer of thanks.

Ophie was of the opinion this little "oopsy" was a sign that it was high time we replenished our stock of dishes and cups. "Brighten the place. No more white. Mixed china, lots of color. That's the ticket. Where is the restaurant supply house you use?"

"On the mainland." I was too worn-out to even consider crossing the bridge this afternoon. Maybe another day.

Even if Ophie didn't pick up that I was dead tired, Bridgy

did. She came up with a brilliant suggestion guaranteed to give me a few hours of peace.

"Let's lock up here, and Sassy, if you drop us at my car, you can hang in the turret while Ophie and I go beg for sample pieces at Royal Restaurant Supply. Who has a better sense of tableware design than my aunt Ophie, Queen of Eclectic Decor?"

Well, that was true. I'd been to Ophie's house. She had a magical way of taking accessories that should never be in the same house, never mind in the same room, and placing them together with majestic flair. The result was always stunning.

While Ophie preened, Bridgy gave me a broad wink.

When we got out of the Heap-a-Jeep, Ophie was holding the shopping bags that she carted back and forth with her each day. I shoved my keys in my pocket and offered to take them up to the turret. I had no idea what Ophie carried around, but she claimed she was a better cook with her bits and pieces nearby. I slung my purse over my shoulder, gathered Ophie's bags and rode the elevator to the top floor.

Standing in front of the apartment door I realized that my keys, which were usually in my hand, were buried. Purse? No. Pocket? There they were. When I pulled out the keys, they dragged along a folded piece of paper, which promptly fell on the floor. I opened the door, kicked the paper through the doorway and stepped inside. I hung my purse on the top hook of the umbrella stand and left Ophie's baggage leaning beside it. Then I picked up the note while I still had the energy to bend.

Chapter Thirty-two ||||||||||

The view from our patio was magnificent as it always was in late afternoon. The sun was not yet ready to set but was sending token streaks across the sky. I could see a couple of powerboats heading to dock on Sanibel. A flock of ospreys hoping for throwaways was circling the fishing boats already tied up at Pine Island.

I sat in one chair and, without Ophie to treat me to a well-mannered ladies lecture, I slipped off my sneakers and snuggled my feet into the soft cushion of the neighboring chair. As soon as I unfolded the note, my feet dropped and my toes began searching for my sneakers. I had someplace to go.

I snatched my purse, and with my untied sneakers flopping, I headed for the elevator. I took out my cell and hit the speed dial for Cady.

No answer, so I left a message on his voice mail.

"Meet me at Miss Delia's right away. I'm leaving . . ."

As soon as the elevator door closed I lost my connection. I tied my sneakers on the ride down, fully expecting that Cady would be calling back by the time I hit the lobby, but no such luck. I jumped in the Heap-a-Jeep and peeled off like a sailor with a twenty-four-hour leave and a hot date waiting. I put my phone on the passenger seat so I could grab it as soon as it rang, but Cady didn't call back.

In a few minutes I turned onto Delia's block, which looked naked without a deputy sitting in a Lee County car in front of Delia's house. Life had started to go back to normal in such a short time.

I parked my car and slid the note out of my pocket, wanting to be sure I'd read it correctly.

INFORMATION ABOUT DELIA BATSON'S LAND IS
IN HER SHED. MEET ME THERE AT 5:30 AND I'LL
SHOW YOU.

The tenor of the note reminded me of those movie scenes where the heroine stumbles upon the entrance to a dark, mysterious cellar, or finds a cryptic message inviting her to meet someone in the cemetery at midnight. Bridgy and I would start chomping hard on our popcorn, squealing, "No! No! Don't go."

I chided myself for sheer silliness. It was dinnertime on a bright, sunny day, and rather than being lured to a cemetery, I was invited to a clandestine meeting in a gardening shed, the type sold in Sears and Ace Hardware. Not much danger there.

Still, I wished Bridgy and Ophie hadn't headed off to

the mainland, and I doubly wished Cady would answer his phone. I left a second message saying I was waiting for him at Delia's, then sipped a bottle of warmish water that had been in my cup holder all day while I listened to a commercial for a new restaurant in Cape Coral that promised a fabulous karaoke night on Fridays. When the clock on my dash said five thirty, I turned off the radio and the car engine, deciding to wait for Cady and my mysterious note writer on Delia's lawn.

The house looked cold and lonely, as though it had been empty for years instead of a few days. I remembered how forlorn the inside looked when Ryan and I came to find Delia's burial clothes. I shook off the melancholy and walked along the side of the house to the rear patio, which was empty save two natural wood Adirondack chairs with a glass-topped table set in between. Toward the back fence was a nice-sized propane barbeque, which I didn't expect. Delia didn't strike me as an outdoor cook. Still, having grown up in the Ten Thousand Islands long before air-conditioning, it wouldn't surprise me to learn that she knew how to cook on a spit over a fire built in a hole dug in the sand.

There was an old, rusted tan and brown shed crooked enough that it was practically leaning into the side of the ramshackle garage. I yoo-hooed, but no one yoo-hooed back. I toyed with the idea of taking a seat in one of the chairs and waiting but decided against it. I walked around to the front yard and looked up and down the short block. Both sides of the street were deserted, as were most residential streets this time of day. A while from now, folks would come out for their after-dinner strolls, but at present they were deciding whether or not to have that second pork chop or another slice of grilled snapper. I paced up and down the driveway, vacillating. Was the note a prank? Didn't matter. As long as I was here, I decided to take a quick peek on the off chance there really was something interesting to see in Delia's shed. If nothing jumped out at me, I'd call Cady again and invite him to meet me in Times Square for ice cream instead.

Decision made, I walked to the shed. An ancient padlock dangled across the side-by-side door handles but wasn't locked. When I pulled it off I saw it was so rusted that it probably hadn't been usable for years. I looped it through the handle attached to the jamb and opened the door.

The inside looked like every shed in Florida. A beach umbrella and sand chair leaned in one corner. A spare propane tank was tucked into another. Rakes, trowels and a broom hung from a Peg-Board, while spray bottles of mold remover, tins of fire ant poison and a bag of garden fertilizer sat on a shelf. The only possible source of information was a stack of newspapers on a moldy, lopsided wooden table. I stepped through the doorway. *Whomp!* I felt a ferocious smack to the back of my head. I dropped forward, landing on all fours. The door closed behind me. There was a vague scraping noise I couldn't identify. For a few woozy seconds I thought a rough wind gusted in from the Gulf and slammed the flimsy door shut, knocking me down. But I knew that couldn't be right.

I tried to get up but my legs were unsteady. Standing wouldn't be an option for a minute or two. I rummaged through my purse and patted my pockets looking for my cell phone. I'd left it in the car. Stretched out on the floor, I must have looked like Gulliver invading Lilliput to the dusty green salamander who stopped to look me straight in the eye before he scurried behind the sand chair.

And then I heard the hiss and noticed the sharper-than-gasoline smell of propane. I pulled myself up, leaning heavily on the old wooden table, which creaked ominously as it rocked on uneven legs. I knew I should check the propane tank, but the door was a couple of feet closer. With one hand on the table I took a wobbly step and reached out to push the door open. It was stuck. I moved closer and, mustering up what little strength I had, pushed with both hands. The door was definitely blocked.

The propane smell was getting stronger, so shutting off the tank became my new priority. I shuffled to the tank and leaned close until I isolated the hissing sound. It was coming from the valve, which, no matter how hard I tried to turn it, was stuck. My lungs began to gasp for air. My head was pounding. Last thing I wanted to do was die in Delia Batson's shed. My brain started to fog and I fleetingly wondered if Bridgy would bury me with Ophie's buttermilk pie recipe.

If I couldn't turn off the tank, I would have to get the door open. I threw my weight against it a couple of times. It moved enough for me to see the smallest sliver of daylight between the door and the jamb, but it wouldn't open.

I pressed my face against the tiny gap and tried to breathe clean air from outside the shed. I imagined I could smell salt wafting inland from the Gulf. I called for help, all the while banging on the door. If any of Delia's neighbors heard me, they must have thought I was someone's television with the sound turned way up. No one came. No one so much as yelled for quiet. I was dog tired and not able to think clearly. Involuntarily I slid to the floor. Then

I saw a window at the back of the shed, too high for me to reach. Its frame was touching the garage, but if I could break the glass, that would let some air in, or at least let some gas out. I struggled to stand up on my rubbery legs.

Finally I was standing. I leaned against the door and looked for something that would smash the glass in a window so high over my head. I wasn't lucky enough to spot a toolbox. The thumping in my head was getting louder. The rake or the broom. Either should do it. I bobbed and weaved my way to the back of the shed, first holding on to the table and then grabbing the broom off the Peg-Board and using it, brush end down, as a walking stick. The few feet to the window seemed like miles. It was harder and harder to breathe.

I'd have to hold the broom in both hands and aim for the pane that seemed to have the most room between it and the garage wall, the bottom left.

I held the broom like a spear and bounced it against the glass. When I pushed, the window moved with the broomstick and bounced back. Vinyl. The windowpanes were vinyl.

I looked around for a screwdriver, gardening shears. I needed a sharp point. No luck. My breathing was shallower and my arms and legs were feeling heavy. Cady. As soon as Cady heard my message, he would come. He'd get me out of here. I turned and in a determined fury stabbed the broom handle at the edge of the door right where the sliver of air and hope was, and shouted, "Cady. Come and find me."

I kept banging until I slid to the floor for what my hazy mind thought might be the final time. I felt a gust of clean air and opened one eye. A man was silhouetted by the sun going down on the Gulf. Cady was here in time to rescue me.

"Oh my God, I smell gas. Lots of it. Let's get out of here before there's an explosion. C'mon, you have to help me. You have to stand up."

The voice wasn't Cady's, but I didn't care. The nice man grabbed my arms, pulled me to a sitting position and dragged me to my feet. As soon as we were out of the shed, my legs gave way and I started to crumple to the ground, but he wasn't having it.

"No way, young lady. Keep standing. You have to walk. We have to get to the front of the house."

He flung my arm over his shoulder, and although you couldn't quite describe my shuffling as walking, I managed to move even if I didn't quite keep up.

As soon as we got to the front lawn, the man let go of me and pulled out his cell phone. I dropped wearily to the grass and looked at my savior.

Tighe Kostos was talking into his cell. "There's been an accident and there may be a gas explosion imminent. Send everyone. Address? Wait. I have it somewhere." He began patting his pockets. I croaked out Miss Delia's address and curled up in the fetal position ready for a nice long nap.

He punched off the phone and pulled me to a sitting position. "Damn, I told you I never wanted to see you again. Now stay awake. Help is coming."

And it was true. I could hear the sirens, but I also heard an imperious, "What on earth is going on here?"

Rowena. Even in my stupor, I said a silent prayer. "Oh please Lord, not now." But there she was.

"Sassy, what on earth? Mr. Kostos, I am so sorry that

you had to be subjected to these . . . shenanigans. I don't know what else to call it."

She leaned over me ever so slightly, "You get up right now. You're embarrassing yourself. No matter what you do, Mr. Kostos is going to complete his deal with the nephews and purchase Delia's island. I'll see to that."

My throat hurt and my voice was hoarse. "Rowena, you can negotiate with the nephews until dolphins dance with manatees in the middle of Times Square. Skully is Delia's heir. He was her husband."

And, delighted with myself for bursting her bubble, I dropped back onto the grass and probably passed out, because I don't remember anything more until, dressed in a hospital gown, I woke up in bed in the Medical Center. A handsome young doctor with a well-trimmed beard was asking my name repeatedly.

Chapter Thirty-three

"Mary Sassafras Cabot," I answered as proudly as a first grader announcing she could spell C-A-T.

"Sassafras?" He started to doubt that I was lucid.

"Parents. Flower power."

Then he asked me to name the month and the year. Then I had to tell him what state we were in. I gave correct answers, but he continued with more questions. Finally, he asked where I lived.

When I answered "the turret," it threw him until I realized he wanted an actual address. He seemed satisfied when I gave him one.

"Now Ms. Cabot—"

"Please—Sassy. Everyone calls me Sassy." I turned my head maybe an inch and moaned. I reached back but the doctor seized my hand.

"We cleaned your wound, shaved your head and put on a sterile bandage. Please don't touch."

I barely heard the "don't touch" part; I was focused on "shaved your head."

"Shaved my head? Am I bald?" Even acknowledging that the recent past was still a bit foggy, the thought of having my head shaved caused more panic than I felt when I was locked in the shed with a gas leak.

The doctor said, "Bald, yes. But only in one spot. The entire area, including bandage, is only two inches by two inches."

I blanched. "I have a giant hole in my hair?"

"A small hole. The hair from your crown will hide most of it." He gave me a tight smile. "You know, the grass and dirt we cleaned out of your wound indicated you were hit by a gardening tool, probably a shovel. Instead of worrying about your hair, you should be grateful you don't have a fractured skull."

A voice from the doorway confirmed, "Definitely a shovel. We found it in the yard. The lab is examining it now, but it had traces of hair and blood, so we're presuming it is the assault weapon." Frank Anthony walked into the room, with Ryan Mantoni at his heels. Ryan gave me a quick wink and a thumbs-up, but the lieutenant was all business.

"Doctor, we don't want to interrupt, but we'd like to interview the victim as soon as possible."

Victim. He called me a victim. I was tired of all his labels. For a while he seemed to think I was a suspect, then I was a witness, now I'm a victim. What is it with this man? Can't I just be Sassy?

The doctor skimmed the folder in his hand pensively. I presumed it was my medical record.

"Sure. I have to order some tests for Ms. Cabot. I'll be at the nurses' station for about five minutes, but when I come back, you'll have to wrap up."

He tucked his pen in the breast pocket of his lab coat and was halfway to the door when I demanded, "Tests? What tests?"

Without turning around the doctor said, "We'll talk about that later."

Ryan came close and gave me a soft kiss on the cheek. "Boy, Sassy, you scared the world. Cady is pacing back and forth in the lobby and stops every twenty seconds to ask when he can see you. Bridgy is crying and, well, you can only imagine Ophie. Drama queen doesn't begin to describe it. They only let us come up because we're, well, us." And he pointed to his badge.

Frank Anthony shook his head and cast his eyes upward, the picture of impatience. "We only have a few minutes. Start at the top. What were you doing at Miss Batson's house? Who hit you and how did you get locked in the shed?"

He took out a pen and his official black book, ready to capture my story. I was certain he'd become deranged if I told him that I went to Delia's in response to an anonymous note taped to the ship's bell, so I decided to start in a different place.

"I walked into the shed and, out of nowhere, something hit me from behind."

I knew he'd eventually come back to why I was at Delia's, but he let that go for the moment and moved on to who else might have been there. "And you didn't see or hear anyone?"

"Not a soul. I was a little surprised that none of the neighbors heard me when I started yelling and banging on the shed door."

Ryan said, "Our canvass indicated that no one was home in most of the houses on the block. Turns out there was a spaghetti dinner down by the bay a couple of blocks to the north. Half the neighborhood was there. Pasta and clam sauce."

I had nothing more I wanted to say, but the lieutenant wasn't letting me off that easy.

"So, tell me exactly why you were nosing around Miss Batson's property."

I gritted my teeth, but even that tiny motion increased my headache, so I decided it was easier to come clean. I didn't have enough brain power left to tangle with him.

"I got an invitation," I muttered, dreading the conversation to come.

"Someone invited you to Miss Batson's house?"

I nodded ever so slightly.

"Who?"

"I'm not sure. Er, I don't know."

"Was it someone whose name you don't know? Perhaps someone you recently met?"

I pulled the blanket close to my chin, thinking I could duck for cover when the explosion erupted, then I answered truthfully in a voice just above a whisper, "I have no idea who invited me."

Ryan grimaced and pretended to put his hands over his ears, knowing the tirade that would come. I shrank down into the mattress, waiting for the blast.

Instead of snapping at me, Frank closed his notebook. "If you can't remember, you can't remember. Head injuries are like that sometimes. We'll check in with you later."

I so wanted to let it go, but in all honesty, I couldn't.

My voice dropped into complete whisper mode. "It's not that I don't remember. It's that I don't know. I never knew. Someone put a note on the ship's bell . . ." I shrugged, and then winced because the shrug hurt my head.

Ryan's face froze, panic-stricken. I could see he wanted to run straight out the door. He actually took one giant step backward, and then caught himself.

Lieutenant Anthony moved directly to apoplectic. He did not pass go. He did not collect two hundred dollars.

"You have elevated dangerously stupid to a whole new level. We have a murderer running loose and you—"

He was interrupted when the door banged wide open and a three-ring circus burst into the room. Aunt Ophie and Bridgy were carrying every toy and trinket the gift shop sold. Cady cradled a bouquet of brightly colored wildflowers in his arms.

Ophie thrust her treasure trove at the unsuspecting Frank Anthony, who, at the last second, understood her intent and opened his arms enough to avoid calamity as she literally threw assorted teddy bears and colorful monkeys at him.

"My darlin' girl. My sweet chile. I'm so grateful you're alive." She lunged across the bed and grabbed me in a smothering hug, so she could whisper in my ear, "Y'all know we're not supposed to be here but I told the charmin' lady at the desk that I was your mama and begged her to let me bring my other children to see their poor baby sister. How she could think I was old enough to have grown children, I'll never know. Bad eyes, I guess. But she let us up, bless her heart."

She put her two hands on the pillow at either side of my head and pushed herself upright. Then she wheeled one hundred and eighty degrees on the narrow heels of her impossibly high shoes, and stopped short.

"My Lord, here we're doing this 'I'm your mother, here's your brother and sister, we're all so worried' piddle, and there's no need." She gave a broad wave in the general direction of the two deputies. "Look here, the hospital staff is letting your friends in for a quick visit. So nice of y'all to come."

It was challenging for Frank Anthony to look official with his arms filled with stuffed animals. Still, to his credit, he tried.

He cleared his throat. "Miss Ophelia, Ryan and I are here on official business." And he tried to push the armful of stuffed animals back at Ophie, who ignored him. She began circling the room, opening doors and drawers as if she were choosing a hotel room for a night's stay, but Bridgy's and Cady's ears perked right up.

Cady honed right in. "What do you mean, 'official'? Didn't Sassy have an accident? Rowena Gustavsen got in touch with Pastor John. He called Bridgy, who telephoned me, but by then my editor was already on the horn because he monitors the police band. When I got to the site, the ambulance was gone. So I came here."

I gave him as stern a look as I could muster given that I had more aches and pains than I had body parts. "I called you before I went to Delia's and again when I was sitting outside in my car. You didn't pick up."

Cady's face reddened and Ryan murmured, "Trouble in paradise."

I turned on Ryan and, without thinking, uttered the one sentence guaranteed to infuriate all the men in the room.

"He made me promise not to do any investigating on my own, but Bridgy and Ophie went to the mainland before I read the note."

Cady asked, "What note?" just as Frank Anthony dumped his armful of cuddly toys on my bed all over my feet and thundered, "Investigating? What were you investigating?"

Bridgy and Ophie were each shouting some version of "you should have waited for us."

Amidst all this pandemonium, the doctor walked into the room, which quieted everyone instantly.

He stepped in front of the deputies as if separating them from the others.

"Okay, I know who two you are, but who are the rest of these people?"

Ophie, never one to be ignored, pushed her way in between Frank and the doctor.

"I'm Sassy's mama. I came as soon as I heard, and brought her darlin' siblings."

Ryan actually smacked his forehead, which I would have done if I thought my head could stand the blow. Instead I rolled my eyes.

The doctor looked directly at Ophie and asked, "Did you have a nice flight?"

"Flight?" Ophie looked around, wondering who he was talking to.

He didn't waver. "Flight. According to Ms. Cabot's chart, you live in Brooklyn. Brooklyn, New York."

Shameless, Ophie amped up a thousand-watt smile. "So happens I'm here for a visit. Lucky as all get-out for my little girl."

I couldn't stand it anymore.

"Ophie, for heaven's sake! Doctor, let me apologize for my friends."

He gestured dismissal with the folder in his hand. "It doesn't matter who they are. They all have to leave. I need to speak with you privately."

Bridgy ran over and squeezed my hand. "We'll be right outside."

The doctor told me he wanted to keep me overnight for observation and had scheduled a CAT scan in the morning. He left an order for Tylenol and said he was sorry but he couldn't give me stronger painkillers until he saw the results of the scan. He suggested that I eat light—applesauce, yogurt, maybe some tea.

"Your body has had a trauma and needs rest. I am going outside to send your friends home. I'll leave a notation that you can have visitors tomorrow after the scan. Sleep well."

Ugh. I looked at the clock. It was hours until bedtime. I clicked on the television, but of course I hadn't arranged for the service to be turned on, so all I could watch was the loop that told me over and over again how lucky I was to be in such a modern medical institution. I looked at the pamphlet titled "Your In-Room TV" and saw that it was too late in the day to contract service. I'd have to wait until the morning.

I started to sort through the plush bears and monkeys that were haphazardly strewn all over my bed. I had gotten as far as naming a pink and white striped sock monkey

"Candicane" and was mulling over an appropriate name for a beige teddy with multicolored spots—Polka and Dot both seemed too easy—when a tall African American nurse wearing pink scrubs and an air of efficiency brought me Cady's flowers arranged in a pretty glass vase.

"How about I set these right here, hon?" And she put them on the dresser opposite my bed. "This way you can look at them while you doze off."

She asked if I wanted Jell-O or juice. I started to shake my head, realized that wasn't a good idea, so I said no. She told me she'd see me in a while.

No matter how I shifted around, I couldn't find a position that would let me fall asleep. Besides, my mind was racing around. Who left the note? Who locked me in the shed? And why?

I shuddered to think what would've happened if Tighe Kostos hadn't come along. Or was that his plan? Lure me. Trap me. Not quite kill me. Then rescue me and be the hero, throwing off any suspicion that he killed Miss Delia.

I sat up, pounded the pillow and tried to wiggle into it, looking for a cozy spot for my aching head. When the nurse came back she was surprised I was still awake. She checked my pulse and temperature, listened to my heart and lungs.

"You're sounding fit." She dropped the stethoscope from my chest. "If you want to get out of here sooner rather than later, I think sleep is the best prescription. Doctor will check your chart in the morning. He'll want to know how well you slept."

She made that sound like a mild threat. When she finished making notations in the same folder the doctor was reading earlier, she checked my pitcher of ice water and chastised me for "not hydrating," which in south Florida means "are you trying to wind up in the hospital?" Of course, I'd already managed to wind up in the hospital fully hydrated; still, I obediently sipped some water from a plastic cup.

After pouring more water in still another plastic cup, Nurse Bossy put the cup on the edge of my nightstand and turned off the ceiling light in my room, which left me only the night-light in the bathroom.

"There you go. That should help you fall sleep. Now close your eyes." Sounding exactly like my mother when I was five, except that she didn't blow me a kiss, the nurse closed the door nearly shut and moved on to the next patient.

I sat up and took slow sips of water, but each swallow was like a hammer blow to my head. I was starting to feel exceptionally sorry for myself but perked right up when I thought to call Bridgy. I slid out of bed onto the cold floor and padded to the closet. I found the note that started all this still in my pants pocket, but no cell phone. Then I remembered. It was still in my car. My car! I wondered where that was. Did Bridgy take it home? Did the sheriff tow it to a car impound lot somewhere on the mainland?

It was an effort to climb back onto the bed, which seemed about three feet higher than it was when I slid out of it. I pulled the solidly heavy landline off the nightstand and onto my lap. A strip of adhesive with faded directions for outside calls was peeling off the base of the phone. Easy peasy. I picked up the receiver and stopped. I was so used to speed-dialing Bridgy that I couldn't recall her number. I hung up the phone. I sat for a while, struggling to remember. The one number that did pop into my head was our home phone at the turret. Even if Bridgy and Ophie were off rescuing my car or having some other grand adventure, I could leave a message.

I dialed and after two rings heard my own voice, "press one to leave a message for Sassy," then Bridgy telling callers to press two to reach her, finally both of us saying, "press three for Sassy and Bridgy." I pressed two, left a message then called back and repeated the message for "Sassy and Bridgy." My message was simple. "I'm lonely. I'm bored. Please call me."

I pushed the phone off my lap but kept it on the bed so when Bridgy called back I could pick up on the first ring. Then I watched the second hand circle round and round on the face of the silver-rimmed clock hanging above the door.

The phone didn't ring.

I was too hyper to sleep, so I decided to see what the night-stand held in the way of entertainment. I opened the top drawer and was pleased to find a tooth brush, tooth paste and some kidney-shaped plastic thing that I'm sure had a purpose although I had no idea what it was. I hoped a previous patient had left a book or a deck of cards, but no luck. Next I opened the cabinet door. I found a freshly sealed plastic bag containing a blue paper robe, which would add some modesty to my cotton hospital gown, and cardboard slippers. I double jabbed the air above me. Pa-pow! I could go for a walk.

I put on the robe, eased my tootsies into the slippers and glanced at the clock. It was ten after nine at night. Where exactly could I go? Stumped for an answer, I decided there had to be a patient area somewhere on the floor. Maybe I'd find some magazines.

The hallway was empty and silent except for the murmur of televisions from behind half-closed doors as the other patients settled in for the night. At the end of the long row of patient rooms to my left was a lounge with double glass doors and a vast picture window. *A Room with a View.*

Since the nurses' station was to my right, I should be able to get to the lounge without being noticed. That was a plus since I didn't think I was allowed to walk around. Still, no one expressly ordered me to stay in bed, or even in my room, so I decided to go for it. I stayed near the walls because the thick metal handrails gave me a sense of security. And I'd be less visible should Nurse Ratched take a fast peek down the hall.

The second I opened the lounge door, I heard a loud snuffling. A middle-aged man dressed in pajamas and a plush robe sat in a corner chair. A glossy magazine had slipped from his knees and lay spread on the floor at his feet. His head was thrown back, his eyes were shut, his mouth wide open. Every breath in was a wheeze, every breath out was a snore. I wasn't going to find my quiet change of scenery here. I swiftly rummaged through a pile of magazines on a coffee table. I had no interest in *Sports Illustrated* or the *Economist*. I almost yelped with delight when I found a threadbare issue of *Cosmo*, an old copy of *People* and, best of all, a magazine I didn't know existed, *Canoe and Kayak*. Ever since Bridgy and I went paddling by ourselves from Tony's dock, I was curious to learn more about the sport.

I rolled the magazines and tucked them under my arm. I'd never be able to sit and read with the snorer in rare form. Feeling sorry for myself, I lamented that Miguel had gone home. If he were still here I'd have some company. Oh great. Only concerned with myself. I shook off my melancholy and decided to be joyful that Miguel was snug in his own house with the adorable Bow for his companion.

Skully. I forgot about Skully. I was on the third floor; he was on the second. Generally he wouldn't be a person I'd want to fritter away spare time with, but ever since he told us the romantic story of his life and Delia's, I'd softened. I grabbed the *Sports Illustrated*. I'd stop in, and if he was awake I'd offer him a magazine.

It took me a minute to remember his room number and then figure out where his room was in relation to mine. I walked past the staircase closest to the lounge. I remembered Skully's room was nearer the elevator bank, so I walked to the next staircase and opened the door quietly. No point getting caught now that I actually had a plan. I tiptoed downstairs. On the second floor I stood in the stairwell and looked through the diamond-shaped window in the middle of the door. A heavyset nurse wearing flowered scrubs and a shower cap walked past, her quiet steps almost as furtive as mine. I credited that to her thick-soled shoes rather than intentional stealth. When she passed from my line of sight, I opened the door slowly, stuck my head in the hallway, looked back and forth and gave myself the all clear. I shuffled along as quickly as my cardboard slippers would allow.

Skully's door was closed. I turned the knob, grateful that it didn't creak, and pushed it open just far enough for me to slip inside. The ceiling light was on, so I could see Skully's roommate, curled in a fetal position, sound asleep. When I moved around the door, I was momentarily paralyzed. The nurse with the shower cap was standing in the middle of the room. We were both preoccupied. She was fiddling with some sort of needle while I was trying to find a way to slide out the door without being seen. As I watched she took a step toward Skully, who was dozing peacefully, and the light glinted on a lock of hair that escaped from her cap. It was the color of lilacs in spring.

"Rowena?" It was out before I realized.

She turned around.

"You. I should have finished you off when I had the chance. You are the nosiest . . ." And she rushed at me, viciously stabbing the needle closer and closer to my face.

I wielded my rolled magazines, using them alternately as a shield and as a sword. And I screamed. As. Loud. As. I. Could.

Skully's roomie woke and groggily asked what was going on. Skully never asked a question. He awoke ready to fight. Lying in bed strapped to machines didn't stop him in the least. If he could reach it, he threw it at Rowena. The water pitcher hit her squarely in the back of her head, knocking the shower cap askew. I don't know which disoriented her more, the hit in the head or the ice water dripping down her back, but she threw the shower cap to the ground and growled like a wounded bear. Before she could recover, Skully threw an apple, the television remote, even the tiny canoe still wrapped in cellophane. He threw that kidney-shaped plastic thing that seemed to come with hospital beds, and followed it with the toothpaste tube and the toothbrush.

Over the loudspeaker a voice implored, "Security to the second floor. Repeat. Security to the second floor. Stat."

The call for help enraged Rowena to the point she wasn't sure who she wanted to kill. She turned away from me and back to her original target. Skully picked up the telephone, but the tangled cord rendered it a useless weapon. Rowena grabbed Skully's intravenous tube and jabbed it with the needle. I jumped on her back, wrapped my elbow around her neck and grabbed a fistful of her hair, jerking her backward.

Two floor nurses came through the door and, seeing a patient attacking a nurse, tried to subdue me.

Skully's roomie yelled, "Not her. The other one."

I looked at them and said, "She injected something into his IV tube."

The nurses ran past me and ripped the intravenous out of Skully's hand. In the confusion, Rowena edged toward the door, inching into the hallway.

"No you don't!" I shouted and grabbed at the gray roots of her purple hair. I held on for dear life. She shook her head wildly from left to right and I countered by shaking her scalp up and down. Rowena elbowed me in the ribs and I kneed her in the back of her legs, trying to throw her off balance. Then strong arms enveloped me and a soft voice whispered in my ear.

"Calm down, tiger. The cavalry has arrived."

Ryan Mantoni had Rowena's arms pinned firmly to her sides. So, who was holding me? I turned my head slightly and looked directly into the big blue eyes of Frank Anthony.

Then I fainted dead away.

Chapter Thirty-five |||||||||||||

It was another two days before I was released from the hospital. Bridgy and Ophie alternated sitting at my bedside, lamenting how close they came to "losing" me.

Even my mother (the real one in Brooklyn) wanted to come down to help me heal, no doubt bringing enough of her various herb remedies to mandate a thorough search by TSA officials. She was miffed but finally agreed she'd wait to come to Florida after the doctor cleared me as totally fit for the evening beach walks she loved so much. That sent her scrambling for the *Farmers' Almanac* to check the full moon calendar.

The best thing about being hospitalized was that it gave me an easy out to avoid Cady's colleagues in the print press, the well-coiffed television reporters and even self-described "murder bloggers" who all requested an interview. Still, I wanted to get back to the turret, the Heap-a-Jeep, the Read 'Em and Eat and my normal life.

The doctor sent me home with a long NOT-TO-DO list. Basically I could stay at the turret, but except for fifteen-minute walks twice a day "sidewalks only; walking on the beach is too strenuous," I was pretty much confined.

A couple of days after I was released, to keep me from going stir-crazy, Bridgy drove me over to Miguel's for a playdate. Between Miguel's leg in a cast and my patched-up head and bruised arms and face, we looked like we'd survived the worst hurricane to hit the coast in centuries. Hobbling around on crutches, Miguel insisted on making *torrejas*, sweet bread similar to French toast. When he picked up the rum bottle, I said, "Whoa. The doctor has me off alcohol for seven days."

"*No hay problema*, only a drop." He snapped his fingers indicating the mere hint of rum, "to give a taste of Cuban nights."

Then he poured a bit more than I would have. What the heck, I wasn't driving. We stood at the stove together and dished out the *torrejas*.

"Just like at the café, eh?" Miguel asked.

He was right; this was comfortable, like a normal workday.

I carried our plates out to the patio, which had a luxurious view of the bay dappled by the shade of sand pines and mangroves.

The *torrejas* were incredible and I told Miguel so, adding that we should put them on the menu at the café. A shadow crossed his face.

"You think Ophelia would like to make them?"

"Ophie? No. She leans more toward grits and hush puppies. You're our international chef. Who else do you know that can make clotted cream?"

"Ah, the British, of course. But you know I can only make it when I am able to find unpasteurized milk. Not easy to come by." He used both hands to move his cast-bound leg slightly to the left. "So, I can come back to work?"

I was aghast. "Well, not today, but hopefully soon. We're hanging on by a thread without you."

"Ah, then it is settled. I am not moving back to Miami."

"Moving?" My voice arched so high I squeaked. "How could we run the café without you? Even with Ophie's help, we're stretched to the max. We need you back."

"*Bueno*. I will tell my sister that I am staying here."

"Your sister?"

"She said you found a replacement so quickly, I must not be necessary to the kitchen of the café."

I laughed so hard that the stitches on the back of my head throbbed, but I didn't care.

"Miguel, you *are* the kitchen of the café. Without you the whole café goes haywire. You should see Bridgy and Ophie battling over whether or not Swiss cheese belongs on a hamburger."

"Of course it belongs. The *Swiss Family Robinson* Cheese-burger."

The indignant look on his face sent me back into gales of laughter, which brought Bow out from behind a planter to investigate the noise that disturbed her nap. Clearly we didn't look interesting, so she walked past us, nose in the air, and settled in a just-the-right-sized circle of sunshine, stretched out with her head on her right paw and closed her eyes.

Although she was unmindful of us, we smiled at her like two doting parents fawning over the newborn window in the maternity ward.

"She seems content." I wanted to pet her but was afraid I'd break the mood.

"*Sí.* I think she is lonely for Miss Delia, but so many of her haunts and her old friends are nearby. It must provide some comfort."

I patted his hand. "I think Miss Delia is dancing in heaven knowing that her beloved cat is here with you, although she might think that green ribbon with yellow polka dots is too bold a color scheme for her sweet Bow."

The rest of the week I hung out on our patio and took my fifteen-minute walks around the parking lot. After days of practicing new hairstyles to cover my bandage with absolutely no success, I wasn't sure whether it was boredom or vanity that made me decide to splurge the day before I was due to go back to work. Either way, I walked over to Creative Hair and practically cried with relief when Nancy said, "No big deal. A little layering goes a long way. You'll be gorgeous."

I so loved my swingy new hair that I turned the splurge into a spree and decided on a mani-pedi in neon raspberry, complete with white daisies on random fingers and toes.

Bridgy and Ophie put their heads together and decided that I shouldn't get up early and open with them on the morning of my first day back, so they arranged for Cady to pick me up and drive me to the café during the lull between late breakfast and early lunch. They weren't taking "no" for an answer.

I was gussied up and ready to go when Cady pulled into

the building driveway. He actually whistled, which flustered me a tad.

"You look wonderful. You're glowing." Then he blew it. "You should get hit in the head more often. Er, I didn't mean that the way it came out." His cheeks turned redder than my hair.

I shrugged it off. "For a reporter you really don't have a way with words. New hair." I waggled my fingers in his face. "And new nails."

"Okay, nice," was all he could manage, probably afraid to move further into foot in mouth territory. He threw the gear shift and off we went.

I'd been away from the Read 'Em and Eat for less than two weeks, but when we pulled up in front I felt at peace the way folks do when returning from an extra-long vacation. I was finally home.

Cady opened the door and, gentleman that he always was, stepped aside so I could walk in first.

I took one step inside and was floored by voices yelling, "Welcome back!"

Bridgy wrapped her arms around me, gave a tight squeeze and whispered, "Don't you ever do anything like that again."

"Like what?" I feigned ignorance.

"Like solving a murder, you dope. Come say hello."

Tears welled up. I tried to brush them away but they kept coming. Then Bridgy started crying, too. Ophie thrust paper napkins in our hands and flipped the sign on the front door from "open" to "closed."

I was thrilled to see Miguel, crutches leaning on the

back of his chair, sitting next to Miss Augusta. I wondered if they were talking about Bow.

Pastor John and Jocelyn rushed forward, each pushing a bouquet of wildflowers at me. Resisting the temptation to annoy Jocelyn by reaching for John's first, I stepped back.

"Why, these are such lovely flowers. Ophie, could you please?" Then I leaned toward the Kendalls, whispering, "Still wobbly, you know."

Pastor offered me his arm and led me to Emily Dickinson. When we reached the table Miss Augusta stood.

"Sassy, I can't thank you enough for tracking down Delia's killer. I was wrong about the wreckers, but you kept your promise. Not everyone does."

I started to cry again and enveloped her in a gentle hug. She squeezed me back.

"Sit down, right there in Delia's seat. Lots of folks want to thank you all proper-like."

And for the next twenty minutes I felt like the Queen of Fort Myers Beach granting audiences to her loyal subjects. More than a dozen of our regular customers and nearly every member of the café book clubs came by to say how glad they were to see me, how happy they were that I was all right. I blushed when Connie and Iris, the two newbies from the Potluck Book Club, presented me with a golden-wrapped box of chocolates. Iris remembered aloud that when they first came to book club they were uneasy about the murder—Miss Augusta flinched at the word—but it turns out they'd met a heroine.

According to Maggie, Holly wanted to skip school and

join us, but since she missed a day for Delia's funeral, Maggie put her foot down.

"She's been telling all her friends you are more than tope." At my blank look, Maggie explained. "As far as I can figure, 'tope' is beyond cool, so you are way beyond cool."

I polished my imaginary crown, which had even Augusta chuckling.

"Don't be surprised if she comes around begging you to start a teen book club. Her friends think you're poppin'— what we used to call 'happening.' "

Maggie gave me a warm hug good-bye.

Judge Harcroft looked sheepish as he stepped up to our table. He told me how sorry he was for my trouble and that he was glad I was feeling better. He started to turn away and then thought the better of it.

"Augusta, I . . ." He faltered and then recovered. "I am sorry for any discomfort I might have caused at the reception for Delia. I had no idea."

She glared at him for a long while and then exchanged a twinkle-in-the-eye look with Blondie. "Some things can't be helped. Any little boy knows that."

Confused but glad to have been given absolution, he turned toward the door, saying, "If you all will forgive me, I must . . ."

"*Dash.*" Augusta completed his sentence for him.

His confusion mounting, he flushed and slipped out the door.

Like the judge, most folks said their piece and left quickly. A couple of regulars were snacking on the courtesy sweet tea and cookies that Bridgy and Ophie had set out. One or two others were looking at the bookshelves, but my reign as queen had come nearly to an end.

When Sally Caldera came in, I heard Jocelyn whispering, "Mustn't tire Sassy. She's been through a lot, you know."

Would Jocelyn remember to be so kind to me at future book club meetings? Oh, but with Rowena gone, who would she tussle with? My face must have clouded, because in an instant Bridgy was hovering like a helicopter looking for the perfect spot to land.

I waved her off, but rather than go away she leaned in and whispered. "It's Rowena, right? All this talk about book clubs. You're having flashbacks."

Getting all huffy about my book clubs being under attack, I said through clenched teeth, "Well it's not like she tried to kill me at a book club meeting."

Bridgy bent down and whispered in my ear, "Seriously? If she'd killed anyone at a book club meeting, it would have been Jocelyn."

And we rolled into one of our fits of hysterical laughter, which had become more frequent now that I was home from the hospital and feeling better.

"Well, you two are in a festive mood." Frank Anthony was standing right behind Bridgy, Ryan at his side.

Ryan stepped forward and presented a shiny silver bag, tied with a half dozen rainbow-colored curly ribbons, to Miss Augusta. It got her so rattled that we were all grateful he didn't insist she open it. She could do that in her own good time.

Without being asked, they swung chairs around and joined our little group, which had dwindled down to Miss Augusta, her neighbor Blondie, Cady, Miguel, his sister Elena, Bridgy and me, with Ophie flitting around offering more sweet tea and cookies. After Jocelyn made a little speech about how happy she was to be of some minor help, which we all knew meant "you couldn't have held a funeral, caught a killer or done anything else without my assistance," she and Pastor walked out with Sally. The few remaining stragglers seemed to sense that it was time to go, and in a few moments we were left to talk among ourselves. I wondered how Augusta would feel about my asking Frank and Ryan a few questions. While I was still trying to decide, Miss Augusta charged ahead full throttle.

"Since Sassy went out and found your killer for you, don't you think you should tell her what in tarnation this was all about?"

"Rowena wanted the commission for brokering the sale of Miss Delia's island." I didn't need the deputies to tell me that much. "But why kill Delia?"

Frank Anthony nodded. "According to Ms. Gustavsen, it was an accident. The trouble started when she convinced Tighe Kostos that a 'local' could seal the deal easier than he could. She wangled a hefty commission agreement out of him. Her visit to Delia Batson was, as she put it, 'to try to talk some sense into her.' When that didn't work, Ms. Gustavsen offered to purchase the island, pretending she wanted it for herself. She actually planned to resell to Kostos. Make a fortune."

Ryan picked up the story. "Miss Delia was tougher than she looked. According to the confession, she refused politely, then not so politely. She showed Rowena the door, but Rowena was seeing dollar bills and grabbed Miss Delia by the arm. Gave her a rough shaking. Miss Delia fell, hit her head and was knocked unconscious. In a panic, Rowena grabbed a couch pillow and . . ." He looked at Miss Augusta, who sat stoically, her eyes fixed on a point somewhere along the far wall. "Well, that was the end."

"Y'all need more sweet tea." Ophie made it sound more like a directive than a question. She went into the kitchen and came back with a full pitcher of tea with lemon slices floating on top and a plate of Robert Frost Apple and Blueberry Tartlets.

"Why did Rowena try to kill me? I had nothing to do with selling or not selling the island."

"You are a snoopy busybody." Frank Anthony chuckled when I glared at him. "Hey, that's not me. That's what Ms. Gustavsen called you, and if it's any comfort, she swears she wasn't trying to kill you, only wanted to scare you away. That's why she locked you in the shed a few minutes before her meeting with Kostos. She was going to rescue you, but he was early. She kept telling us that she's really not a killer. Miss Delia was an accident and you and Skully were . . . threats needing to be tempered."

"Threats?"

"You were getting in the way of her potential commission on the sale of the island. She considered that a threat."

"What about Skully? What did he do?" Bridgy had a soft spot for him, and I have to say after our time together in the hospital, so did I.

"When Rowena found out that he'd been seen lurking around Delia's house, she was afraid he knew she'd been there the night Miss Delia . . . that last night. So she asked him to meet her at the Point on the pretense of paying him for some jewelry. He's a trusting guy." Ryan shook his head. "When he reached into his canoe to lift out his bag, she hit him in the head with an oar. With him bent over, she had gravity on her side and knocked him cold. The Gulf tide was coming in and she thought it would finish the job. She wanted it to look like an accident."

I shivered at the thought.

Frank Anthony said that Skully was down but not out. Lacerations on his scalp but no fracture. "He's a sailor and knows these waters. He'd automatically pulled his boat a few feet above the water line, so when he fell and the tide came in, it didn't come high enough to drown him or drag him out into the Gulf.

"Ms. Gustavsen had an insulin pen her sister left behind after a visit. It was sitting in her fridge and came right to mind as a solution to the Skully problem. As soon as she found out he was in the hospital, she tried to sneak into the room to stab insulin into his intravenous tube, but for a while his roomie had a private duty nurse 24-7. When Skully came out of the coma, he couldn't remember what happened, so she thought she had time. But once you"—he pointed directly at me—"told her that Skully was Delia's heir, not the nephews, she knew he'd be impossible to negotiate with, so he had to go." He gave me a nod. "You put a stop to that."

"How is he? Does anyone know?" I looked at blank faces and a few shrugs of shoulders. "I called him a few days ago at the hospital but of course his phone was turned off. Or, more likely never turned on. And then yesterday when I called the nurses' station to check on his condition, they said he'd signed himself out."

"Sounds like Skully." Ryan looked at Frank. "I guess we could keep an eye out for him. Check Tony's boat dock, like that."

There was a loud bang on the door and then the ship's bell clanged.

"Lord a'mercy. What part of 'closed' do these folks not understand?" Ophie steamed toward the door like a Key West sunset cruiser trying to outrace a lightning storm. When she peered outside, she surprised us by flinging the door open.

"Y'all, look who's here."

And in came Skully. I jumped up and ran to greet him, but when I saw the wary look on his face I stopped dead, not wanting to overwhelm him with hugs.

"Good to see you." I reached out a tentative hand for a shake and was surprised when he took it. "We're having some sweet tea and tarts. Come. Have a seat."

"Thank ye, but I have a job waiting on Matlacha—help rebuild a boat dock. Need to shove off, get there before dark." He took an envelope out of his pocket and started to hand it to me. "I wonder if you would . . . oh, Miz Maddox, didn't see you there."

He brushed past me, walked to the table and placed the envelope in front of Augusta.

"This here is for you; help fend off those nephews."

Augusta opened the envelope and took out some official-looking papers.

"Don't have my cheaters. Could you tell me . . . ?"

Skully thought for thirty seconds or more and decided he could.

"I went to see the government man. Turned out to be a

government gal. Didn't expect that. Anyway. I signed papers. When all is said and done, and the lawyers and the courts do what they do, Delia's islands will stay open and free." He took a deep breath, unused to talking so much and to such a large crowd.

"Told the government gal about the nephews, and she said that once my claim as Delia's husband is set right, I can deed the land to the government. While we're awaitin', I get to pick who can act for me in case something happens. I pick you. I made her put it in writing 'til the other paperwork is fixed. She did and that there is the paper. Notarized and all. It'll make Delia happy."

He looked at the clock over the counter, picked up his bag and headed for the door. I rushed to catch him. I touched his arm and whispered, "Thanks for saving my life."

"Little Miss, we saved each other." And he was gone.

Everyone started talking at once, except for Augusta, who was unnaturally still. Noticing how quiet she was, we settled down.

Ryan slid the present he'd brought up close to Augusta's glass of sweet tea. "Miss Augusta, I do believe this cause for celebration requires you to open your gift."

Augusta yanked the ribbon and both it and the silvery bag fell to the tabletop, revealing a tall bottle filled with golden corn likker.

Buffalo Trace.

Aunt Ophie's Buttermilk Pie

||||||||||||||||||||

1 unbaked 9-inch, deep-dish pie crust
4 eggs
1 cup sugar
2 tablespoons flour
4 tablespoons softened sweet (unsalted) butter
1 ¼ teaspoons vanilla
1 cup buttermilk

Preheat oven to 400 degrees.

If pie crust is frozen or refrigerated, let it warm to room temperature.

Crack eggs into a small bowl, hand beat with a fork until yolks are broken. Set aside. Measure one cup of sugar and sprinkle flour on top. Hand stir until well blended. In a large bowl, beat softened butter with mixer set on low and slowly add sugar/flour. When well creamed, continue to beat while adding eggs and vanilla. Then dribble in the buttermilk a little at a time while still beating. Continue for one or two minutes until well mixed. Pour into pie crust shell.

Bake for 15 minutes at 400 degrees, then lower temperature to 350 degrees without opening the oven door. Bake for 45 additional minutes. Pierce center of pie with a knife. If it comes out clean, pie is done. If not, bake for a few minutes more.

Cool and refrigerate.

Serves 8

DON'T MISS THE FIRST NOVEL IN
THE BOOKS BY THE BAY MYSTERIES FROM

Ellery Adams

A Killer Plot

In the small coastal town of Oyster Bay, North Carolina, you'll find plenty of characters, ne'er-do-wells, and even a few celebs trying to duck the paparazzi. But when murder joins this curious community, writer Olivia Limoges and the Bayside Book Writers are determined to get the story before they meet their own surprise ending.

M769T0910